Praise f

"*The Chamber* is the ultimate locked-room page-turner. Six saturation divers trapped in a hyperbaric chamber are dying one by one under mysterious circumstances and don't know who to trust. The isolation and fear are palpable, and the impending dread thrums along with a steady, heart-hammering intensity. Dean's meticulous research into the day-to-day duties of saturation divers lays the groundwork, but it's his ability to thrust readers into the metal chamber and slam the door behind them that makes *The Chamber* a haunting, unforgettable thriller."

—Heather Gudenkauf, *New York Times* bestselling author of *The Overnight Guest* and *Everyone Is Watching*

"A highly original thriller set in the claustrophobic, high-risk world of saturation diving. The tension is almost unbearable. A master class in suspense—I absolutely loved it!"

—Shari Lapena, *New York Times* bestselling author of *The Couple Next Door*

"If you look up the definition of locked-room mystery, don't be surprised to see the cover of *The Chamber*. Saturation divers dying inside a locked hyperbaric chamber with no way out for four days is one of the most unique and compelling premises I've read in a long time. It was claustrophobic, intense, and as the pressure built and the countdown to the surviving divers' freedom was on, I couldn't put the book down for a single second. *The Chamber* is perfection, Dean's writing and research are flawless, and I can't wait for whatever new mind-blowing gem he comes up with next."

"It takes locked-room mysteries to new depths like never before. If someone had told me to read a book set in a decompression chamber, I would have passed but I went in blind and found all of the meticulously researched facts absolutely fascinating. Once you start to read the book, the pressure is on to finish it, which I did in two days. It is a tour de force. If your daily job can kill you in multiple ways, you certainly don't expect to be targeted by your colleagues. Chilling, intriguing, and educational in a most entertaining way."

THE
CHAMBER

THE CHAMBER

A Novel

WILL DEAN

EMILY BESTLER BOOKS
—
ATRIA
NEW YORK   LONDON   TORONTO   SYDNEY   NEW DELHI

EMILY BESTLER BOOKS

ATRIA

An Imprint of Simon & Schuster, LLC
1230 Avenue of the Americas
New York, NY 10020

First Emily Bestler Books/Atria Paperback edition August 2024

EMILY BESTLER BOOKS/ATRIA PAPERBACK and colophon are trademarks of Simon & Schuster, LLC

Simon & Schuster: Celebrating 100 Years of Publishing in 2024

For information about special discounts for bulk purchases, please contact Simon & Schuster Special Sales at 1-866-506-1949 or business@simonandschuster.com.

The Simon & Schuster Speakers Bureau can bring authors to your live event. For more information or to book an event, contact the Simon & Schuster Speakers Bureau at 1-866-248-3049 or visit our website at www.simonspeakers.com.

Interior design by Kyoko Watanabe

Manufactured in the United States of America

1 3 5 7 9 10 8 6 4 2

Library of Congress Control Number: 2024936209

ISBN 978-1-6680-2117-0
ISBN 978-1-6680-2118-7 (ebook)

For deep-sea divers and booksellers.

You are rock stars. You work under immense pressure and need to decompress after a long shift. You are vital, underappreciated, and extremely knowledgeable. You multitask on a whole different level. Without you, things would go wrong in a hurry. Thank you.

By the pricking of my thumbs, something wicked this way comes.

—WILLIAM SHAKESPEARE, *MACBETH*

GLOSSARY

Saturation diving is a hidden world. Technology moves on over time: protocols and equipment improve. Diving systems vary one to another, from country to country, ship to ship. This account relates to the technology and systems of the early 2000s. Here are some commonly used terms:

Air Diving   Diving with an umbilical (as opposed to SCUBA), but not in saturation.

Bellman   Standby diver inside the Diving Bell.

Bends/Bent   Decompression sickness. Bubbles form in bodily tissues after hyperbaric exposure.

BIBS   Built-In Breathing System. Gas supply available to give chamber occupants breathing gases other than the gas used to pressurize the chamber.

Blowdown   Pressurizing a diving chamber or bell.

Boyle's Law   The relationship between pressure and volume (at constant temperature).

GLOSSARY

Chamber A sealable diving chamber with hatches large enough for people to enter and exit, together with a breathable gas supply to increase air pressure.

Clump Weight A concrete weight deployed to ensure the Diving Bell remains tensioned and aligned.

Decompression The dropping of pressure experienced by divers at the end of a dive, or chamber occupation. The process of inert gases leaving the bodily tissues during this period.

Delta P Flow caused by a pressure difference.

Diving Bell A smaller chamber suspended by cables, used to transfer divers to and from the DSV.

DPS Dynamic Positioning System. Maintaining a DSV's position using thrusters.

DSV Diver Support Vessel.

Equalize Rebalancing pressure in a gas-filled space (e.g., ears, sinuses).

Equipment Lock Medium-size lock in TUP used to transfer hot water suits and equipment.

Hat Diver's helmet (providing gas, light, comms).

Heliox Mixture of helium and oxygen used as a breathing gas.

Hot Water Suit A special wetsuit with integrated hoses supplying the diver with constant hot water.

HSE Health and Safety Executive.

GLOSSARY

Lock-on   The connection of one pressurized chamber to another (e.g., Diving Bell to TUP).

LST   Life Support Technician. Operator of life support systems of the saturation chamber.

Medlock   Small-size lock in chamber used to transfer food, medicine, laundry, menus, etc.

O-Ring   A mechanical gasket used to create a seal between two contact surfaces.

Reclaim System   System to reclaim helium-based gas used by divers so it can be recycled.

Sat Diving   Saturation diving. Where divers remain pressurized for long periods, often weeks, with their tissues saturated with gas. They decompress once at the end of the job.

Scrubber   A canister used to remove carbon dioxide.

SCUBA   Self-Contained Underwater Breathing Apparatus.

TUP   Transfer Under Pressure. Also known as the Wet Pot. Transfer chamber to move from living chamber to Diving Bell or lifeboat. Also serves as the bathroom.

Umbilical   Life support hose bundle (gas, hot water, comms, electricity) connecting divers to the Diving Bell, and the Diving Bell to the DSV.

Unscrambler   Electronic device to make words spoken by divers (breathing heliox) intelligible.

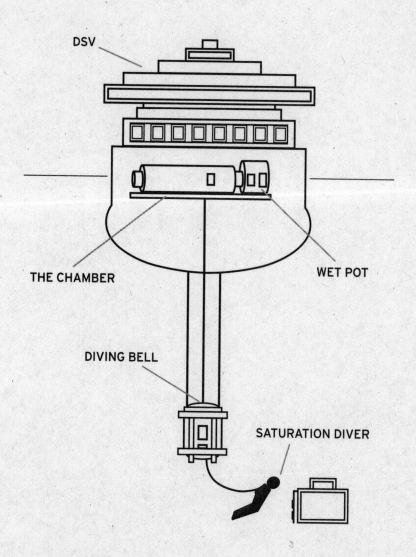

DSV

THE CHAMBER

WET POT

DIVING BELL

SATURATION DIVER

1

THE SEA DOES not care for your lost loves or your heartache. It is ambivalent to your fears, your trauma, your mortal desires. The sea knows only itself; sprawled across the world, smothering the depths, concealing both truths and horrors. The sea does not know love from hate.

The sea merely is.

I leave Aberdeen behind and step up onto the gangplank of the *Deep Topaz*, our *DSV* or *Diving Support Vessel*. I have already said my goodbyes. Salt breeze in my eyes, wind stinging, I climb on board with my bag. Mike Elliot is waiting for me, sun illuminating his weathered face and green eyes, picking out the silver in his eyebrows.

"So foul and fair a day I have not seen." His San Diego accent has been softened by a decade of North Sea life.

"Dickens?"

"The other guy. How's life?"

"Same ship, different day."

He smiles and I catch sight of the military tattoos on his forearms, some of them undisturbed, others camouflaged by fresh ink. Regrets and mistakes. *Reinvention.* I pull out my camcorder and he makes his excuses and leaves me alone.

I aim it awkwardly at myself, the flip-out screen displaying my pale, pointy face. No makeup or hairstyling. Home-dyed hair almost too short for a ponytail. My mother used to call me *pretty, if you make a real big effort*, and she was being generous. "This is our home for the next month," I say self-consciously. "Twenty-eight of those days will be at pressure, or *at depth,* as we say, at least it will for Mike and me and the other four saturation divers. We will live on board this ship, in a small pressurized chamber, and then we will descend in pairs via a Diving Bell to work shifts on the seabed. The pay is five or ten times what we might earn onshore doing construction work. We are well compensated for the risk."

I end the recording. The footage, which will be edited into a short film by one of the largest diving firms in Scotland, might help bring more women into the industry. I feel it's my duty to at least try.

Deep inside the vessel I discover Jumbo, a veteran Sat diver from Liverpool. Some might call him my *Sat Daddy*—an experienced diver who once took me under his wing—although he and I have never used that term. Jumbo is short and dark and muscular, and he has the eyes of a much older man. His mother is Irish and his father is St. Lucian, and he is one of the most respected divers working British waters.

"Ears," he says, his accent still strong despite living in Cawdor, east of Inverness, for decades. "Have your ears ready, Brooke."

I greet the medic, Gonzales.

"Ellen Brooke?"

I nod and she asks me to take a seat in a chair. We are most likely the only two women on this ship. Long curly black hair and a serious, uneasy expression. She uses an otoscope to check my ears because they are particularly vulnerable to changes in pressure. One thing Jumbo told me years ago: *Sat divers need guts and good ears.*

Gonzales measures my blood pressure and checks my breathing, her frown intensifying.

"All good?" I ask.

She clears me and we exchange a glance and I am not sure what to make of it. She seems ill at ease. When Jumbo is looked over he pulls off his shirt. Evidence of a life of work: scars, inside and out. Removing his shirt isn't flirtation and it isn't bragging; it is Jumbo proving he isn't too old yet for the job. I have never doubted him in this respect, but I fear he may be starting to doubt himself.

Medics wield a surprising amount of power over us saturation divers. They decide if we work or if we go home. They have access to extremely potent drugs. They have authority with little oversight, at least on board the ship.

I have known one or two to relish that power.

A gull squawks.

The *Deep Topaz* is steaming out into the North Sea past Buchan Deep, east of Aberdeen. A desolate horizon devoid of landmarks or reassurance. The world out here appears blank and untouched, but crisscrossed along the seabed beneath us is an extensive labyrinth of wellheads and pipelines, manifolds and connectors. This is an unseen universe, and only saturation divers have access to it.

I am not permitted to film the briefing from the captain, Lennox. He instructs us, in serious, gruff tones, to stay safe. He says anyone can call an "all stop" at any time. That is technically true, but you had better have a darn good reason considering how the ship costs over a hundred thousand pounds each day to run, and the only reason it is running—and the ninety or so crew are being paid—is to keep us six divers alive. The captain reiterates that safety is paramount. He instructs us all to take our time and avoid injuries.

The other divers are on either side of me. Mike and Jumbo—rugged, long-limbed American and compact Brit—are the oldest and most experienced. Both military men, they are followed in age by me and André and Spock. Then there is Tea-Bag, our resident rookie.

"I'm Ellen Brooke," I say, holding out my hand, although I doubt he needs the introduction. "What's with the nickname?"

Tea-Bag shrugs.

André, named after the vertiginous wrestler of the 1970s and '80s, says, "Lad keeps his bag in his mug, don't you, Tea-Bag, mate? You leave it right in there."

I would guess Tea-Bag is about a decade younger than me. Thirty or so. Olive skin, big brown eyes, square jaw. I overheard him talking to his mother in a different language from the docks before we stepped aboard. You can tell when someone is talking to a parent, reassuring them, no matter what language they are speaking. He says, "I like stronger tea than you, André. I won't tolerate a weak brew."

André smiles a big toothy grin—he has a significant gap between his front teeth—and with a broad Nottinghamshire accent, looks down at the rookie and says, "Third time in the bin, is it?"

Tea-Bag swallows, pulls back his shoulders. "Second."

André's smile flattens somewhat. He looks more circumspect. "You'll be all right, lad."

We don dive company overalls and hard hats and head out on deck. Gusts of squally wind; the sound of waves crashing. The deckhands are checking valves and cables, and the crane operator is running through his checklist. A tall, upright man with a tidy white beard and piercing blue eyes steps over to us. I smile as soon as I recognize him.

"Should be straightforward," says Halvor Magnussen, soft-spoken in spite of his build. He is a man devoid of small talk, and a legendary Sat diver himself back in the days when life expectancy in this profession was far shorter than it is now. "One-and-a-half-ton lift bag."

Halvor talks us through the work, his Norwegian accent stronger on certain words than others, and we listen. The sea isn't calm but it isn't stormy either, and the last of the gulls from land up and leave as we head out into deeper waters. All, that is, except one. Behind my colleagues I catch sight of a large black gull spread-eagled on the timber boards, its wings extended. The bird's neck is broken, its head loose and set at some ungodly angle. Its beak is slightly ajar. I should be paying attention to Halvor's technical directions, but I watch on as a young deckhand in a hard hat picks the gull up gently in his gloved hand, primary feathers splaying in the breeze, gemstone eyes shining, and throws it unceremoniously over the starboard side of the ship.

"I said, any questions?"

"No," I say, snapping back to the brief, to Halvor. "All clear."

"Like I am saying, it should be straightforward. First dive at zero five hundred hours. Weather might be a problem. We will take it one day at a time."

The six of us set off to the gear room and Halvor returns to his base for the next month: Dive Control. On most ships the Bridge is the nerve center and the captain enjoys unrivaled authority. Not so on a DSV. When the divers are in the water, Dive Control is the nerve center and Halvor is, effectively, God. The Bridge's job, and it is an extremely important one, is to keep the ship motionless, regardless of conditions, using GPS and a dynamic positioning system via thrusters. If the ship moves, then the Diving Bell moves with it and any diver working on the bottom will have their umbilical snapped. They will be left utterly alone, with no comms or hot water or flowing air, in the unlit depths.

I ask the lads if I can film us doing gear checks.

"No, not me," says Spock, offering no apology or explanation, which comes as little surprise. A superb diver and ultra-marathon runner, Spock, real name *Leo*, prefers to keep himself to himself. He has the most pronounced cowlick in his hairline I have ever seen: a quiff to rival any boy band star. Smooth-skinned and always calm, he takes his diving as seriously as he does his parental responsibilities as a father of four young girls. Whereas many Sat divers work too hard, he makes sure he has enough time onshore each year to share the responsibilities and key moments with his wife. If there is an enigma on this ship, it is Spock.

"No problem," I say.

After I check my own helmet, something we call a *hat*, a yellow object that weighs over forty pounds and keeps us alive at working depth, I film André and Jumbo running through their comms checks.

André ducks as he moves into Dive Control, ten or so yards from the saturation chamber system, the locked environment soon to be our home. He says, "Test camera" and Jumbo moves his helmet.

"Testing camera."

"Camera clear."

Jumbo says, "Test hat light, mate."

André presses a button, one of hundreds arranged into panels in Dive Control, and the helmet's powerful light switches on and off.

"Lights working," says Jumbo, upbeat.

"Going off comms," says André.

These two are close. Not only because they have dived together for years, but because they drink together when back on dry land. André is a foot taller than Jumbo, and his skin is ten shades paler, but apart from that they could almost be brothers.

I sit my camera down on a shelf and film myself checking my own hat. I tighten the bolts and check the seals. We do this ourselves, like paratroopers packing their own chutes. There are no shortcuts when you work at over three hundred feet below sea level. You rely on your training, your buddies, your gear, and your nerves. If you panic, you perish. The key is to think, not to react. When things go wrong, you must fight your primal instinct to surge up to the surface. The surface is no escape. We assist ourselves and each other. Six of us. If one of us loses a hand or a digit on a hyperbaric welding job, which happens more often than I care to think about, the other lads sew that diver up and provide opiates.

I look up at the camera. "I'm happy with my hat."

We select our boots and hot water suits. Most of us have favorites. André selects the largest size, Jumbo the smallest. I am not sure Spock cares which he uses. He doesn't seem the type to let nostalgia or superstition affect his thinking. I am the opposite. When I used to work in the Gulf of Mexico we often used hot water suits like these, but it wasn't a matter of life and death out there if they failed. It is here, have no doubt. At the bottom of the North Sea we work six-hour dives at about three degrees above freezing. If the hot water stops running through my umbilical I will succumb to hypothermia in minutes.

"You gonna film us in the Wet Pot taking a shower, Brooke?" asks Jumbo, pointing at my camcorder.

"Not worth the battery," I say.

He smiles, dimples forming on either side of his lips, and pulls off his overalls.

The chamber is almost ready to swallow us whole. I point the camcorder at the system. Pipes, valves, steel rivets. My voice doesn't sound as confident as it should. "This is our new home. We will live at approximately the same pressure as the seabed, about 330 feet on this dive. The chamber is cramped; imagine the size of the back section of a bus, the rear seats, and the six of us locked inside for an entire month. Six beds in bunks, a table with benches, and a Wet Pot chamber attached that serves as a bathroom, gear room, and transfer capsule. Food, medicine, and clean laundry will be sent in via a small hatch after the pressure has adapted. We're not too far from the kitchens on this ship, so meals should still be hot when they reach us. We won't breathe air, we will breathe a mixture of helium and oxygen, so this might be the last time you can understand me without subtitles."

"I can't understand you now," says Mike. "Too much Cajun in you, Brooke. Too much Louisiana."

I ignore him. Mike can look menacing at times, but he's a sweetheart. "The six of us will live, eat, and sleep here in this cramped pod on the ship. There are small face-size windows in the living chamber allowing our Life Support Technicians and their assistants to look in, and for us to look back out. In the States we call assistants *Bettys*. They stay on the vessel while the six of us go up and down each day to work on the seabed. We'll work in two-man shifts, each shift lasting eight hours with six hours bottom time. We eat and sleep in the chamber on the ship and we reach the seabed each day via the Bell."

I stop recording. The *Deep Topaz* bucks with each wave, but as we are in the center of the vessel the movement here is less violent. Outside the thick steel chamber hatch is a disorderly pile of soft bags. They are all named. Jumbo, or, to give him his real name, Gary Pritchard, ex–navy clearance diver, is the oldest of our team, and, along with Tea-Bag, is one of the only non-white divers currently working in the North Sea. Fell-runner and decent cook, Jumbo is our seasoned elder, and his dark green duffel bag has seen better days. Mike Elliot, retired US Navy, our resident petrol-head and calisthenics fanatic, is a Corvette enthusiast and motorcyclist. He has a gym bag. I've met his long-term girlfriend, Emily, a well-spoken British architect, and liked her a lot. The pair don't look like they'd make a good fit but somehow it works. Not unusual in this line of work, Mike is missing most of his left thumb. Spock, the quiet family man with an unintentional hairstyle, is entirely emotionless, hence the name. Even his holdall is forgettable: a soft, gray Puma bag. Spock has the build of an NFL quarterback but, despite this, he doesn't show an ounce of bravado. He once canceled a lucrative dive in the Mediterranean because his daughter needed to have her tonsils removed. I don't know many other divers who would have made that decision. André, wiry expert welder, ex–rugby player, and inveterate gambler, is almost as old as Jumbo, but less wise. His bag is expensive tan leather, and because of his height he gets teased that it looks like a purse when he carries it. And then Tea-Bag, or, according to his bag's name tag, *Javad Assar*, is a relative mystery. Here on his second-ever saturation dive, he's brought a brand-new rucksack which, as often happens with rookies, is far larger than the others it sits with.

He hasn't yet adjusted to just how cramped and austere our living conditions will be.

The Diving Bell is a smaller pod operating at the same pressure as the chamber and the seabed. It connects via a short tunnel above the Wet Pot and is raised, moved, and dropped through the ship's moon pool on steel cables. We run Bell checks, inspecting our umbilicals and backup gas tanks. Standing in a circle, we then draw straws to ascertain who will win the lower bunks. Nervous energy: anticipation and dread. I, naturally, draw a short straw. Upper bunk for me, meaning less space and less privacy. The lads go off and do whatever they each do in the five minutes before we lock ourselves inside. André will smoke one last cigarette. Jumbo will likely call his girlfriend to say goodbye. Mike will stand on deck to take a final breath of fresh air, or any type of air, for four weeks, and do some basic stretches. I have no idea what Spock does. I check my diving helmet one last time and text Gilly, my sister-in-law in Harrogate.

"Look after them for me, sis. The big one as well x."

Gilly replies instantly, because even after all these years she is nervous every time I do this.

"I'll look after them. You just focus on staying safe. Sunday roast in the new pub when you get back home. Don't do anything too dangerous. Love you xx."

Tea-Bag climbs into the chamber first and we each pass through our bags, netted Bell hammocks, and *Dopp* kits. I am wearing a sweatshirt, jogging bottoms, and flip-flops because I know exactly what is to come. The last one in, I slide through the hatch into the confined chamber holding two pillowcases: a Spider-Man one from Henry's bed, and a blue-and-white-striped Laura Ashley one from Lisa's.

A Life Support Technician asks, "Everything inside?"

"Everything's in," I say.

"See you in a month."

A metallic clang.

The hatch closes.

2

JUMBO, SPORTING bright white socks and Reebok pool sandals, grips the steel handles and pushes his foot against the hatch.

It seals.

The blowdown process—pressurizing the chamber—begins.

Our home for the next four weeks, something resembling a mini-submarine, a chamber the size of a family bathroom, begins to hiss and creak. In Dive Control they slowly increase pressure. Nitrogen, principal cause of the *bends*, is purged and replaced gradually by another inert gas: helium. The bunks are unmade. The Life Support Technician I met for the first time an hour ago walks around the exterior of the chamber checking for leaks. Once he is satisfied, the pressure continues to build.

Thirty feet.

"You OK, lads?" asks Halvor from Dive Control. His Norwegian accent carries through a microphone to our integrated speaker. Our voices can travel back to him via a microphone and an unscrambler device.

"Yes, boss," says Jumbo. He speaks for us not because we have nominated him leader or because he has any official seniority over the rest of us, but because it is natural for him to reply.

We make up our bunks. One key principle of deep-sea diving is *leave it how you found it*. In many ways we live by a watered-down military code. We speak in *Roger* and *Over* and *Copy That*, at least when we're not face-to-face. Many of us need to decompress, if you'll forgive the pun, for a day or two before returning home to our loved ones after a monthlong job. It is not easy to speak for weeks on end in military abbreviations and then go back to full-on civilian life chatting about relationships and emotions and the school run. The transition can be jarring for everyone involved.

One hundred and fifty feet. We are still on board the ship, but we don't live like the rest of the crew.

The gas man knows not to rush this or he will boil us alive. I am probably not the only one to have nightmares about oversize out-of-control pressure cookers. The gauge on the wall ticks higher and we reach the kind of temperature you encounter when stepping off an air-conditioned plane in a tropical country. That blast of heat and humidity when the doors open. The rapidity of that change.

A loud *pop* noise and Tea-Bag runs, two paces, to his bunk.

His shampoo has exploded all over his bedding.

"Rookie move, Tea-Bag, mate," says André, reaching up to touch the ceiling.

"Clean it up," says Spock, his expression flat.

"I did the same thing on an early dive," says Jumbo, grinning, a droplet of shampoo on his cheek. "Nobody does it twice. Uncap every bottle next time, captain."

It isn't easy making up a bed with broad men either side of you doing the same. We are more confined than submariners, more cramped than lovers inside a Tokyo hotel capsule. And yet somehow we know how to inhabit this space. We are acutely aware of how much room we take up and so we rarely bump into each other. This is a humid, blue-collar ballet; an unlikely dance performed by welders and ex-navy divers, each impatient to create their own private space.

Tea-Bag sits on the hard dining bench outside the sleeping area flapping a blue towel to waft air onto his face. Not *air*, not anymore. *Gas.* We are breathing *heliox*, a mixture of helium and oxygen, saturating our bodily tissues with it, and from this point onward, thanks to our high-pitched voices, anything I manage to film on my Sony camcorder will require captions.

I look at Tea-Bag and gesture thumbs-up and he returns the gesture. He has a date tattooed on his forearm. I need to keep an eye on this young diver. I want to ask him how long his first Sat was and where he worked and who he worked with, but he doesn't need that kind of attention right now. He needs to focus on resisting the almost overwhelming urge to panic and grasp for the hatch handle.

The gauge's progress is not as smooth as you might imagine. The needle sticks a little as it shows pressure increasing, and I can deduce from the whites of his eyes that Tea-Bag is fighting some animalistic survival instinct, an instinct I am familiar with even though I have learned to supress it.

In these conditions even the most seasoned and mild-mannered professional can spiral out of control.

Mike sits opposite Tea-Bag reading a copy of *American Iron Magazine*. He reads slowly and methodically about motorcycle racing in the Red Rocks of Utah, the magazine at arm's length. I spotted him onshore one time wearing reading glasses and he took them off immediately. Sweat drips off his nose and he cleans it from the stainless-steel table using tissue paper and antibacterial spray from a bottle—the motion a reflex, autonomic—and then he places the paper in a transparent bag hanging from a hook on the curved metal wall. *Make a mess, clean it up immediately.* Bacteria grows rapidly in these damp, fetid conditions. We have each suffered ear rot and athlete's foot. Serious infections take hold with terrifying rapidity. Germs spread. They multiply and mutate. A team of six can be wiped out in hours in these confined, airless chambers. Mike knows it. We all do.

"Everyone comfortable?" asks Duncan, our Scottish Superintendent, Halvor's boss, through the speaker on the wall. He's in Dive Control, the next room, monitoring us.

"Yeah," says Mike. "All good, Chief."

The pressure gauge reads two hundred feet and I have to wipe sweat from my face every minute or two. The beds are all made up and the steel table is extended to its maximum extent. It is covered in newspapers: mine and Spock's. That is one of many things the life support assistants help us with. They charge our digital MP3 players and they bring us reading material and they feed us. Every whim catered for. Some of them joke that we are lazy, but most wouldn't change their liberty and fresh air for our humid incarceration. We rely on them, and the greater team outside, for *everything*. If they so wanted they could cook us alive, freeze us to death, starve us, and gas us. With the lack of control we have and the enormous list of ways they can each inflict harm upon us if they so desired, it is in some ways similar to an academic experiment that could get out of hand. There is an inherent imbalance here, and the only reason we tolerate it is the money.

We are paid well, you see. There are no other manual jobs that pay anything like what we bring in. Despite this, most Sat divers, or *sat rats*, as we are sometimes known, never grow wealthy because, like pirates and sailors and other outlaw misfits, we tend to live each day as if it is our last. Because, as my Floridian mom used to say: *one day, honey, you'll be right*.

Our home is round like a tank of propane. Our walls are that particular shade of gray-beige you find in asylums and mortuaries. Institutional *greige*; every surface wipeable.

Tea-Bag turns to Mike like he has been building up the courage for a good ten minutes and asks him, "Were you a Navy SEAL?"

Mike doesn't look up from his bike magazine. "I wasn't anything, son."

"What?" says Tea-Bag.

Mike knows the young diver can't understand him easily with the amount of helium we are now breathing. Cartoonish voices take time to acclimatize to. The gauge on the wall displays 230 feet. Mike says again, slower this time, "I said I wasn't anything."

Tea-Bag doesn't know where to look after that response.

I walk to my bunk.

One and a half paces.

This, for the next month, will be my only private space, and I use that term loosely. I have a thin mattress and a pillow and a blue sheet. A privacy curtain. And then another bunk, Jumbo's, directly beneath mine, complete with a miniature Liverpool FC flag and a photo of his family. My bed hangs above his, from the ceiling, on chains. Headphone sockets and space for a paperback novel. If we want to watch TV we have to do so through a tiny porthole, huddled together. When I lie down I can stretch to touch each and every other bunk here. It is preposterous, really. Back home, in our sleepy village north of Harrogate, Yorkshire, my bedroom is four or five times larger than this entire chamber. Steve and I designed it that way: with plenty of air and light. He also built himself a small timber cabin with a living roof—somewhere for him to work servicing and repairing wristwatches. He chose the wooden floorboards in the house and I chose the wallpaper. Here, when I lie flat, my feet almost touch Tea-Bag as he sits on the bench wiping his face.

I take out my camcorder and press record. "Three bunks in a U-shape. Six beds. The rear bunks, home to Spock and André, cover the hatch we came in through. André's has hand cream and reading glasses because he's getting old." I turn the camera the other way, facing our living space. "This is it." My voice is squeaky; I can't do anything about that. Lisa calls it a *shrimp voice* and Henry says I sound like Donald Duck. "Bench on the left, bench on the right, table in the center. Usually we keep it folded down and away so only the central section sticks up in the middle of the chamber. We can add on extensions if we eat together."

"Happy families," says Spock, his eyes blank as always. I heard how his early Sat buddies felt deeply uncomfortable around him until they had completed a few dives together. Then they realized he was not only rock-solid reliable and calm under pressure but also one of the most physically capable, and honest, divers they had ever worked with. He is currently reading the *Financial Times*.

"Any investment tips?" I ask.

He looks up, scratches his jet-black hair, and says, "Buy oil."

It is why we are here. Oil is the reason this vast DSV with over ninety on board, running at a hundred thousand pounds per day, is motoring out north of Devil's Hole, for a month's offshore work. We are here because oil must keep flowing. We report to Halvor, the Supervisor, although Jumbo and Mike might contest that notion, and he reports to the Superintendent, Duncan, and the Night Super, the latter being a somewhat controversial figure in the industry, and they in turn report to the Operations Manager and eventually everyone reports to the oil company and its shareholders.

Jumbo looks at Tea-Bag and says, "You all right, lad?"

Tea-Bag nods.

"You sure? Tell us if you feel rough. We don't keep secrets in here."

Jumbo doesn't instruct him to keep equalizing, rolling his jaw and popping his ears, because that would sound condescending. Instead, Jumbo completes the action himself, somewhat performatively, and then Tea-Bag follows his lead. An unspoken education. This is partly because Jumbo is a fair man, paternalistic, and kind, and partly because he knows that while Tea-Bag is a rookie in our world, he is already a highly experienced commercial diver on the outside, excelling at air work for many years to reach this point. Sat is the apex of the diving industry, you see, a pinnacle only a few dozen achieve each year. I had to work air-diving jobs for eight full years and collect all my certifications and courses, all my tickets, before I was even considered for saturation work. Air diving (breathing air instead of specialist gas mixes) is still commercial diving, still tough work, just not quite as extreme, or well compensated, as Sat work. Even then it took a long time, partly because people were hesitant to lock a woman in the bin. Many people hated the very idea of it.

We are, to this day, an extremely rare sight.

I watch as Jumbo continues to keep a close eye on our newest pal, our newest brother. He asks him questions and laughs at his jokes.

My pillowcases are doubled up. I can lie down after a tough dive and a shower and a meal, and then sleep breathing in the scent of my children. That comfort keeps me going through tough times, and there are always tough times working offshore.

I attach their photos, together with one of Steve and me in Rome, his tanned arm around my shoulder, to the curved metal wall by my bunk using magnets. We lean on each other through the unavoidable troughs of life. I wasn't sure I'd ever meet a man like him. I had almost given up all hope.

Halvor announces, "Blowdown complete. Everyone feeling good?"

Mike replies for us. "All good."

We have another twelve hours under steam before we reach our featureless destination: a set of coordinates that show we are three hundred feet or so above a particular manifold.

"Menus coming through," says the speaker on the wall.

I walk over and open what we call the *medical lock* or *Med-lock*. Ninety-nine times out of a hundred this conduit is used for pots of hot water and nets of freshly laundered T-shirts, nothing remotely medical, but it is nevertheless what we call it. A small air lock where items can be passed in and out after the pressure has been adjusted. I open the hatch and retrieve the menu card.

Jumbo takes it from me and, in his broad scouse accent which seems even more indecipherable with helium, announces, "Bread rolls. Steak. Chicken thigh. Haddock bake. Usual sauces. Peas. Cauliflower. Fruit salad. Cheese and biscuits. Chocolate sponge."

We each tell him what we want for dinner and he uses a pencil to mark the grid. He grips the pencil daintily, as if this was a calligraphy exercise. This is a process we will go through multiple times a day over the next few weeks. I estimate I eat about five or six thousand calories in Sat compared to less than half that back home.

The heat is up to ninety degrees or so, like a cool summer evening in Lake Charles twenty years ago. I would sit among the cypress stumps at Contraband Bayou with a six-pack and a portable radio listening to KBYS and daydreaming about what a successful diving life might look like.

I couldn't have imagined my life now.

The food comes through an hour later in aluminum foil containers with cardboard lids. We eat shoulder to shoulder. Jumbo, the smallest of our crew, then Spock, Mike, Tea-Bag, André, and me. We each have our own bottles of vitamins and our own pre-selected hot sauce. When you breathe helium it has physiological effects in addition to our cartoonish voices. One: we can't regulate heat well. We need the chamber to be stuffy and hot so we don't freeze. Two: for some strange reason we can't taste much. To combat that we have created an unofficial hot-sauce aficionado club.

"Hot Gator again?" says Mike, squinting at my bottle.

"Gator Hammock, you mean?" I say. "Not anymore. Not enough Scovilles."

"Pappy's Hillbilly Hooch?" he asks, his voice deeper than everyone else's, the thick veins in his hands and forearms pronounced.

I shake my head. "Pappy's? Amateurs only. I got me some Satan's Blood Chile Extract. Bona fide rocket fuel."

We shake sauce from small bottles onto our bland food. I'm not saying British food is bland, though it often is. I'm saying it tastes bland to us at pressure.

We each take a shower because when you are cooped up like this there is an unwritten rule: no body odor will be tolerated. Some people haven't read the memo but thankfully this bunch, on the whole, have.

I hit record and say, "Bathroom. Let me walk you through the process." I take two towels and slide through into the Wet Pot, also known as the Transfer Under Pressure chamber or TUP for short. "The Wet Pot is the midstage between our chamber and the Diving Bell. It is where we put on our gear and also where we shower and go to the bathroom." I point to the stainless-steel toilet. "The guys will request water and then they will shower and dry off and walk back in topless wearing a small towel. Not so straightforward for me but I have developed a method. By positioning one towel strategically like so, I can ensure no Betty outside will stare at me. Against the rules but so far nobody has complained. Then I request water. They turn it on. I shower quickly and dry off and change into my joggers and shirt, then hit my bunk." Being a woman in Sat is something rare and unknown; heck, being a *man* in Sat is rare and unknown. It is part of the reason I am making the video recording, although I haven't told the guys that. I would like to see more women in this line of work. I would love to dive with one or two excellent women before my Sat days are over.

The chamber walls creak.

The life support systems hum as myriad pipes and ducts carry gases away from us or toward us. We have to trust the men outside won't mix those two things up.

Shifts are organized and I learn I am to be on the first outing at 4:00 a.m. with André as Bellman. I am delighted; keen to escape these confines, to stretch out and explore the seabed for a swim and a stroll. He will likely be even keener to stretch as he can't stand up straight in here, not even close.

The light dims and the chatter winds down.

Curtains are drawn.

We tend to rest and sleep when we can. Which is most of the time.

I stare at the photos on the wall and snuggle into my pillow, into their beautiful individual scents: subtle to the point of being imperceptible, but nevertheless comforting to me. I begin to drift off to sleep with their faces and their voices in my thoughts.

And then, as my mind turns vague and thick with dreams, a piercing alarm rings out.

"To the lifeboat, right away."

3

WE MAKE OUR way into the Wet Pot. Even though we know this is a drill, albeit a poorly timed one, I can see the anxiety etched on their sleep-addled foreheads. Escaping to the hyperbaric lifeboat is onerous enough when it is a practice run, your imagination spinning out in all directions.

"Could have done this three hours ago," mumbles Mike as he clenches and unclenches his fists.

No voice comes back through the speaker.

"I had already dropped off," says Jumbo. "I need my beauty sleep."

"You need a beauty coma, mate," says André.

"Two divorces and counting," says Jumbo. "You'd need one as well."

I consider filming this drill, but I realize it won't be possible due to the tight climb we'll need to complete.

We have to open a hatch in the ceiling and take it in turns to climb up a ladder into kinked steel trunking, a vertical tunnel of sorts—all under the exact same pressure, our working depth—higher and higher until we reach the lifeboat. Six worms shuffling up through a narrow tube. Once we are inside the lifeboat there is no space between us. No air. My shoulder is squeezing into Spock's hard back and my leg is being pushed by André's bony hip. Sardines in a hermetically sealed tin. We stand up-right, as far as that is possible, while the Supervisor runs through checks. I am five eight and my neck is bent, so this is far worse for Mike and Spock, and André is the most hunched of us all. Foul breath: the exhalations of men who were asleep or else on their way there.

I slow my own breathing. One of the basic but vital tricks and mantras of deep-sea diving: never get ahead of your hat. There are many such phrases. You panic, you die. There is no surface. The Bell is your only hope. Leave it how you found it. Don't fol-low your instincts, follow your training.

"Lovely trip so far," says Jumbo, grinning, his squeaky voice almost unintelligible. "You enjoying it, Tea-Bag, son?"

"Had worse," says Tea-Bag, giving his best attempt at bravado.

"Why do they call you Tea-Bag, fella?"

"We've been over this."

"You haven't told me, have you?"

"What?"

"I said you haven't told me why."

Tea-Bag nods. He was born in Britain but his parents are Kurdish. "When I was air diving in the Red Sea I left my tea bag in my mug and drank it with the bag still in. Name stuck."

That makes sense. Last year I met an ex-diver called Peanut who coughed up a peanut he was choking on back in 1973. Thirty years stuck with the same nickname.

More checks and protocols from Dive Control.

"We all good?" asks Jumbo.

We nod and grunt to show we are.

As terror-inducing as this so-called lifeboat is, older divers still remember the days when we didn't have them. I have heard so many anecdotes. I don't like to dwell on them when I am *in the bin*, as we call it, but occasionally they come up in conversation. DSVs sinking in storms. The ship's crew leave in their own lifeboats, but if there is no hyperbaric lifecraft on board the divers in the chamber have no such option. They observe the ship tilting and they feel it. They accept their fate, I suppose, because they have no other choice. Life support would scurry around the chamber or chambers, frantic, worried, for as long as possible. The divers might be told their fate or they might be left to work it out for themselves. Alarms and sirens. The infamous *Abandon Ship* announcement. But, again, divers don't have that option. We have no options whatsoever. If someone opens the hatch we all die instantly. *Raspberry jam*, as my first supervisor called it. So, the divers wait. The voices stop coming through the speakers. The racks of towels and spare sheets outside the chamber begin to fall over, visible through our small porthole windows as the ship upends. Perhaps the divers watch seawater enter the deck, pouring down stairs, rising up around the curved walls of their chamber. The ship goes down and they go down with it. The power might then fail. Complete and absolute darkness. Six divers saying their last words and thinking their last thoughts. If the bottom is deeper than the pressure they're held at then the hatches will pop open and they will drown down there. If the hatches hold they will die from hypothermia.

Such was the fate of many brave divers who came before us.

Nowadays, in the event of a sinking, our destiny would be different but equally horrific. Some would say more so. We would be strapped into a tight, rigid seat with nowhere to go. We would each succumb to severe seasickness on a lifeboat this size. There are no toilet facilities, no washing facilities. Six of us vomiting and urinating, and worse, in a sealed chamber, strapped into our seats. We would be dehydrated and lost. No windows or help, no Dive Control, nobody to give us water or blankets or answers, no contact with the outside world whatsoever. We would be entirely on our own. Then, if we are eventually found by the wrong people, by people who don't understand the laws of pressure, people whose instinct might be, despite all the warning signs painted on the outside of the lifeboat, to open a hatch and help surviving divers, each one screaming protests in squeaky voices, well, then they would kill us all and they might perish themselves in the process.

We are packed too close.

We breathe the same gas we just exhaled.

Saturation diving is, despite the apparent risks, statistically safer than scuba or cave diving. Ever since Piper Alpha, the 1988 rig fire that claimed 167 lives, the whole North Sea oil industry has worked to tighten up protocols and upgrade kit.

I cannot wait to exit this lifeboat. Our usual chamber is cramped but I don't mind it. At least it has windows. This lifeboat is no such thing.

A steel casket.

"Drill complete. Thanks, lads."

I don't mind that they call me a lad. In fact, I quite like it. We file down the ladder we came up on, squeezing through the trunking, the metal tube, back down into the Wet Pot. Sweat drips down my face.

We each go to bed without another word spoken.

The wall above my head says *Drass*, the specialist Italian company that manufactured this system. I say good night again to my beautiful children and dear husband, and then I turn to face the curved metal and, as if stepping out of a Bell into deep water, I try to escape the confines of this place in my mind.

My bed is still warm from before the drill. We live a monastic life in many ways, although most of us are about as far removed from monkhood as it is possible to be. There is no phone reception inside here. The Wi-Fi, for laptops, is patchy at best, and oftentimes it is nonexistent. There is a headphone socket with piped music, but this varies from system to system. We have a wired phone, but most divers do not use it because our friends and family can't understand a word of what we are saying. The last time I called Steve from Sat, on our tenth wedding anniversary, he couldn't make out a word of what I was trying to say and we both left the call frustrated. It took an hour of Gilly mediating before I could venture home. So, for long stretches of each job, we stay quiet. The bin is a place for thinking, working, and sleeping.

My joints ache from the pressure and the helium. But, vitally, my sinuses are fine. You see, any confined air pocket will be affected by pressure changes, causing tissue damage. We must avoid such barotrauma at all costs. This is why ears and sinuses are the key to any successful diving career.

I know I will be awoken at four. I desperately need to sleep but I can't stop thinking about the lifeboat. We have all lost people. That's diving. Jumbo was in the Falklands and he has lost more than the rest of us combined.

I asked him once if he suffered from PTSD.

He told me never to ask him that again.

His eyes burning, he told me to never again ask anyone a question like that when offshore.

4

"OK, SO NOW it's 4:00 a.m. and you guys are on shift," says Malcolm, the rather nasal Night Super. "I'm told breakfast is coming through. Over."

The Night Super was investigated a decade ago after a gas mix-up incident in Norwegian waters. He was eventually exonerated but his name still carries, fairly or unfairly, the baggage of that near miss.

I stretch and climb out of my bunk, careful not to make any sudden moves that could wake Jumbo beneath me, or any of the others mere inches away. André is already moving the curtain aside to enter our living quarters, his head bent to clear the ceiling. I rub my eyes with my fingertips and follow him out.

The yellowish lights are harsh and they don't do André any favors. He looks gaunt and I probably appear much the same. Heliox thick in my lungs. You might expect me to want to go back to bed at this ungodly hour, but the truth is I am eager to climb through into the Bell and escape the confines of this chamber system. I yearn to walk on the seabed and swim and do backflips on the mud.

I am looking forward to being alone in space.

We open the Medlock and retrieve aluminum foil containers and stainless-steel tea caddies. Fresh milk and delicious ice-cold juice with pulp. Food is important, for fuel, but also for morale. Much of the work the guys outside do is to support our morale. Good food served hot. Diving suits delivered bone-dry. Music and news through our headphones; football matches on screens through the porthole windows. Letters from home and fresh reading material. And then there is what we provide for ourselves: black humor, wild tales, banter, and friendship.

All to keep ourselves balanced.

After the table is extended we begin eating right away as we only have an hour before work commences. Quietly, I devour bran flakes and a bacon roll, then fruit salad and two plain yogurts. André eats a sausage sandwich and All-Bran and scrambled eggs. We need the energy. We also need the bran because, as an experienced Canadian on my first dive so eloquently stated, "The most valued skill of any deep-sea diver is being able to poop on command." What he meant was we can pee on the job whenever we like—only role I am aware of that will permit that behavior—but anything else is *complicated* at depth. It is possible but it isn't pretty.

André uses the Wet Pot first while I check our dive plans one last time. Then I place our dirty plastic cups in the transparent bag, and the used containers in the Medlock, and I thoroughly wipe down all the surfaces. We cannot become sick in here. We must do everything we can to minimize the risk of infection or disease.

André emerges in his XL hot water suit and harness. He won't be diving today unless something goes seriously wrong. As Bellman he will be in charge of feeding me my umbilical, making sure I have enough hot water, but not too much—I don't wish to parboil on the seabed—and he will be ready in case we hit trouble. In reality he will keep an eye on gauges and, once I'm at the worksite, he will probably read half a paperback seated in his rope hammock above the open hatch. Six hours is a long time to spend in a Bell the size of a small lift, crammed full of pipes and survival gear, with a gaping hole at the base to the dark depths of the ocean.

We don't say much to each other because André can be cranky in the morning. I haven't filmed him eating his breakfast but I say, "You OK if I join you in the Bell for the checks so I can film?"

"They OK with that?" he asks.

He means Halvor and the Super.

"Yes." In truth, I have no idea if they're OK with this. A Bellman usually completes all checks before the other diver, or divers, join him in the Diving Bell.

André sighs. "All right, fine."

I take some time in the Wet Pot to scrub my face and brush my teeth. Turning on the water in the small steel sink is a process that requires help from outside. Flushing the toilet is an even greater ordeal: six stages in total, involving multiple valves. It is a weak point in the chamber system, one of many.

I use the hose to clean everything down. *Leave it how you found it.* Cleanliness and safety. Pay attention. Take your time. Don't panic, think.

Mantras to survive by.

I dress in my jogging pants, long-sleeve sweatshirt, then hot water suit and Wellington boots. I pull on my harness and attach, using climber's carabiners, my spanners and knife. Then I open up for André and we check each other's gear before hearing the words "Bell in place" from Halvor through the speaker. This is the weakest junction of any saturation diving system and we both know it. The Bell has been locked on to our Wet Pot via a short piece of trunking above our heads: essentially a metal tunnel around three feet long. The seal is guaranteed by a rubber O-ring. Our lives, and the lives of whoever may be standing outside the chamber, depend on that one O-ring.

We open the hatch.

5

YOU WOULD BE surprised, or perhaps appalled, by the rust in here. Seawater eats away at anything metal. Everything offshore has a life expectancy, the six of us included. I once described the working parts of Sat diving systems as NASA technology crossed with a 1970s construction site.

State-of-the-art life support and sledgehammers.

André climbs the final rung of the ladder and uses the knotted rope inside the Bell to heave himself up. After a dive shift on the seabed, this lower section of the Bell can be flooded to help us back up, but no such assistance at this point. His height doesn't help him. I am a good half foot shorter than André and even I feel like I am confined within a refrigerator.

I secure my bottle of water and climb up the ladder after him. I want to film this process but I realize it will be impossible for me to hold the camera steady while I rise, and I don't want to burden André with it while he's Bellman. He will have enough on his mind.

Once we are both in, the cramped conditions go from bad to far, far worse. Rusted metal, multiple pressure gauges, gas bottles, first aid kits, and umbilicals so long and unwieldy they take up much of the interior space even when neatly coiled, which is an art in itself. Jumbo and Mike like to dive together and as they're both very particular about Bell tidiness we tend to leave them to it. I begin filming, muttering something about how not to worry about the amateur-looking duct tape repairs. It is all thoroughly tested and approved. André gives me a concerned glance.

We are still locked onto the system. Usually it would just be the Bellman inside running through checks with Dive Control. I keep my mouth shut and film him doing his work. Tomorrow it will be him working in the water and me in charge of the Bell.

One shift wet, one shift dry.

"You've seen a copy of the dive plan?" asks Halvor, slow and clear. "You understand the dive plan?"

"Yes," replies André. The unscrambler device in Dive Control is working well. Our family members have no such equipment.

"Confirm your hyper-gas monitor reading is status green."

"Confirmed."

"Bullhorn working?"

"Yeah."

"You've checked the diver recovery winch?"

"Yes."

"Tools?"

"All good."

"Umbilicals?"

"Roger, roger. Umbilicals checked. Gas checks and standby checks also complete."

"Very good, Bellman. The Bridge says fifteen minutes."

"Roger that."

"We'll test through-water comms," says Halvor. He pronounces his *w*'s as *v*'s.

André winds up the device. "Testing, testing."

"I can hear you loud and clear," says Halvor. "Once again, fifteen minutes from the Bridge."

We check our gear again, close the hatch, and André rigs up

in his hammock. It is made of thin rope and it is comfortable compared to standing with your legs on each side of the Bell exit pool, or sat perched on a narrow bench.

The clump weight, a multiton, white-painted chunk of concrete that sits a few yards above the seabed and stabilizes the Bell while we work at depth, goes down through the ship's moon pool, a hole in the center of the vessel, before us.

André appears composed. I have rigged up the camera on the wall of the Bell using electrical tape and string, and he doesn't seem to notice or care.

We begin to sink down through the water.

"Eighty feet down," says Halvor through the speaker.

I squeeze my nose and equalize even though changes in pressure are minimal. André does the same. I lift my yellow helmet into place, which is never a very pretty sight as it weighs as much as an overstuffed long-haul suitcase. André helps me into it. I will do the same for him tomorrow when we repeat this operation. If you think living inside a pressurized chamber with five men is claustrophobic, try being locked inside a small Bell as it rapidly descends deeper and deeper through freezing seawater, all while squeezing your head into a heavy, rigid helmet.

"One hundred and sixty feet down."

André checks my umbilical, my light, hot water, comms. He clips and secures my hat. It is not designed to be worn outside the water.

It is so heavy it could break your neck.

"Two hundred and fifty feet down."

I slow my breathing. A sense of the immensity of water outside these cold metal walls. André is wearing an almost identical hot water suit but he keeps his helmet staged in case he needs to rescue me on the job. We are heading toward working depth. In some areas of the North Sea that can be almost double where we are now, which means eight or more days to decompress instead of four. The most I have ever done is nine days and that was a mental and physical challenge to say the least.

"That's 320 feet," says Halvor. "Everything good?"

"All good," says André.

"I can see you both on the camera nice and clear. OK, Bellman, open the door."

André works the hatch open and I stare down at the small pool of water, a glimpse into the depths, a view seemingly impossible. We are dry at the bottom of this body of water, and I am mentally preparing myself to enter, to drop down into nothingness, trusting I will find the seabed twenty feet below and not a thousand.

"When the hot water's coming through, she's clear to leave, Bellman," says Halvor. "Check for leaks as she goes."

I take a deep breath and step down onto the first rung of the ladder.

My head is dry but my boots are wet.

I descend.

6

WEIGHTLESSNESS.

I climb down onto the clump weight and check my umbilical. *Always* check your umbilical. It is as essential to life as the anatomical cord it is named after.

I'm here to work on a manifold, a structure where multiple junctions converge into a single channel. Undersea oil infrastructure requires constant maintenance. Luckily for us, the work never ends.

"Reclaim is good," says Halvor through my helmet.

He means the ship is recovering the helium I exhale. I have been told helium costs over ten bucks a breath, so they recycle it and pump it back into the living chamber. Sat divers produce no bubbles. We are closer to marine life than human.

"Confirm no leaks, Diver One."

"Confirmed."

"Make your way when you're ready. Over."

I take a jump from the clump weight and float down gently to the seabed below. A smile breaks out across my face. Freedom. Solitude and open space. Indescribable serenity. I swim with my arms as I make my way down, smoothly, ephemerally, through this undersea realm.

The water is like gin. Sparkling clear. Deeper than this and it becomes dark. South from here, where the currents blow like undersea winds, visibility can drop to a few feet or less. But in this place, today, for this moment at least, I can see an unknown world laid out in front of me.

"Are you ready for a morning of work, Brooke?"

"As ready as I'll ever be."

"That's the ticket. We've got the connector and coil coming down from above, just so you are aware. Crane's dropping it to you now. Over."

"Roger that."

I walk along the seabed, occasionally looking up for signs of the gear. A stroll. A Sunday constitutional as my husband once called it. This is not how *you* experience the underwater world of snorkeling on vacation, or swimming a few feet beneath the surface in a pool. I am neutral in terms of buoyancy. As graceful as a blacktip shark. OK, not quite that graceful, but I am more peaceful and relaxed than I have been since I boarded the DSV in Aberdeen. Emptiness: all around me. A thousand starfish, or as my young son calls them, *sea stars*, clustered together on the house-size manifold. Eels and plain, gray fish. Shoals, shimmering. I walk around, utterly alone, and watch on as the connector and coil fall gently to the seabed from the crane above.

Space, inverted.

The reality of life as an aquanaut.

"Received," I say.

"Roger that. I see it nice and clear through your hat camera. Make your way to it in your own time, Diver One."

I walk over, hot water spraying out at my hands and legs to prevent me from succumbing to hypothermia. The coil might weigh twice my bodyweight, but down here in the water I can manage it. For heavier structures I would have a lift bag, but I manage to drag the coil toward the manifold.

"Relax on your breathing, Diver One."

"Roger that."

I slow myself.

"Watch the coil doesn't mess with your umbilical. Take a moment if you need one."

I take a moment. I have already been down here for an hour, because, on the seabed, with ten atmospheres of constant pressure, everything takes time. I relax for a while and then I move the coil the final few yards to the structure. The water around me fills with sand.

"Do you have your tools, Diver One?"

"Affirmative. I have my tools."

"Very good."

Henry drew me a card for, I think it was my thirty-eighth birthday, and he colored it pale blue with plump orcas and squid and a woman on the seabed wearing a snorkel and long, split fins. He draws for me after he's been mischievous because he thinks I'll forgive him instantly. He's clever that way. I still have the card and I keep it in my bedside table at home. I will cherish it always. He didn't write it to *Mum*, he wrote it to *Ellen Brooke, Sea Diver*.

People compare us to astronauts. But the truth is our world is far more mysterious and haunting than theirs. Imagine being on a spacewalk, only the space around you is thick with sand so you can't see the shuttle you emerged from. Then imagine working in those conditions in your NASA suit, only you are not weightless, you are merely neutral, so when you swing a tool or lift a piece of gear, you encounter resistance and pressure rather than the ease of a vacuum. We have it tougher. Inside a space station, a slow leak can be patched. You have time. We, on the other hand, do not have that luxury. We would all die instantly and the cleanup operation would leave the team responsible with nightmares and years of therapy. They may never recover. Astronauts versus aquanauts: no contest. Now imagine you are on that same spacewalk and the visibility is poor instead of crystal clear, and you are sweating with all the exertion, and then, out of the blue, when you are completely alone, you feel a massive living thing brush past the back of your thighs. Imagine the intensity of that panic, that terror.

Like I said: no contest.

The DSV is hovering far above. Its GPS-operated dynamic positioning system is holding it steady. If it were to malfunction I would be dragged around across the seabed, smashing into pipelines and wellheads, cutting across anchor chains. I should not think of such things but at the same time I cannot help it. Sometimes your thoughts go rogue; I know mine do. The image is already clear in my head.

"Easy on your breathing, Diver One."

I shun the unwanted image.

Take a moment.

"Look to the right for me, Diver One."

I do as he asks.

"Look up, please. That's it. Clear the area for me so we can take a better look."

I use my gloved hands to move mud and silt from the connectors—a series of bright yellow cables attaching to the manifold—and they come into view. Visibility has worsened from fifty yards to two or three due to me dragging the coil across the mud.

"We are waiting for the OK from the platform to make the swap, Diver One. It might be a little while. Take some time for yourself."

This is common. Safety checks and double checks. Confirmations. They do not want oil flowing before connections have been secured and valves closed, and they do not want thousands of volts being discharged at the wrong time.

"Might be awhile, Diver One," Halvor says again. "Could be thirty minutes, I'm hearing."

My extremities are blissfully warm from the hoses squirting bath-temperature water to my hands and ankles and neck. My breathing is slow.

"Could you switch my light off for a while? Over."

"You sure? Light off? Please confirm. Over."

My breathing slows even more.

"Light off, please."

"Switching light off now. Over."

Everything turns to purest black. In utero: some reflex or memory. Then, once my eyes acclimatize, slate grays and rich, dark blues. The emergence of it all. A quiet world absent of war or corruption. A silent cathedral; a miraculous, hidden universe. Whales passing in the far distance: unseen and unheard. I let my body go limp, supported by the water. I hang, fetal, breathing calmly, and then I close my eyes.

7

REVERTING TO AN earlier time. Mom, living in rural Ohio, south of Columbus, pregnant with me, crazy in love with Dad and his rough, leather-clad ways. Me floating. Them, happily together, for a while at least. Perhaps I was vaguely aware of there being something else out there, a world, while also being utterly content with what I had inside her womb. Perhaps not. Warm, thick amniotic fluid like the water being pumped through my suit. A physical connection to my mother and her bloodstream. Layers of insulation and protection. Me, hanging limp, soothed, safe.

I do not sleep on the seabed although I have done so in the past: in the Caspian Sea, the Gulf of Mexico, off the coast of India when I was trying to work toward my North Sea career. Rather, I daydream with my eyes closed. Steve, Henry, Lisa. *Family*. The trio I think about when I wake in the middle of the night. My thoughts are of them. Always. My breathing has softened as much as it can and my heart rate is that of an adult minke whale: slow and strong. This, here, is what I do and who I am.

Halvor knows not to interrupt a precious moment of peace and solitude. He is a fair man, a diver with many years in Sat, and he has walked in my boots before.

I think back to an early date with Steve, him surprisingly nervous and skittish, stumbling over his words, me entranced by his bright eyes and the fine laughter lines on each side of his lips, each wrinkle pale against his skin. It was July and we were in a pub garden outside Ripley. Wind, and occasional squally showers. He brought his arthritic Labrador, Finn, who wouldn't leave me alone. Lovely old Finn. He was one of a litter Gilly and her partner bred. I wish Finn had lived long enough to meet Henry and Lisa. How he would have adored them both.

I swallow saliva but it goes the wrong way and I have to inhale deeply.

Everything changes all at once.

Can't catch my breath.

Hat too tight.

My back stiffens, straight like a rod, and I cough into my helmet, and then I wheeze again, my eyes bulging in their sockets.

Pressure.

Too much pressure.

The world outside shrinks as my peripheral vision darkens.

"Checking you're OK, Brooke?" says Halvor.

From serenity to dread.

I cannot reply to him.

"Diver One. Come in. Over."

I splutter and wheeze and then my coughing subsides.

"OK," I say, strained, my voice a croak.

"Your gas working, Brooke? Your hot water OK? Your umbilical?"

I clear my throat. I need to equalize my ears, but you can't pinch your nose using your fingers when you're wearing a helmet, so I push my face hard into the section of mask designed for the task and equalize.

"I'm OK," I say, gasping for gas. "Wrong hole. Fine now."

"Very good."

I had a grouper appear once from behind a well when I was

working for an outfit from Louisiana who usually stick to the deepwater fields of Mad Dog. Grouper the size of a darn mini-van. I turned from my welding and its eye flashed past my helmet, an eye the size of my head, and I yelped. That was the first and last time I yelped in Sat. The lads would not let me forget it.

I spend the next two hours removing nuts from the connector. That doesn't sound like a two-hour job, but this deep, in poor visibility, with each nut as tight as it will fit, it is exactly that. My arm is aching and burning by the time the connector finally works free.

"Move your head to the left, Diver One."

I do as he asks.

"More, please. Look down so I can see."

I look down.

"Very good, Diver One. Take a minute for yourself and then we'll connect."

The connection process takes another hour. Everything is unwieldy underwater. Imagine swinging a sledgehammer at the bottom of an ocean, dragging it through water, pushing against all that resistance. It is no wonder we eat as much as we do.

Years ago when I was working in Asia in a three-man Bell, we were swarmed by jellyfish as we climbed back up our umbilicals. At almost five hundred feet deep, the Malaysian diver and I were covered in a cloud of them, and we were both stung all over through our suits by their trailing tentacles. On the ascent, squeezed inside the old-style Bell, I was convinced I was going into anaphylactic shock. The pain was all-consuming. After we locked on and climbed through to the Wet Pot, I requested adrenaline or antihistamines but the only thing they passed through the Medlock was a bottle of chilled Stolichnaya vodka. It did the trick and made the final days of Sat, that grueling period of slow decompression, all the more tolerable. You will not find that form of medical intervention on North Sea ships and rigs, not these days. The only downside was a fellow diver made a pass at me. He wasn't pushy or assertive, but it was out of order. I decided not to take it to management but, once back onshore, I made sure he knew exactly how I felt.

He quit the industry for good the following year.

"Make your way off the manifold, Diver One. Platform has confirmed they're going to test flow in five minutes' time. Off the manifold to a safe distance, please."

If a problem occurs, they don't want me standing right in front of it. I jump off the structure so I can float back down ten or so feet to the seabed.

But something snags.

I spin.

My helmet jerks higher, wrenching my neck so violently it feels like it'll pull my head from my torso, and suddenly there is freezing cold water rushing over my face.

"Everything OK, Diver One?"

I turn to climb back up the manifold, to gain purchase, to relieve the tension on my umbilical, but I keep on falling into the silt below.

Ice-cold water up my nose.

Salt burn.

"Diver One. Everything OK? Please come in. Over."

Darkness.

Nobody to help me but myself.

"Umbilical stuck," I blurt out, my mouth filling with water. "Need to purge . . . hat."

I look up with my helmet light to check what's wrong with my umbilical but I can't see far enough. I have kicked up too much silt and sand from the bottom.

Seawater in my eyes.

"Diver One, take your time. We'll pause on the connection. You take as much time as you need. I can send the Bellman out if you need him."

Gag reflex. Water up to my eye level. Hat filling. I drag myself up my umbilical and then pause, clinging to the side of the structure.

Water creeps higher inside my helmet.

8

I BLOW DOWN my hat with gas.

A sudden, urgent breath.

I gather myself and take back control from whatever dark force stole it from me.

My tube snagged on a junction. When I realize what happened, I smile to myself and work it free and then I can move normally again.

The neck dam must have been pried off during that umbilical snag.

"Hat purged," I say.

"Say again."

"Hat successfully purged. All clear. Over."

"Good work, Diver One. Take a few minutes. Don't get ahead of your hat, now."

I take a series of deep, calm breaths and move higher, pulling myself up by my umbilical, arm over arm, like I am in a tug-of-war battle.

Starfish, everywhere. Orgiastic piles of them.

I take time to rest.

"Your hat feel OK, Diver One?"

"It's good now."

"Umbilical clear? Hot water OK?"

"All fine."

"You want to head back to the Bell now? We can test the connector on the next dive. Almost six hours in. Over."

Dark, thick, cloudy water in every direction. An undersea world the size of France, completely uninhabited. Well, not completely. There might be half a dozen of us down here right now, many miles apart.

"No, let's do it."

"You sure? Happy for you to head back to the Bell if you're worn out."

"Leaving the manifold now."

"Careful with your umbilical. Watch your fingers and your feet, Diver One. Take your time."

I jump free of the structure, making sure my umbilical is clear.

"Walking away now. Over."

"Very good, Diver One."

"I'm clear."

A tangle of rusting metal and yellow cables.

"Testing now, Diver One. Stand by."

My heart settles to something like its usual rhythm under all this water, all this weight. There might be a dozen people on the whole planet in deeper water than I am at this moment, walking around, working. Might be two dozen. I knew a supervisor once in Nigeria. Dutch man, he was. Smart and serious. He had been a Royal Netherlands Navy clearance diver, common enough story. One day off the coast, his offshore career came to an end. One of his divers, an experienced man from Seattle, five years into his Sat career, panicked or lost his mind down on the seabed changing out a pump. Visibility was good. No technical hiccups. He was thirty yards away from the Bell in the middle of his shift when madness grasped him. I do not want to think of his name.

Not because it might be bad luck, I just don't want to think of him too closely while I am down here. The diver, a veteran himself, started babbling and shouting. His Dutch Supervisor tried to calm him, talk him down, but he couldn't make out what he was saying. *Helium screams*, is how he described it to me. The diver squealed and yelled and the Supervisor told the Welsh Bellman to put his helmet on immediately and prepare for a rescue. The diver cried and screeched like he was afraid of something at the south of the Niger Delta. At a depth of three hundred and fifty feet the diver walked farther away from the Bell, and he told the Dutch Supervisor, his voice steady, that he must remove his hat for a while. The Supervisor tried to talk him out of it, tried to tell him help was on its way, reminded him the Bellman was suiting up, he'd be in the water in a few seconds. But the diver took off his hat and drowned. He died with the Supervisor's voice still transmitting desperate pleas through the helmet speaker yards away on the seabed. He died and nobody will ever know what it was that he was so afraid of.

An octopus pushes itself up through the sandy seabed and propels away from me.

I should not think of such things when I am at depth. It is important for me to manage my thoughts. The Dutchman could no longer supervise divers. That experience left a piece of him on the seabed. I should not think of such things in the chamber, either. Like I said, sometimes you are not entirely in control of your own mind.

"Connection test concluded. Flow has resumed. Well done, Diver One."

"Good. I'm exhausted."

"Make your way back to the Bell at your own pace, please."

I had to complete this job today. I have had a dozen worse incidents, half a dozen since I came back from my career break.

They are par for the course as my golfing diver friends would say. Jumbo once told me: *some jobs are smooth and some are rough.* It is not possible to avoid stressful incidents but it is possible to deal with them professionally. Panic is our constant enemy and there is no option to go up on your own.

That primal instinct must be denied.

I climb my umbilical and my forearms are burning from loosening and then tightening the nuts. On the clump weight I unclip tools and stash them in the mesh box for the next diver.

Never leave tools on the seabed.

Never leave *anything* on the seabed.

As I face this three-ton weight, with the stunted ladder up into the Bell mere yards away, everything darkens. A shoal of finger-size fish dart away and hide behind the Bell. A sensation of something behind me. Something even larger than the Diving Bell. The fish are skittish. I walk, my heart in my throat, to the base of the ladder. I am in its shadow now, something gray and prehistoric, something colossal with unblinking eyes.

The gravity of whatever it is.

The immense shadow it casts.

I force myself to speak. "Entering Bell now."

I sense it move.

Somewhere behind me: a heart, a brain, a *mouth.*

9

HALVOR'S VOICE. "DIVER One coming up now, Bellman."

I make my way up the ladder rungs quicker than I usually do and stand up—half in the Bell, head inside; half in the wild undersea world, legs in the water—that shadow still moving effortlessly around me.

I cannot see but I sense it by my boots.

"Up you come," says André.

I grab hold of the two knotted ropes I used earlier to access the Bell from the Wet Pot below, and heave myself up. From weightlessness to extreme lethargy, the heavy hat causing my neck to bend. André disconnects the clips and pins holding it in place and lifts it off my shoulders. The relief of that. I climb in fully and help drag up what remains of my umbilical.

"You look dog-tired, Brooke."

"Well, you look old."

He grins and I notice how straight and white his teeth are, even the front ones with the gap in between. Many saturation divers live fast and loose, many are borderline alcoholics, but we all look after our teeth. The last thing you want on a monthlong saturation job is an acute toothache.

He passes me a large bottle of water and I drink it down in one go.

"Eels?" he says.

I shake my head. "Something much bigger."

He nods and we say no more about it.

"Leaky hat?"

"Yeah."

He passes me a towel to dry my hair. Most of it is sweat but I don't tell him that.

André's hair was red when I started diving in the North Sea. Then it turned gray. These days it is chestnut brown from a bottle.

"Close the hatch, Bellman," says Halvor through the speaker. He sounds tired himself after that dive.

We do as he asks.

"Hatch secured."

"Roger that."

"Well handled, Brooke," says André. "Good dive."

I lean against the wall, the gear, the gauges, the coiled umbilical. "Wasn't a good dive."

"You got the job done."

I close my eyes and breathe the stale, thick gas inside the Bell. Imagine a cup upside down in a bowl of water; that trapped pocket of gas. Now imagine the cup pushed down to the bottom of the sea.

"I want a shower," I say. "A hot shower."

We begin our ascent.

"You ever been rushed by a triggerfish?" asks André.

I shake my weary head. "No. I've seen plenty but never any aggravation."

"Territorial little bastard wouldn't leave me alone. Western Australia. Kept ramming me, rushing me. He was intimidating because I was in his environment, you know. Like an angry, short man in a pub you're not familiar with. Nearly drove me to panic."

"Jellyfish is the worst I've had."

"They're bad, but the triggerfish got inside my head. Like he was the predator and I was the prey down there. Kept on probing, never backing away. He was chasing me around the seabed, couldn't have been more than two feet long if that."

"You got in his face, man."

"I swam off, best I could. Wouldn't leave me alone for two seconds."

"Thought you were after his woman."

He shakes his head and laughs at the memory, but then his face turns serious and he looks up as if to the hull of the ship. "I didn't lose it but I actually got close, if I'm honest. Almost snapped. Just from a small fish."

I drink more bottled water and André turns up the heat in the Bell for me because I am not as warm as I should be. More exhaustion than anything. He wants to chat but I don't have it in me. The reality is as Bellman you become quite bored and lonely. The first two hours are a relief, having some space to yourself, regardless of how steampunk-dystopian and cramped it might be. You are busy prepping the diver and feeding out the umbilical and checking gauges. But then your saturated mind can start playing tricks on you. The pressure, the helium, the blackness outside the tiny porthole. It is not good to be alone with your own ideas and memories for too long in a situation like this. Better to keep busy. Best to be out in the water with arduous work to do.

We both rerack the umbilical neatly for the next divers and then something begins to hiss.

"What is that?" asks Halvor, gruffly, over the intercom.

The hiss intensifies.

"I don't know," I say.

"Fucking leak," exclaims André. "Fuck."

"Close the valves now," yells Halvor. "Shut the valves off."

The Bell is steaming up.

Rapid decompression.

A breach.

The undiluted fear in André's eyes as he hesitates for a split second.

Panic taking root.

10

THE HISSING INTENSIFIES.

We are losing pressure fast.

"Blow yourselves down," says Halvor, his voice urgent.

André shouts something but I can't make out his words through the noise.

I check the lower valves. André does the same with the upper ones.

"Close off those valves now, lads," says Halvor. "Right now, please."

I am lightheaded.

"Fucking hell," says André.

Pain in my ears.

Fog inside the cramped bell. Some kind of mist.

I know what comes next.

"Blow down!" booms Halvor.

It doesn't matter if we are closer to the surface or the bottom. Rapid decompression will kill us both in no time.

"The valves," shouts Halvor. "Concentrate. Shut them off."

I turn off two more and then the hissing stops. It was André who found it. The bilge drain down by the hatch. He saves us both.

"Blow yourselves down right now," says Halvor over the speaker, his voice firm. "Repressurize. Do it immediately."

André blows us down. He is almost convulsing with the exertion and the relief.

"What happened?" he asks, his helium voice even squeakier than usual.

"Keep blowing yourselves down," says Halvor. "You both all right?"

"Yes," we say in turn. But when we catch each other's gaze we both see that glazed veneer of stale terror, that knowledge that we escaped by seconds.

"Keep blowing down," says Halvor, relieved. "Well done, both of you." And then I hear him mumble "*Jaevla*" to himself, cursing in his native tongue, followed by "*Helvete.*"

I have worked with enough Norwegians, on enough Norwegian ships, to understand what he means.

"I thought we were raspberry jam," says André, smiling manically, cackling. "Raspberry jam, mate."

I laugh back equally manically and smack him on the arm.

We both know the details of Byford Dolphin. I think we all ponder that accident from time to time. The way the chamber hatch was opened prematurely in 1983 on a drilling rig, causing explosive decompression. The violence with which one man was sucked through the narrow sliver of an opening; his body torn apart in a fraction of a second, his spine found thirty feet away. We know the diver's liver was discovered all on its own as if placed down. He and his fellow divers were killed instantly, their blood boiling in their veins.

The air warms and we each take a moment.

Silence.

The reflection of two people who almost met their maker.

The Bell emerges up through the moon pool in the center of the vessel and it jolts and swings around due to the rolling seas.

We are not in a storm but one might be brewing.

This is another reason I prefer working in the water to being Bellman. In the water you have to contend with currents, you have to tense your body some days to stay in place and weld. But you are not dangling from a cable, rising and falling with each swell on the surface. Six hours of that can make anyone nauseous.

Checks are done and redone and then the Bell is transferred into position above the Wet Pot.

"Open the door," says Halvor.

We open it and watch as the water in the base of our Bell falls through into the Wet Pot below. Seawater in our bathroom.

We made it back.

"Shut down the valves," says Halvor. "Close the equalizing valve when you leave."

Unwanted images of these valves malfunctioning and us not reacting in time. The resulting carnage. Bone fragments and raspberry jam everywhere.

I purge the picture inside my head.

Deep breaths.

I head down first, my legs not as steady as I want them to be, and then André passes down the helmets to me one by one, his hands shaking. He passes down all our empty plastic water bottles, the sitting hammock, his book. *Leave it how you found it.*

Finally, André steps down the ladder and we close the hatch and secure it.

We stand drenched in sweat, staring at each other.

Just another day.

11

THERE ARE DIVES when you don't feel like you have worked for six hours at the bottom of the sea and then there are dives like today. The adrenaline is draining from my bloodstream and I am left shaken. What I really need is a firm hug from Steve. A coffee made by him. To feel his familiar arms wrapped around me and to smell his neck. The fact I can't have any of it stings.

"You all right, mate?" says André. "That was rough. You look a bit pale."

"That was my fault."

He frowns at me. "Nah. *Life's but a walking shadow.*"

"Sorry?"

"It is what it is. That's what I'm saying."

"The bilge drain valve. The dead man switch wasn't right. I must have knocked the valve with my boot. I nearly killed us both, André."

"No, mate," he says, assuredly. "Bollocks to all that, Brooke, I mean it. Shouldn't be possible, should it? Dead man switch should have been in place. I'll talk to the Super about it, and we'll go over it with Jumbo and Mike and the others. There's no way that was your fault."

I nod, unconvinced, and remove my yellow rubber boots. He does the same with his Wellingtons.

"And when it is our turn, it will be our turn. You know what I mean? Better to go out with a bang than a whisper, that's what my dad used to say. Won't be a bilge drain that does us in."

The rust bothers me. Diving systems are becoming safer and safer. Companies like Kirby Morgan and Gorski are designing, building, and testing gear and intermodular systems with superior materials, safer protocols, and improved flanges. The hardware is so much better than when I started. We have sophisticated ROVs on most of the vessels, multimillion-pound underwater robots capable of filming and completing ultradeepwater work, deeper than we could ever go in Sat. And yet there is still rust. I'm not sure it bothers any of the others. But every connection point to seawater is a reminder of the unrelenting corrosive force of Mother Nature. We can be as futuristic as we like; salt water will always win in the end.

I gesture to his paperback. "You reading how to get rich, André?"

"I'm already rich," he says, a twinkle in his eye. "We all are, aren't we? What I'm learning about is how to become *wealthy*. Subtle difference."

"Investments?"

"Exactly," he says, flicking through the pages of *Rich Dad Poor Dad*. I suspect he saw one of the client company reps with a copy and followed his lead. "Putting our offshore money to work for us. Not relying on a stream of endless jobs, but on passive income. Long-term planning and tangible assets."

"I need a new TV," I say, almost too exhausted to crack a joke. "That count?"

"I'm serious, Brooke. You're late thirties, right?"

"I wish."

"I'm forty-four," he says. "But I look fifty-seven. Eleven years in Sat so far, which must be about double the average. It has taken its toll, in more ways than one. We can't do it forever like Jumbo and Mike, can we? Those fellas are made out of different stuff. And we can't all become supervisors, either. Got to think ahead."

"All right. I liked you more when you spent all your money on beer and Porsches."

"I still have the Porsches."

"I tip my hat to you, André, honest I do. When I got my ticket my instructor told me one in fifty saturation divers become *lifers*. And now I know that lifer really means ten years or more. The ones who survive longer are the exception, not the rule. Might borrow that book after you're done with it."

"I'm only thirty pages in. Give me a week or two."

"You had six hours!" I say.

"I was flicking through *Autocar* for most of that time. What do you think I am, an intellectual?"

"I wouldn't call you that."

In the Gulf of Mexico, or *GOM*, we'd call each other *dude* or *bud* or *brother*. They'd even call *me* brother. In Asia and the Med it was much the same, depending on the crowd. In Nigeria, Australia, and the North Sea *mate* tends to be the norm. But we are brothers and sisters in a strange, dysfunctional way. I had no brothers or sisters of my own growing up, but this rabble are more like siblings than anything else I have known.

"Raspberry jam," says André. "With bits."

I shudder. "Don't you dare."

"Pips and skin."

A loud bang from outside. Either from the deck or Dive Control.

"Need a drink, Brooke, after all that. Proper drink."

"You'll get a strong cup of tea if you're lucky."

A man shouts something unintelligible from the living chamber on the other side of the door. I think it's Mike.

Odd.

Mike never shouts.

"Less eventful dive tomorrow, eh?" says André, approaching the hatch to our living quarters.

If we were two guys we would both strip off our gear here in the Wet Pot and then one would take a shower while the other one waits in the chamber. But we are not two guys, so we have to face opposite walls and change discreetly.

I push our suits into the equipment lock while André opens the hatch.

The vision on the other side stops us both in our tracks.

12

"MEDIC!" YELLS JUMBO.

It takes me a long time to understand what is happening to whom. Spock is standing in the living area, keeping out of the way. He looks unaffected. Jumbo and Mike are crammed into the narrow walkway between our bunks. When I say narrow I mean barely enough room for one person. The curtain has been ripped off the wall. Bedding is strewn all over the floor, and I spot my MP3 player smashed to pieces near Mike's bare feet. At first I thought there had been a fight. We have seen fights before; I have even heard of divers headbutting each other in the Bell.

But this is much worse.

This is Tea-Bag.

My first instinct is to run in and help. I am a trained medic. We all are, I think, at least four of us. But there is no room for me. André and I keep back with Spock.

"What happened?" I ask.

Spock still doesn't look rattled. "We let Tea-Bag sleep late." Even on helium his voice is robotic and flat. "After the lifeboat drill last night he and Jumbo slept in. We thought they were both asleep."

"Trauma shears," says Mike, gruffly.

Jumbo retrieves the first aid kit. I can't even see what is happening never mind get involved. We are constrained by the extreme physical limitations of our environment.

"Status update, please, lads," says Halvor through the speaker.

Mike slices through cotton.

"No pulse," he says.

Spock repeats to Halvor, "No pulse," through the microphone.

"Medic's on her way," says Halvor. "Any second now."

I thought it might be a fire. When André and I returned from the Wet Pot I sensed smoke for some reason. A diver friend from Italy told me once how he thinks that would be the worst way to go. It is a constant possibility. We can't bring hair oil or aftershave into the chamber for that very reason.

The Banned List is extensive.

Mike counts as he performs chest compressions, his tattooed forearms rigid, pushing down hard into Tea-Bag's sternum. He will likely break several of his ribs today.

Come on, young man.

"Twenty-seven, twenty-eight, twenty-nine, thirty," says Mike, removing himself from Tea-Bag's lifeless body.

Jumbo replaces him immediately, pushing a bag valve mask firmly over Tea-Bag's mouth and nose. Jumbo has already connected the valve mask to *BIBS*, our *Built-In Breathing System*, and he squeezes twice to give the young diver two deep breaths. Then he moves out of the way.

Mike continues chest compressions. Our chamber feels smaller than ever. I could reach out and touch any one of these five men. I am shoulder to shoulder with André and Spock, but if I lean I will touch Tea-Bag's socked feet, each sock jerking violently with every chest compression, or Mike's shoulder, his tendons and muscles protruding, or Jumbo, the smallest and oldest of our number, standing by with the mask, his face a picture of both hope and despair.

Five complete cycles of thirty chest compressions followed by two bag valve mask breaths. I know the protocol. We have trained for this a hundred times.

"No pulse," says Mike, again, as he resumes compressions.

"No pulse," repeats Spock to make sure Halvor understood.

Halvor does not reply because he knows what we are doing. There is no window or camera pointing into the bunks section of the chamber—they afford us that limited degree of privacy for the month we are locked in—but he knows. Halvor does not speak when there is nothing more to say.

Gonzales, the medic, pushes her face up against the glass of our porthole, the one by the Medlock.

"Any pulse yet?" she asks.

Spock replies through the microphone. "Not yet."

Gonzales replies, "Passing epinephrine shots into the lock now."

This is the next protocol. Defibrillators do not work in saturation chambers. Maybe they will develop something next year or maybe it will take a decade. But for us, defibrillators haven't been signed off as either safe or effective.

Spock opens the Medlock and retrieves the syringe.

"Give the shot after the next cycle," urges Gonzales.

Spock stands upright holding the needle as Mike continues to work.

"Come on, damn it," grunts Mike through gritted teeth. "Stay with us, brother."

Jumbo joins in. "Come on, lad. Keep fighting. Come on, matey."

Seconds pass by like hours, hours like seconds. There is no sense of scale inside this airtight capsule. Perspective: abandoned. I imagine the lifeless blood inside the patient's vascular system, a portion pumping incrementally around his body thanks to Mike's actions.

Artificial circulation.

A worthwhile farce.

"You want me to take over?" André says to Mike.

Mike shakes his head without looking back at us. He is drenched in sweat, droplets falling from his nose and the whiskers on his chin. His sleeveless Metallica shirt is saturated.

Jumbo uses the mask again.

They repeat the cycle one more time, and then André and Spock take over.

They check for a pulse.

"No pulse," says Spock, because we always say things out loud. Communication is key. "Adrenaline now?"

Gonzales says, "Affirmative. Give it."

"Epinephrine administered now."

Spock pushes the needle into Tea-Bag's bare chest and then he recommences chest compressions. Mike sits opposite me with his head in his hands.

He already knows.

We all do.

The chamber is eerily calm. After a while I take over the bag with Jumbo doing compressions, his green, decades-old tattoos bulging and stretching with each push. We continue for twenty minutes. For forty minutes. For an hour.

Gonzales has run through to Dive Control to consult with Halvor.

"I think that's it," says Halvor, his voice deep and slow through our speaker. "You can stop now, lads. Time to call it."

Mike stands up and checks Tea-Bag's neck for a pulse.

We take it in shifts to do CPR for another forty-five minutes.

No talking.

We do not give up on our youngest diver.

Eventually we glance at each other and then at Tea-Bag's gray face.

His young, smooth, gray face.

We don't discuss the decision. We do not utter a single word.

We simply stop.

13

MIKE PUNCHES HIMSELF hard in the thigh.

We congregate in the cramped living area and Jumbo says, "Boss, can I put the curtain back up?"

I understand what he means. We are too close to the body. The proximity is horrific because we have nowhere to run, no opportunity to put any meaningful distance between us and the young deep-sea diver we have left on the floor. Imagine being locked inside a small box room with a corpse and five other adults. We need a curtain, however flimsy: a barrier to afford him some dignity.

"Leave it as it is for now, please. The Superintendent is on the phone to Aberdeen for instructions."

We sit, dejected, on the rigid benches that flank our chamber. Any memory of my umbilical being trapped, the Bell valve failing, feels like a lifetime ago.

In this world, everything can change in an instant.

I know this only too well.

Halvor's face at the porthole. His neat white beard. "I am very sorry," he says, with all the gravitas and quiet stoicism of a grandfather or town elder. "You did everything you could."

I stifle tears, pushing my face into the crook of my arm, squeezing my eyelids tight to deny myself the release of crying.

We say nothing.

"You OK?" asks Jumbo.

I sniff and remove my arm and then I nod.

"They are talking to the Procurator Fiscal onshore. We will know how to proceed in the next several minutes. Hang tight, please, lads."

I have seen dead bodies before. We all have. Mike in Iraq. Jumbo in the Falklands but also in the North Sea. André on the *Estonia* wreck. Spock had to stay in Sat once at the end of a job and then steam east to go search for a helicopter and its passengers at the bottom of the sea outside Shetland. I first saw a corpse in Nigeria on the deck of our ship. A crane accident. Next one was on a platform in the Mexican Gulf, somewhere outside South Marsh Island. One deceased and another guy in a coma. Each incidence adds scar tissue to what you had accrued before. This day will scar us all again.

"Just started," says Jumbo, cutting the silence, his voice unsteady. "Was a good kid, was Tea-Bag. Just got his ticket. Hadn't paid off his course fees yet."

Nobody says anything.

Jumbo has been known to lend his own money to divers so they can pay for their courses. He even helped me and Steve dig out our garden pond by hand. He has been known to help divers in many different ways.

Five minutes later the Life Support Technicians ask if we would like some hot water to make tea and we tell them we do not.

"What's a Procurator Fiscal?" I ask, aware of the title but vague on its exact meaning.

"Like a coroner," says Spock, without emotion. "Scottish version of a coroner, similar to a DA."

Mike rubs his eyes with his knuckles.

"Lads," says Halvor, now back in Dive Control. "We've heard

back. We are to leave Javad where he is for the time being. Don't cover him or change anything for now. I am going to start decompression. You will all be out in four days. I am sorry it ended this way."

Our faces: the emotions complex and changing, but poorly mixed. *Oil and water*. The two substances we live by. I look around. Expressions of relief that we will be out soon. Four days. But also anxiety that we may not be paid. I know that must sound heartless but it is what we are thinking, part of what we are dealing with. We are usually paid a daily rate for each day *in the bin*. People have bills to pay, alimony they are behind on, gambling debts to settle, loan sharks who won't listen to excuses, not even this one. I look around. Other, more subtle emotions. Happiness that they will see their families soon and disgust that they can embrace that same happiness at a time like this. Reflection, sadness, horror, guilt.

The full gamut.

Did he have a preexisting condition that wasn't picked up through medical checks? A congenital heart defect or a partial blockage in his brain? It could happen to any one of us. Scientists still don't fully understand the myriad effects of pressure changes on human physiology.

Gonzales appears at the fist-size porthole. "You did everything according to procedure as far as I could tell."

I frown. *As far as I could tell?* What does she mean by that?

"I'm here with you," she says. But she is not. Far from it. "Anyone need anything? A mild sedative? If so just let me know, please."

We do not let her know.

I remember being in Sat years ago, in my early days, with a man called Big Jim. He was as tall as André, and he never married or had children. He was extremely close to his Irish parents, who had moved to live in Portsmouth, and he spoiled them with his paychecks. Then one day, working on the Norwegian pipelines, he was told by our supervisor that his mother had been killed in a train derailment. Big Jim was the most reliable man I had ever seen underwater, as cool and collected as Spock, as experienced as Jumbo, but he spun out of control at the news. He demanded an accelerated decompression but that request was turned down. Jim spiraled. He was in no danger himself, but that was the moment he lost control of his own psychology. I wasn't a qualified diving medical technician back then but three of the other divers in the chamber were. One of them sedated Jim, against his will, and he stayed like that for the rest of the decompression time. It was painful to see him moaning in his bunk, slurring and crying.

Sometimes we are forced to take actions that would seem unthinkable, or at the very least disproportionate, to anyone unfamiliar with our line of work.

"He was fit," says André. "Young lad. Looked fitter than me, that's for sure. Could do dozens of pull-ups."

Normally there would be insults and jokes back and forth. Construction site humor.

Not today.

I look beyond into our disheveled sleeping quarters.

He lies among bedsheets and syringe wrappers. His skin is dark red. That could be the effect of the pressure, or it could be from whatever medical condition killed him.

I do not wish to push Halvor, but if he doesn't receive instructions soon about what we should do with the body I don't think I will sleep a wink over the next four days.

I am not sure what would be more unnerving: seeing him down there, lifeless and unmovable; or sleeping a few feet away from a stripped, empty bed.

14

GONZALES TALKS THROUGH the speaker. "Are the rest of you feeling OK physically? Any chest pain or breathing difficulties?"

Jumbo touches his throat.

Mike stretches his shoulders.

Autonomic responses.

The crew outside are concerned about the gas mix we are breathing. If you saw the tanks room you would worry too. Old metal tubes full of high-pressure concoctions, the exact ratios created specifically, by a man, for each trip. The elaborate pipework seems to be ancient and decaying, the gauges analogue rather than digital. An analogue gauge—a needle moving around a dial—is more reliable than a digital equivalent, which is why we use them, but they do not inspire confidence in an era of screens and computing.

"I feel physically normal," says Jumbo, tears in his eyes.

"Same," says Mike.

André looks at us all, then at the cooling corpse a few feet from where he sits, and then he says, "My lungs feel OK."

Spock rubs an eyebrow with his fingertip and says, "I am fine."

I say, "No pain or discomfort. Do you guys know what happened to him?"

She does not reply to my question. Eventually Halvor's voice appears. "We are talking to the onshore authorities right now, guys. Health and Safety Executive are on the line. I will do my best to keep you informed. Right now this weather system is building steam so you may experience some movement. The Bridge will work to stay as far away from it as possible." A long pause. He's probably talking to someone else. "Medic suggests you all have a hot drink at a minimum. Tea, coffee, sugar. We are sending two pots of hot through."

They mean one or more of us could go into shock. It is not merely the tragic loss of life, of *young* life, it is the fact we must sit in such close quarters with the body and we cannot leave. Someone dies in a hospital or in a workplace accident and the survivors are separated from that cadaver immediately to receive care, attention, police scrutiny. We are not kept with our dead, and for good reason.

The two pots of hot are pushed through the Medlock.

Jumbo makes us tea and coffee because it is his turn and nothing will change that.

I think about the training we have all received. Extensive and repeated protocols for how to deal with a hot water suit failure at depth, how to deal with a crushed diver, an emergency Bell ascent, a slow leak, hypothermia in the Bell, the loss of a digit and how to sew up the wound, blown eardrums, rotting feet. The most haunting, for me at least, was training to give CPR in the Diving Bell itself. I have trained for this many times and it is never less than harrowing. A Bell has no flat, hard surface to lay someone down on. It is round and packed full of gear. The best solution they've come up with is less than ideal, to put it mildly. The unconscious diver is hung from the ceiling by his harness. A cervical collar is placed around his neck, and a pharyngeal airway is inserted. Then the Bell is flooded with seawater to reduce the pooling of blood in the injured diver's body. Following that the healthy diver must perform CPR by holding the unconscious diver firmly and pushing his head into their chest. You literally headbutt them back to life in a flooded Bell because that, apparently, is the best available option. If the unconscious diver is slumped or your head is too high relative to their chest then the protocol is to use your knee to perform chest compressions. You have to knee your strung up pal in the heart over and over again as hard as you can.

I would be lying if I told you I haven't had nightmares about it.

Four of us: me and Spock, André and Jumbo, all drink strong tea with extra sugar. Using glances, and subtle pats on arms and shoulders, we check in with each other. Jumbo looks the most shaken, but I can also detect that André is chewing at the inside of his mouth or grinding his teeth because his cheeks are bulging. The stainless-steel water pot they sent through is dented from the pressure change. Mike, inherently resistant to change, sips his black coffee. It has been a decade since Steve urged me to try Yorkshire tea. He did it stealthily. I drank strong drip coffee back then and cappuccinos in the morning from a machine near our stove. He would bring me up tea in the morning on a tray, sometimes with a candle and a chocolate chip shortbread cookie. It was a joke at first but I grew to love it and now, even when I travel back to the States to see family, I pack a box of Yorkshire tea bags.

The chamber creaks.

Exhaustion hits me in waves. Usually I would rest in my bunk after a strenuous dive, having first showered and eaten. We tend to rest a lot. But I cannot eat yet and there is no way I can rest on my bunk with him still in that position, lifeless on the floor.

"You know what they're going to ask us to do next," says Mike.

"Lifeboat," says Jumbo.

"He was a big lad," says André, concerned.

They are right. We will soon be asked to place him in a

body bag and attach him to a stretcher and then maneuver him through tight vertical, kinked trunking into the hyperbaric lifeboat above the chamber system. We know this is coming because, again, we have repeatedly trained for it. But we have never actually done it for real. There is a significant difference between training with someone who will adjust themselves or help you out along the route, knowingly or unknowingly, and lifting genuine *dead weight*.

"Lads, listen up, please," says Halvor. "We are passing through a new camera in the Medlock. We are going to need one of you to photograph Javad from as many angles as possible, urgent request from onshore. It is a digital camera with a large memory card and we need you to take as many pictures as you can without touching or disturbing him. Any volunteers?"

Spock says he will do it.

I recall how he has an underground darkroom at home. Spock doesn't speak much about his hobbies, but he did tell me one night last year about his passion for photographing castles and ruins, and bleak landscapes. He mentioned Forres, Dunsinane, and Fife.

Spock opens the hatch and takes out the camera, familiarizing himself with the settings and dials. Unlike the rest of us his fingernails look manicured. He takes ten minutes to photograph Tea-Bag from every conceivable angle, some shots with flash and others with harsh yellow-tone chamber lighting. We watch as he looms over the body, one white-socked foot on either bunk, careful not to touch him. Then Spock passes the camera back through in the Medlock.

"Lads, you all still feeling OK physically?" says Duncan, the Superintendent.

We all say we are.

"Aye," he says, with a thick Argyll accent. "Before we go

ahead and transfer the deceased to the lifeboat for accelerated decompression, I'm told we're going to need to do something else, something we haven't ever trained for. I'm going to hand you back to Halvor for the briefing. Over."

Mike and Jumbo look at each other, then they both look at me.

"The Super is on the phone to Aberdeen now," says Halvor. "They have an incident room set up. In this weather they cannot get people out to us on the ship and as we cannot get Javad out of Sat quickly enough we are going to have to do something . . . irregular."

"Tell us," says Mike. "And we'll do it."

"It is not the norm but I am told there is no alternative. It has been signed off on by the top."

"Tell us," says André.

"There is no alternative, I am afraid."

We wait.

"I am going to talk you through specific details so you can conduct what I have been told is called a remote autopsy."

15

WE STARE AT each other.

"Repeat that, please, boss," says Jumbo. "We didn't catch what you said."

A long pause.

We hear the tail end of him double-checking with the Super, who himself is most likely asking for confirmation from someone senior in Aberdeen.

"Because the hyperbaric lifeboat will take days to decompress, even if we accelerate the process, we will have to take several samples immediately. I am being told the extended time under pressure, and the deco, will affect the chemistry of Javad's bodily tissues."

We do not answer.

What is there to say?

Mike sits looking down at his feet, at his black Reebok flip-flops, and he shakes his head.

"Gonzales is going to help walk you through the procedures step-by-step." Halvor is doing his best to make this seem normal. "I am told it is the only way. We need this done quickly, respectfully, and carefully. We have been told repeatedly, from several officials, that we must do everything we can to minimize contamination."

Gonzales appears again on the other side of the porthole. She has bags under her eyes and a sore developing on her lip.

"We will send through the evidence collection kit we keep on board. I am also sending extra wide–bore pipettes, nitrile gloves, disposable hypodermic syringes, face masks, and sterilized containers."

The five of us use alcohol wipes to clean our hands.

A few seconds later Spock opens the Medlock.

"Please put on the gloves and mask up before you touch the other items."

The Super's voice in the background. Duncan and Halvor have worked with each other for many years.

We do as Gonzales asks. It is lucky we don't tend to suffer from claustrophobia because wearing skintight gloves and masks while locked inside an already cramped pressurized chamber, with a body, in a storm, breathing thick gas, is enough to turn anyone deranged.

Halvor and Gonzales talk through procedures, with a brief interlude as the onshore pathologist guides them. They explain over and over about sealable evidence bags, how to handle swabs, how to deal with Tea-Bag's personal belongings, how to ensure the chain of custody is kept as clear and transparent as possible by completing steps in the correct order.

The chain of custody.

I suspect that nomenclature is used in relation to all forms of physical evidence collection, and Halvor wasn't referring in any way to *humans* being held in custody, but still it puts me ill at ease. Did something happen when André and I were down in the Bell?

Halvor asks for one of us to volunteer to take the samples. He says this is important to minimize the risk of cross contamination. Spock volunteers. He does not mention that he is the most medically qualified because he does not need to. We all know it. Once again, he is the right man for the job.

I sit on the bench, hungry, cursing myself for acknowledging my base needs at a time like this.

"Should the rest of us wait in the Wet Pot, Chief?" asks Jumbo.

"No, I am told we are to keep the hatch closed until the evidence collection has been completed. Unless it is an emergency you four remain on the benches. Brooke, we need you to film the procedure on your camcorder."

"I don't feel comfortable with us, you know, cutting the lad open," says Jumbo, clearing his throat. "Honestly, I don't. Not inside here. I think that should wait."

No reply from Halvor for a few seconds.

"I am told we will not be doing anything like that inside the chamber," he says. "Just collection." His voice goes away for a moment. "Nothing more invasive than drawing fluids."

Mike looks relieved.

We all do.

Spock takes out the needles, swabs, tools, bottles, and bags from the collection kit and places them all down on a bunk itself covered with a thin plastic sheet.

"Are you ready, Leo?" Halvor asks Spock.

"Ready."

"I will pass you to Gonzales now."

She speaks as she watches through the porthole. "The most urgent sample is blood, I'm told. We need to access the blood least affected by postmortem distribution, which means the venous or femoral blood from Javad's leg. Do you understand?"

"Roger that," says Spock.

Gonzales's face is glistening with sweat. "Use the trauma shears to cut the remainder of his pants leg. Take a sample when you're ready. Do you require further details or instruction?"

"No. I'm good."

"We need approximately thirty milliliters."

He cuts through Tea-Bag's pants and then removes a syringe and needle from the wrapper. Mike keeps his head down. He looks strange with no cap. Mike always wears a cap; he removes it at the last possible moment when putting on his dive helmet. Jumbo stares up at the ceiling. André has closed his eyes tight. But because I need to film, I also need to watch. I have no other option.

Spock finds the vein or artery immediately and pulls up the syringe plunger. Tea-Bag's dark red blood fills the barrel. I imagine the blood continuing to come, overwhelming the syringe, pouring onto the floor, up the walls, spraying the ceiling, covering us all. I force the thought away. Spock removes the needle smoothly and bags the sample and seals the bag.

"Blood secured."

My camcorder is filming everything, as per instructions.

Gonzales sounds like she is in control. "Use a cotton swab to collect a sample of any vomit, bile, or saliva excreted from the mouth of the deceased."

Spock is quiet for a while. He does as he is asked and then says, "Swabs collected and sealed."

"Nice job, Leo. Now if you could do the same, please, *inside* the mouth."

Spock takes a deep breath and proceeds. "Mouth swab taken and sealed."

"They are asking if you can use the designated nail scraper on each of his fingernails and then place the scrapings inside a fresh container. If you start to run out of any piece of equipment let me know and we will have more sent down."

Several minutes pass.

Mike and Jumbo check in on each other in the most discreet way imaginable, nodding solemnly.

"Nail scrapings taken and secured."

"Very good. Can you now take approximately a hundred hairs from the head of the deceased, roots and all. I am being told, if possible, you should take from several places on his head so not to leave a bald patch."

Mike looks up now and grins sadly. "I don't think he'll be too bothered."

We all smile.

"Hair samples collected and sealed," says Spock, no emotion in his voice.

I am reminded of a course I attended once in Seattle. It was much of the standard classroom training about Boyle's law and US Navy diving tables. Safety protocols following Piper Alpha, when the whole world's offshore safety measures changed almost over-night, especially in the North Sea. We had an infectious diseases specialist from the University of Washington come to give a guest talk. Spiky black hair and green eyes like a cat. She warned about the almost incomprehensible rate of spread of bacteria in a humid environment like a Bell or a chamber. How repeat cleaning of our hands and surfaces was of paramount importance. We must never share cutlery or utensils. Old food was never to be left around, it was to be removed as quickly as possible via the Medlock. She said she could not imagine a situation where rapid spread of bacterial or viral infection was more likely, and couldn't imagine a situation where catching such an infection was more dangerous. She was brought in to reinforce how important hygiene is during Sat.

It is strange how we are all more at ease now that we have each donned gloves and masks. The scene has been transformed back into what it should always have been: a place where protocols are followed and someone with authority, albeit remotely, is in charge. Control has been reestablished and Spock is performing well.

Halvor comes on to say we should leave Tea-Bag's clothes as

they are. Then Gonzales asks Spock to take a urine sample by plunging a needle deep into the deceased's bladder.

Spock retreats half a step and knocks into the other bunk.

"Is there another way?" he asks. "A catheter?"

Silence. Five seconds. Ten. Then Halvor says, "We're being told this is the only way."

Spock eyes another needle.

"No," he says. "I'm not comfortable with this."

I stand up.

"I can do it."

16

I TAKE SPOCK'S place in the sleeping area and as I do so I nudge Tea-Bag's socked foot. I freeze for a moment. Spock does not meet my gaze as we pass each other, our arms rubbing.

Bedding on the floor. A pillow. My MP3 player. This young man was alive earlier today. He had his whole life ahead of him, a career underwater, perhaps children of his own, perhaps grand-children one day. All those potential lives destroyed.

Some of his skin is pallid and some is still dark red.

Gonzales talks me through what I need to do.

I do as she asks and place the urine sample inside a sterilized container.

Jumbo is filming with my camera.

Halvor then talks us all through the procedure to transfer the containers out via the Medlock. It takes a long time. Each lid needs to be loosened enough so it won't distort from the pressure differential. All of a sudden: another unwelcome image inside my head, this time of a pot of fluid spraying out in all directions, tar-nishing us all, infecting us, and then the aftermath, the cleanup, the never-ending disinfecting. I focus on the task at hand. I do the transfer alone, again, to minimize contamination. Sealed envelopes and cotton swabs in tubular pots. On the other side: the Life Support Technicians, all gloved, help Gonzales tighten lids and organize samples. Methodically, while being filmed, they bag and tag them.

Halvor says, "Well done, all of you."

"What now, Chief?" asks Mike.

"We will be sending through a body bag," he says, his Norwegian accent more noticeable than normal, his voice heavy. "It will take a couple of you to, how do you say, place him inside."

We do not speak. We sit in our gloves and our masks and we say nothing.

"Next of kin?" says Mike.

"We will deal with all that," says Halvor.

The body bag is passed through the equipment lock. It is my understanding that ships of this size have several stored away for such tragedies.

Mike and Spock volunteer to move the body into the bag. It is an extremely awkward process, confined as they are between the bunks, and it takes them some time. Much of the work is done with Mike and Spock perched on the lower bunks. They work quietly and smoothly, trying hard to preserve Tea-Bag's dignity, so far as that is possible. When the zip is moved up and the body enclosed we all breathe a sigh of relief. It is human to crave distance from our own inevitable fate. The barrier between us and what will ultimately become of us, no matter how illusory, is a comfort.

"Shall we move him to the lifeboat, Chief?" asks Mike.

"Not yet," says Halvor. "Awaiting confirmation from Aberdeen. Stand by."

"Can we take off our masks and gloves, at least?" asks André. "It's boiling in here. Breathing isn't easy."

"First I will ask you to place all of Javad's personal belongings in sacks and seal them. We are loading special bags into the Medlock now. Stand by." He talks to someone onshore. "Then we would ask you to strip his bed and process his sheets and pillowcases. All into bags and sealed."

His English is less effortless than usual.

Halvor is shaken like the rest of us.

We do as he asks. A Chelsea FC shirt, a Moleskine notebook, a trio of unopened letters. The process takes longer than I expected because we have no space to work and we do everything we can not to touch or disturb the body bag.

I feel a little unsteady, my blood sugar too low, and as if reading my mind Jumbo asks, "When do you think we can get menus in, boss?"

A crackle through the speaker and Halvor says, "As soon as we're done with this." His voice softens. "Not long now."

Jumbo's request may seem callous, but if we do not have sufficient energy we will not be able to action emergency protocols in case of a storm, or transfer Tea-Bag up into the hyperbaric lifeboat. We need fuel the same way our ship does.

"Camera's dead, Brooke," says Spock.

I check it and he is right. No battery. I thought it had several hours left.

"Camera coming through for a recharge, please, lads," I say.

"Standing by to receive."

"Halvor, will we need to wait for the camera batteries to be full so we can record moving Javad up to the lifeboat?" I ask.

"Checking that with Aberdeen," says Duncan. "Stand by."

Jumbo says, "I could eat a rotten horse."

I don't know if anyone else smiles at this because they are all wearing masks, but I would put money on it.

"Negative," says Halvor. "No need to wait for the camera to transfer the body bag to the hyperbaric lifeboat. It will not be possible for you to safely film that process anyway. Far too tight. You can begin right away. Acknowledge."

"Understood," I say. "Roger that. We'll begin."

"I should be in the water now," mutters Spock, who takes the strain at the head end of the body bag. "I should be taking a nice little swim. Stretching my legs. Doing a backflip off the manifold." He sounds almost whimsical and that is disconcerting in itself. I have never heard Spock sound anything other than matter-of-fact.

To hear him like this is jarring.

Mike takes the feet end. André, Jumbo, and I clear away any obstacles, mainly ourselves, and open up the hatch to the Wet Pot. When they are in there preparing the stretcher, securing the body bag to it, Jumbo says, "I think we can take all this gear off now, can't we?"

"Can we take the PPP off, boss?" asks André.

"Affirmative."

We all pull off masks and gloves and place them in a transparent garbage bag, Hygiene is key. We look like ghouls. Deep mask lines across our faces, hands sweaty and red, eyes tired. Dive Control continues to run through checklists with us to open the hatch in the ceiling up to the lifeboat trunking, and I recall more details about the only time I have ever had exposure to a Procurator Fiscal. It was a decade ago so procedures may have changed since. I expected a pathologist or detective but the Fiscal I saw in court was more like a judge. They seemed to run everything. I was there as a witness. One of our dive crew had been exposed to toxic hydrocarbons at depth and passed out in the Bell on ascent. I wasn't on the dive itself; I was fast asleep in my bunk. When they locked on and came through to the Wet Pot his pulse was faint. He needed a lot of interventions, most of which were orchestrated via telemedicine from an ER doctor onshore. The diver survived decompression but later died in the hospital. A wife and newborn at home in Gateshead. I recall the detailed information we worked through in court. The logbook entries from Dive Control. The exact coordinates of the ship at the moment of the accident. Expert witness statements and recollections from the Life Support Technicians. Annotated photographs of our Bell's interior, and the contaminated hot water suit. The chemical composition of the hydrocarbons. Every single detail of every single medical intervention in Sat: the drugs, how and when they were administered, who administered them, the vitals at different times, the precise gas mix. And now, I expect, all these same details are being meticulously recorded outside the chamber again.

Scrutiny and due process.

Lessons to learn.

"All right, lads," says Halvor. "Take a minute for yourselves. This will not be easy."

17

WE ARE ALL used to *muscling* jobs. On the seabed Dive Control will ask us to carefully jimmy out a connector, or they might ask us to gently push in its replacement. We will give that a try. But then, once they have seen on their screens that it isn't working, we will ask them if we can give it a good kick or a swing from a sledgehammer. They will usually check this diligently with the engineer and offer us a somewhat tentative go-ahead. Then we will get the job done. This, today, will be similar. Moving Tea-Bag to the self-propelled hyperbaric lifeboat is a task that will require technical know-how, teamwork, and, perhaps most importantly, muscle.

We are all physically fit enough to do our jobs. Mike and Spock are the strongest, in that order, and then me and André and Jumbo are all about equally capable. We have to keep in shape because our lives, and the lives of our fellow divers, depend on it.

"You fellas want a Coke or a Red Bull before we tackle this?" asks Jumbo.

We order them through from the Bettys and drink them standing in the chamber, shoulder to shoulder, the body bag still on the floor of the Wet Pot. The drinks are completely flat.

Carbonation does not cope with pressure. But flat Coke is still caffeine and sugar energy.

"I know you lads have been through this, but I am going to guide you on the intercom to make sure," says Halvor.

We all nod.

"Two of you set off to the lifeboat, please."

Jumbo and André start climbing up the ladder through the trunking. I can see Jumbo's Sonic the Hedgehog ankle tattoo, which he got last year to please his granddaughter.

Mike and I make double-sure the strapping on the flexible, narrow-gauge emergency stretcher is secure. We do not want this load falling when we are heaving it up inside the narrow trunking. It would compromise the body but it could also severely injure one of us. The stretcher is bright orange, ready for ship-to-ship transfer or helicopter rescue—the ultimate survival options for everyone except us divers—and it is built from lightweight polymer and aluminum.

We hear Halvor ask André and Jumbo to open and secure the access hatch to the lifeboat.

Mike climbs up the ladder inside the trunking. Like a broad man climbing through air-conditioning ducts above ceiling panels, he squeezes through, wriggling and writhing, and meets up with André and Jumbo. He takes the Maasdam rope of the pulley rescue system. Mike guides the rope down through the trunking until it reaches Spock's outstretched hands.

My training kicks in and I almost check that the injured diver's head is stable and braced. I skip the procedure and we attach the rope to the head end of the stretcher.

I slow my breathing, pursing my lips.

"You feeling OK?" asks Spock.

"Fine," I say.

"You look faint. Want a breather?"

"Long day. I'm good."

He nods, acknowledging with his eyes that I completed a full six-hour dive before all this happened.

When we run through this drill usually one of us is strapped into the stretcher and we are not at pressure. The whole process is exhausting even when breathing air: lifting a full-grown adult using a rope up through a kinked tube, the conditions cramped and close, can be panic-inducing. Imagine wriggling up into a tight cave or drainage culvert. The worst part in an emergency would actually be having to board the lifeboat and close the hatch behind you. The finality of that action. A lifeboat like this one is designed to support divers for seventy-two hours. No more Life Support Technicians to keep an eye on us. No Bettys bringing us food and hot water and laundered clothes. No being at the center of a reasonably large DSV like the *Deep Topaz*, the skilled operators on the Bridge working to avoid storms. We would be rising and falling on a never-ending roller coaster. The seasickness alone would be life-threatening: six of us strapped tight into plastic seats. No porthole or experienced voice through a speaker to reassure. No idea if we'll be picked up or if we'll ever be safely decompressed. The vomit alone would be unfathomable. Everything we've eaten and then the bile and stomach acid. Darkness. A substantial risk that our gases will become out of balance. No gas man to monitor us, you see. No Dive Control. Methane could be an issue. Carbon monoxide and dioxide could end us. Urine and feces. Thick gas, no air, no escape, no space to move. Creeping madness. The boat bucking and diving, spinning in gigantic waves. To avoid deep vein thrombosis from immobility we are trained to perform calf raises and rotations every hour. We would not leave our seats. We'd rely on scrubbers to clean the gas and we'd take anti-muscarinic tablets in a vain effort to prevent the worst of seasickness, that's if there is time to do so. I heard a diver remark once, quite seriously, as though he had given the subject a great deal of thought, how survival at that price might not be worth it.

18

WE DOUBLE-CHECK THAT the Maasdam rope is connected securely to the head end of the stretcher. Like so many tasks offshore, especially in deep-sea diving, this is a joint effort. We are guided by voices from outside, men who once worked inside chambers like this one, but it is up to us to save ourselves on a daily, often hourly, basis.

Mike climbs up through the trunking, his arms scraping the sides. Spock stays down with me. Together we manipulate the rope system to propel the stretcher, in a vertical axis, up through the space. If we hadn't trained for this when things were good we wouldn't be able to do it now when things are not.

Spock looks tired and emotionally drained. I have never seen him like this before.

"You good?" I ask.

"I am."

We work together as a team to ensure the stretcher doesn't get caught on the trunk ladder.

Once the stretcher is up I climb the ladder behind it. The lifeboat is cramped and gloomy when we are here for a drill, crammed in, windowless, but this is extremely challenging. I fight to stay calm. No room to move. The gas is thicker than usual. It is hotter. The space feels impossibly small, like being trapped inside a car trunk or an underground bunker with a caved-in entrance. Pressure from all angles. The constant instinct to scream and run for an exit. There is no exit. The lads manipulate the stretcher and push it to the port seats as per protocol. Reps and sets. You never rise to the occasion; instead you fall back to your level of training.

"Everyone doing OK?" asks Mike.

We each grunt and nod.

"Almost done," says Jumbo.

We stand, stooped, our heads bowed not in reverence but necessity due to the curved ceiling of this pressurized lifeboat. André has sweat dripping off his nose.

"Anyone want to . . . say anything?" asks Jumbo.

We stand, hunched together, looking down at Tea-Bag's body bag on the stretcher. We all have things to say, questions to ask, peace to make with someone or something, but we remain silent.

"Close and secure the hatch on your way out, lads," says Halvor, his voice solemn.

We make our way down the ladder inside the trunking.

"Watch your footwork, please," says Halvor. "Feet and hands."

We arrive back in the Wet Pot and then transfer via the short tunnel into the main chamber.

"Menus in the Medlock," says a Life Support Technician.

Halvor might be on a break now. Or else he is making the necessary arrangements to have the body transferred from the DSV once the accelerated decompression is complete, and once this storm has settled down.

Ordering food is usually a jovial affair. Banter about who orders a salad or a well-done steak. Ribbing each other like schoolchildren because anxiety can often present as juvenile humor.

Mike, Jumbo, and I order steak. All rare, although I doubt we will receive it anything less than medium-well. Spock orders the pork and André opts for chicken. Five orders. Again, there is an empty space on the menu grid staring us all in the face.

We scrub down surfaces and tidy up before the food comes in. We do this for the same reason we had to move the body as quickly as possible. Hygiene. Cleanliness. The constant and meticulous task of disinfecting metal surfaces. We live in a humid bubble and we breathe each other's gas. Make no mistake: this is not air. There is no air for any of us.

Jumbo extends the table, slotting in steel sections, and we sit three on one bench and two opposite.

Out of kilter.

"In the old days," says Jumbo, "they'd sew you up in a sailcloth for a burial at sea. The last stitch would go right through the flesh of your nose to make sure you were really gone."

"Well, that's reassuring," says Mike, straightening his ball cap.

"Lots of people were buried at sea," Jumbo goes on. "More than I expected. H. G. Wells, Alfred Hitchcock. JFK, even."

"Bull," says Mike. "Those folks were dealt with on dry land, at a hospital or base, and then cremated, and then their *ashes* were spread at sea. Not the same thing."

"Did you ever see a proper burial at sea in the navy, Mike?" I ask.

He shakes his head. Then he looks at Jumbo.

Jumbo squeezes his eyelids together and then, with his eyes still closed, asks, "When's that grub coming through?"

Nobody says anything. Not even the Bettys.

Jumbo says, "I was a kid. I didn't see much."

Spock stares at him, his dark eyes intense, his brow furrowed. Then he runs his hand gently over his cowlick.

"We sailed down from Portsmouth, led by *Invincible*, our flagship," Jumbo goes on. "We were a very small part of the taskforce, really. Thousands of civilians waving Union Jacks to see us off. Never actually thought we'd go to war. Not war, proper. After Ascension Island, we steamed south. The Chaplain talked to some of the boys, helped them work through stuff. Demons, I suppose you might say. Decent man, that Chaplain was. Black Country lad. Anyway, in the thick of it I remember being on deck for a burial, sunny and calm, I was standing close to the action, and the Chaplain said something like *we commit his body to the deep*. Then he said some other biblical words and verses I can't remember, but he left us with *when the seas shall give up her dead*. I remember the hairs on the back of my neck standing up. Me, a young kid from Liverpool, third of six lads, no real education or talent, watching history in the South Atlantic."

"Two pots of hot in the lock," says a voice.

André opens the small hatch and brings through the hot water. He makes tea and coffee for us all because he is closest and it is his turn.

"I never saw anything like that, not in combat, not even close," says Mike. "But we had a retired officer buried at sea off the coast of North Carolina, somewhere east of Cedar Island. I didn't hear the liturgy, but I remember the Officer of the Deck calling out *All hands bury the dead* and that hit me like a ten-ton wagon. *All hands bury the* goddamn *dead*. The ship's flag was at half-mast. Cloudy day in the East Atlantic, ring-billed gulls squalling as they battled against the wind. Bugler started up. The gulls looked stationary up there in the sky, battling not to go backward. You talk about goose bumps and hairs standing up, brother, I felt the exact same thing. Firing party. And then the burial itself."

We don't say anything for a long time.

The food is passed through in aluminum foil containers. We have five cans of flat soda. They pass through six sets of cutlery by mistake and we have to sit there with a knife and fork and spoon on the table where our young friend should be seated. André covers it respectfully with a paper napkin.

"Lads, I don't want to disturb your chow, but two things," says Halvor. "One, we've lost live radio for your bunk headphones but the music still works. We're working on a fix, and if you need your MP3s charged just let us know. Second, we have a tele-chaplain service via the phone for anyone who needs to talk. I will leave that with you."

We begin eating; we don't even look up from our containers. Sometimes you forget that every word you say inside this place is overheard and scrutinized. Some of the things said will even be noted down in a logbook in Dive Control. They have a responsibility to look after us while we are at pressure.

That extends to our fragile minds.

The last thing you want in a saturation chamber is a diver going berserk.

19

I AM NOT sure if it is the pressure or the delayed shock that makes us eat so much. Perhaps it is merely the fact that this is what we do in here. Eat, work, sleep. At least I have earned it being the only one to actually make it into the water.

You wouldn't believe me if I described the portions. Square containers, the kind of things you might cook a party-size lasagna in, loaded with mashed potatoes, string beans, steak, meat sauce, chicken wings, and french fries. Bread rolls on the side.

We eat like this might be our last meal.

André pushes away his fruit salad and says, "I'm stuffed. Any objections if I take the first shower?"

We all shake our heads. Mike says, "Don't take all the hot water, eh."

He is joking. One thing we do not have a shortage of on board a DSV is hot water. André asks for a stack of fresh towels, large, and they are duly provided for us via the Medlock. He takes one for himself and disappears through the hatch for some *relatively* private time.

And then there were four.

Two on each side of the chamber, the table in between covered with food containers, cans of flat soda, and a fresh copy of *Time* magazine.

Spock turns to Jumbo and says, "You had burials at sea in the Falklands conflict? I never knew that."

Jumbo says, "It's a forgotten war, Leo. I still have mates who never got over the trauma. Lost other mates for the same reason. My pals can't forget it. Civilians can't remember it."

Mike keeps looking at his food and chewing each mouthful slowly, thoughtfully.

"How many burials did you see out there?" asks Spock.

Mike stops chewing for a moment. His breathing deepens and his temples throb. He keeps on eating.

"Just one. There were a few burials at sea that took place, on various ships. It was a long time ago, mate. Not dozens or hundreds, not like in World War II. But one is too many." He opens his eyes wide to stifle whatever emotion is welling up. "Seeing lads wrapped up like that and then shunted into the water. There's something about working your whole career to avoid people going overboard and then one day making that same thing happen. The officers keep it as respectful and dignified as possible. I don't reckon the cloth gets stitched through the lad's nose anymore, but I did hear a rumor they still weigh the body down with a cannonball or two. I don't reckon that can be true; where the hell would you find a cannonball on a modern warship? But you never know with the Royal Navy, do you?" He smiles. "Makes you think."

"Stitch through the nose," I say, shuddering.

André comes through wearing his towel around his waist. "Shower's free."

"Yes, we noticed," says Spock. "Anyone mind if I take it?"

We let him take it.

André sits down. It is not unusual for me to find myself on a bench like this one wedged between two divers wearing nothing but a towel. I came to terms with this years ago. I never had any problems with my fellow divers, but I did once have an inkling I was being watched by a Betty when changing in the Wet Pot. I will never know for sure, but after that day I started using a Post-it on the porthole glass. Finally, when a supervisor told me I couldn't do that anymore, they needed to be able to see in at all times in case of an emergency, I taught myself how to rig up an extra towel and then shower facing the wall. *Make the best of what you have with what you've got* as Steve and Gilly's dad used to say. *Don't let perfect get in the way of good.*

"What were you guys saying about *nose stitches*?" asks André the Giant, pouring from the water jug the Bettys just pushed through the Medlock. "Someone's been in a scrap?"

"Not those kinds of stitches," I say. "Old navy tradition. Last stitch on the sailcloth through the sailor's nose to make sure he isn't just taking a power nap."

"If I fall over you guys have permission to put a needle and thread straight through my face," says André. "Make double sure I'm not just knocked out, OK? I can look pretty dead when I'm fast asleep, so my ex-wife says. Stitch it. Cross-stitch to make sure."

Mike, without lifting his chin, says, "It's said folks in the old days were buried alive from time to time."

"At sea?" I say.

"It's possible," he growls. "But I meant on land. It's known caskets were dug up years later with fingernail scratches all over the insides. I read about one that had a message drawn in blood right on the wooden boards above the face of the deceased."

André puts his water down. "Have you been reading the *National Enquirer* again, Mikey?"

Mike takes a spoonful of fruit salad and swallows it without much chewing. "It was a genuine concern. If people had enough money they'd order a custom casket with a hole and a cord up to ground level connected to a bell. They'd even pay night watch-men in advance to sit by the bell."

"Bullshit," says Jumbo.

Mike looks up at him, his eyes barely visible in the shadow of his cap.

"I never heard of grave bells," I say. "Bells?"

Mike looks down at his fruit salad. "Some folks, we are talking nineteenth-century Europe, rich noblemen and merchants, some of them installed staircases down to their crypts with a small window. Again, they'd pay a servant to watch out for any breaths clouding the glass."

"I think," says Jumbo, "we should talk about football. Liver-pool, in particular."

The yellowish lights flicker on the wall. The bulbs don't last long at this pressure.

"I read about a mother who lost her young daughter," Mike goes on. "Installed stairs down to her child. Used to go sit down there and read bedtime stories to her girl, and comfort her, if that makes sense, during thunderstorms. Then, when the mother died herself, they buried her close to her child and bricked up the window, leaving just the stairs. I saw a photo of it. Stairs down to nowhere."

"Lads," I say, pushing the remainder of my cheese and biscuits to one side on the narrow table. "Maybe Jumbo's right. Maybe we should change the subject. I can't handle this."

They look apologetic.

Spock opens the hatch and walks through in his towel.

"What subject?" he says.

"Little Victorian girls," I say, sternly. "Dead ones."

Spock frowns.

Mike takes off his cap. "Time for my shower."

20

I REQUEST THEY switch the hot water on so I can shower. My Dopp kit, or wash bag, is no larger than Mike's or Spock's. I wash my hair with Head & Shoulders and scrub down with an unscented shower gel. This is a survival technique. It may be cowardice of some sort, I'm not sure. I have always been aware I need to fit in with the lads and not stand out. I decided early on I'll volunteer for the toughest tasks nobody else wanted, and I'll work as hard, if not harder, than my fellow divers. It's not fair, but as my mom never failed to remind me: *life's not fair, honey*. If there was another female Sat diver in the North Sea I would ask her if she avoids scented lotions and gels like I do. I would ask her how she deals with her period when she's in Sat and if the pressure makes any difference to her cramps. But there is no other woman working at depth in the North Sea right now so I adapt and get the job done.

After I wipe down the Wet Pot I pop the hatch, and, holding the rail above the opening, slide myself through the short chute into the living chamber. Jumbo and Mike are in their bunks but their curtains are open. There is a low-level background hum. It is akin to white noise, I suppose, and that, in combination with strenuous manual labor, means we generally sleep like clubbed seals. That is a distasteful idiom I picked up from a Norwegian air diver and for some reason it stuck.

André is playing a game of Snake on his new Nokia cell phone, his thick-framed tortoiseshell reading glasses perched on the tip of his nose. Spock is reading the *Financial Times*. I consider cracking a lame joke, something about investments and bond portfolios, but I am too worn out.

"Lads, don't get too comfortable," says Malcolm, the Night Super, through the speaker. André and I look at each other. This usually means we have an emergency drill to tackle. BIBS, or an imaginary fire to extinguish, or similar. At least we know we can't have a lifeboat drill as it is already decompressing. "We have Detective Chief Inspector Adrian MacDuff on the phone from Grampian Police. He needs to talk to you all individually. Standard procedure. He wanted me to tell you that the Procurator Fiscal has requested him to investigate but that no determination has been made that Javad is the victim of a crime." We glance at each other. Jumbo's eyes widen. The Night Super goes on, as if reading from his notes, "This procedure is followed when a death is unexpected or sudden. We're going to conduct these conversations from the TUP chamber one by one and have them done as soon as possible so you can go to bed. The Chief Inspector would have preferred to do these in person, he says, via the porthole of the chamber, eye to eye, so to say, but the storm is delaying his transit so he will talk to you via our unscrambler so he can understand your answers. Make sure to speak closely and clearly because the unscrambler only gets us halfway, as you know. We're going to do this in alphabetical order. Joe Atkins first." That's André. "Then Leo Babic." Spock. "Followed by Ellen Brooke." Yours truly. "Then Mike Elliot. Then Gary Pritchard." He means Jumbo. "Joe, make your way to the Wet Pot, please, and I will set up the call."

André stands up.

Mike and Jumbo remain in their bunks, reading. Spock looks at me as I dry my hair with a towel. His face is impassive.

André opens the hatch and slides himself through to the Wet Pot.

"Standard bullshit," says Jumbo in an effort to allay our unspoken concerns. "I must have been through half a dozen of these over the years. HSE and all that. This is how they're making it safer for us, I guess."

Ten minutes later André emerges, ashen-faced, and says to Spock, "You're next."

Spock disappears through.

"Pot of hot, please," says André to life support.

"Coming up."

"Long bloody day," mutters André, his head bent against the ceiling. "Wish I was working in the morning. Should be my turn to get wet."

"At least you've been down, bud," says Mike. "Rest of us never got to leave the ship."

Spock emerges after five minutes and I am asked to go through.

"Close the hatch, Ellen."

Of course I'm going to close the hatch. Night Super is a piece of work. I take a breath. I am exhausted but I cannot lose my cool.

Another deep breath.

"Patching through the call now. Next voice you hear will be DCI MacDuff's."

"Ellen Brooke?"

"Yes," I reply, half expecting him to say, *I am arresting you on suspicion of the murder of Javad Assar, you do not wish to say anything but . . .* I take another long, slow inhalation. I really need to keep my head in check. *Don't get ahead of your hat, Brooke.*

"My name is DCI MacDuff of Grampian Police. Sorry to do this so late on what must be a difficult day. I merely have a few questions."

"OK."

He has a slight lisp.

"Talk me through what happened when you arrived up in the Diving Bell after your shift, if you could."

"André, that's Joe Atkins, and I finished our dive and ascended. We had a problem with a valve, it was my fault, and—"

"Sorry to cut you off but it's hard to understand you. Did you say *valve*? What *exactly* was your fault?"

I bite my lip. "The Bell started to decompress. I had nudged the bilge drain valve and we had to shut it off manually and blow down. We weren't hurt."

"Go on."

"André and I entered the Wet Pot, as we call it, or the TUP chamber and put our helmets and suits into the equipment lock. And then we opened the hatch to the living chamber."

I pause.

"Go on, please."

"We found them doing CPR on Javad."

"When you say *them*, who was doing CPR?"

"It was Mike at that time. Mike Elliot."

"Chest compressions or mouth-to-mouth?"

"Chest. Jumbo, sorry, Gary Pritchard, was helping with the mask. Like we've been trained to do."

"And Javad was unconscious the entire time? You didn't see him dip in and out of consciousness?"

"I didn't see that, no."

A pause.

"How long did the chest compressions continue for?"

"I'm not sure. They completed five cycles, standard procedure, then checked for a pulse."

"Was there any sign of a pulse?"

"I wasn't the one checking at that point but I don't think we ever detected one, no."

"Had Javad vomited during this time? Any convulsions?"

"I'm not sure, I couldn't see clearly from the benches. I noticed later on there was some vomit or similar between his face and the chamber wall."

"Were any drugs administered?"

"Adrenaline. Epinephrine. The medic was assisting us through the porthole. She can give you the details."

"Gonzales?"

"Yes."

"Could Gonzales *observe* the patient from the porthole? I'm not familiar with the exact layout of the chamber, you see."

"No, she couldn't see Javad directly. The sleeping quarters, our bunks, aren't covered by the camera or the porthole."

"I understand. Would you say procedures were followed as they should have been?"

I pause. *Were they?* I am reminded of something Mike once told me on another dive in deep Norwegian waters. We had twelve divers in Sat, a big vessel, urgent work to a pipeline, and then the thrusters of the positioning system malfunctioned before the first dive and the whole thing was called off. He said *everyone has a plan until you're punched in the face.* He also said *no plan survives first contact with the enemy.* "Yes, everybody did as they were trained. We're all qualified dive medics, all except Javad."

"How did Javad seem last night, before you went to bed?"

"Seemed fine. I didn't really know him very well."

"No worries or anxieties expressed to you or your colleagues?"

"Not that I am aware of."

"No pains or health complaints?"

"Again, not that I am aware of."

"After you went to bed did you hear him again? Did you notice anything in the night?"

"We had a hyperbaric lifeboat drill."

"Sorry, could you repeat."

"I said we had a hyperbaric lifeboat drill. Took maybe thirty minutes."

"Did Javad seem OK during the drill?"

"Yes, I think so."

"And then what happened?"

"Then we went to bed. All six of us."

21

THE DETECTIVE ASKS a barrage of further questions.

"Repeat that, please," he says.

"I said I have never dived with him before. I believe this was only his second or third time in Sat."

"If you remember any other details that might be useful," he says, "no matter how small, day or night, ask to be patched through to me."

"Roger that."

"Thanks, Brooke. Can you ask Mike Elliot to come through next, please."

When I open the hatch to our chamber I am overcome with tiredness. We will endure almost four more days of this. Being questioned, stepping past Tea-Bag's empty bunk, brushing arms and legs against it, waiting as the pressure gauge ticks down: our version of a countdown timer.

"Only the veterans to go," says Spock.

I don't think he means *military* veterans. That would not only include Mike and Jumbo but also Tea-Bag. He means the older divers among us. The elders. Even though they are only a few years older than myself in Mike's case. Back in the Gulf of Mexico bunk choice would be decided by seniority. When I worked those waters I was usually the last to pick, and so more often than not I would be left with a top bunk, undesirable because I would be woken up more often and I would smash more of my gear when it fell in the night, and usually a top bunk at the back of the chamber, undesirable because you are then penned in with your head behind someone's bunk and your feet behind someone else's. Here in the North Sea we draw straws, as with this trip, or take pieces of numbered folded paper from a Styrofoam cup. It is democratic. In other places I have known it to be decided on the outcome of a game of Bourré; or a system of bribe payments; or even on a first come, first served basis. When you endure these conditions, constantly, without respite, your choice of bunk is of paramount importance.

"Fresh pot of hot," says Jumbo. "Warm yourself up."

"I'm done," I say, rubbing my eyes. "Long day."

As I approach the bunk area I have an overwhelming compulsion to pull off bedding and open the hatch. I have to brace myself against the walls to resist.

Open it.

I smile through gritted teeth because this is stress talking. It isn't me.

Just open the hatch and leave.

Stop it.

You'll be out in minutes. Free.

I grit my teeth and breathe.

The sensation passes.

André is in his bed already, as is Spock. I wait until Mike and Jumbo are done being questioned and then I slip through into the Wet Pot to brush my teeth.

I have had these unwanted thoughts since I was a young girl. They surface when I am overtired and under too much pressure. I understand them and I know how to deal with them.

When I lie down on my bunk it is as if it has transformed into a king-size bed in an expensive hotel. Steve and I once stayed in the Balmoral Hotel in Edinburgh for two nights while Gilly and her partner looked after Lisa and Henry. We needed some time together. It was a wonderful few days and that is still the finest, firmest bed I have ever slept in.

Curtains are drawn and personal bunk spotlights switch off one after the other. We don't say good night because we are not boy scouts and there is nothing good to speak of. A chamber is more akin to a multibunk prison cell than a camp dormitory; only prisoners live in better conditions. They are able to visit the exercise yard and buy food in the commissary. They are permitted to have phone calls with people who can understand their voices. That is a grossly unfair comparison, I know it is. We choose this life and we are paid handsomely for the work we do. There's a queue of air divers snaking around the block ready for a chance to take any of our places, even after a tragedy like this. I suppose one of those experienced air divers, courses completed, tickets acquired, will now have their chance.

I can't settle.

Everything is out of kilter now that we have lost Tea-Bag.

Some weeks in the bin can pass in what feels like days. The routine of the work, having all your meals cooked for you with no washing up to do. And then some days can pass like weeks. This is one of those. As I sniff my pillowcases and say good night to the photos attached to the chamber wall, I have to bite the inside of my mouth not to fall apart. I miss them both so much—washing their hair, reading them stories, nagging them to finish their dinners. I push my face into the cotton pillow and breathe them in. This chamber is hot and humid and locked, but it is not as bad as a prison cell.

Ask me how I know.

22

A PRIVATE, CURTAINED space. I lie with a curved metal wall to my right, Jumbo's bunk beneath me, curved metal ceiling, flimsy curtain to my left. I could reach out and touch the others. I am in a bunk inside a pressurized chamber inside an aging DSV somewhere in the middle of the North Sea.

If I had to guess I would say Mike and Jumbo are both already fast asleep. Spock, André, and I are usually the ones tossing and turning, reflecting, worrying. Mike and Jumbo seem to be able to sleep through just about anything.

I guess they have clear consciences.

It is discombobulating the way offshore life can interfere with your circadian rhythm. A month inside here means twenty-eight missed sunsets and sunrises. No air for four weeks. No breeze or exposure to the variabilities of weather. We do not have the privilege of seeing the moon, a most base human need. One diver in the Gulf of Mexico told me it was like being trapped in a casino in Las Vegas with no windows, no natural light, and oxygen pumping out of the vents to keep us all gambling. I guess that is what we're doing, only with heliox.

Gambling with our lives for the sake of our livelihoods.

Money, thrills, and comradery, in exchange for poor odds.

When I told André last year about my brief stint in the Oklahoma county jail he told me he's never even been in a real fight. I scowled at him. *Seriously?* He told me he could always talk his way out of trouble. His salesmanship, combined with his towering height, was enough. My brawl was in a dive bar off the I-240. I used to go there to decompress after decompression. Had a Cuban, bass-playing lover back at home waiting for me after my offshore weeks, a boyfriend, I guess you could call him, a decent guy, young widower, but each time I was done with a stint in the oil fields I needed a night or two all by myself to adjust. You go from *Roger That* and *Say Again, Over* to talking about feelings and take-out options. You go from *Three Hots and a Cot*, which is code for all the basics covered, and I have heard the phrase used by ex-cons, veterans, and offshore workers alike, to real life with all its unavoidable complexities. The fight was regrettable. I was drinking too much tequila back then, and I watched a guy in an expensive suit try to walk out of the bar with a drunk girl he'd just met. He had a terrible look in his eyes, like he'd already decided she would be his prey. She was semiconscious at this point. So, I supported her, tried to help her out to a cab, and he became livid. He ended up with a split lip, a broken nose, and a ripped jacket. I fought dirty and I injured my hand so badly I could hardly give the police my prints after I was arrested. The one thing I learned in jail was that as much as I relish the confined working conditions of a chamber like this one, I cannot abide being locked up against my will.

That was a lesson I will never forget.

The belly of the ship rolls with each wave and I can imagine the men on the Bridge holding steady, steaming head-on into each cresting wave, leaning forward and back rhythmically to cope with the motion. We are insulated from the worst of any rocking here in the center of the DSV. The moon pool will be closed over and everything loose strapped down tight. We are insulated from the risks outside but we have our own danger, and loss, to contend with.

Losing a diver is difficult. I adjust my pillow and think about his family and friends, but I also think about the other men in these bunks. How they are dealing with this in their own ways. Mike might have said a prayer before he fell asleep because, despite resembling an action hero, he is a churchgoing Christian. André will have written his thoughts down in his journal, something many divers do. It helps him mark the passing of time in the absence of celestial markers or natural light. He might have written a matter-of-fact chronology of the day or he might have written about his own fears and thoughts. André writes more than the rest of us put together. Spock told me last year that he often counts himself to sleep. His Croatian grandmother taught him the technique. He thinks of his wife, a primary schoolteacher, soon to be deputy headmistress, and their four young daughters, and then he counts, rapidly, silently, inside his own head, until he dozes off. Unfortunately, Jumbo is well known for self-soothing to fall asleep each night, if you understand what I mean. This is something they don't warn you about on saturation diving courses, but, in truth, many divers do it. Some develop a technique to make the process private and quiet. Thankfully, they are the vast majority. Jumbo is discreet. The outliers who make a lot of noise, their bunk shaking, tend not to stick around too long. If you do anything that gets on people's nerves in this line of work your days will likely be numbered.

More rolling and pitching.

We cannot enter the hyperbaric lifeboat because it is being decompressed with Tea-Bag inside. If the ship suddenly sinks—which is unlikely but not impossible—then we would be blown down to match or slightly exceed the maximum depth of the sea here, and then we would hope there are other divers close by to come rescue us. The diving family extends beyond this chamber and this DSV. We are a network of Brits and Malaysians and Norwegians and Indians and Americans and South Africans and Australians at the bottom of this body of water, each able and willing to help the others if asked. Such is the brotherhood of deep diving.

Jumbo snores, wakes himself up, then goes back to sleep.

I am not always keen on sleep. When I sense my recurring nightmare raising its ugly head inside my subconscious I often jerk myself awake, sometimes sitting bolt upright, struggling to breathe. I wait for a while, so the dream passes safely by. The visions are always the same. The beach. The horizontal rain. The realization of what I had done. Digging into coarse, wet sand with my bare hands to uncover the remnants.

When I was a deckhand off Louisiana, working near *Garden Banks*, we were caught in hurricane-force gusts on a vessel smaller and less capable than this one. Eighty-foot waves, eighty-knot winds. Most of us were floor hands, deckhands, grunts, and laborers. Old divers still remember those early days and those risks. You start at the bottom and work your way up, and if you're lucky, very lucky, you'll end up in the bin. There are poorly paid lads out on deck right now as I lay warm and dry in my bunk. They are part of the team that keep us all going. In many ways, they are the real heroes.

One consolation to this awful day is that we wouldn't actually be diving in these conditions, even if Tea-Bag had been fit and well. The Bell would be dragged up and down because of the surface turbulence, which wouldn't affect the diver in the water too badly, but could cause severe seasickness for the Bellman.

I sleep. No dreams, thank goodness. I wake up wondering if it is day or night. Is it sunny or cloudy, breezy or still? Is the world still functioning onshore? I fall asleep for a few hours more then wake with a start. I am sweating. The grainy residue of the nightmare drains away and I am left panting. As quietly as I can, I slip out of my bunk and land on the cool metal floor. Spock is in the eating area reading his novel and drinking chamomile tea.

He looks up at me.

I don't say anything. I wouldn't want to wake the others.

Spock has a pack of indigestion tablets on the table together with a photograph and my camcorder. I think he is using the photograph as a bookmark. It is of his wife and four daughters on a beach, each of them wearing coats and scarves and gloves. His wife is holding a shorthair terrier.

"Lovely photo," I whisper.

He goes back to his book.

23

OUR DSV OPERATES twenty-four hours a day. That is in no way unusual offshore. Anyone who has worked on rigs or ships knows the score. The advantage of long days—most people do twelve-hour shifts—is you have an extended period of time back home to compensate. I have felt guilty a thousand times for choosing this life. I still feel guilty now. I have missed birthdays and school plays and sports days. I even missed Christmas twice. The worst part is always the goodbyes. And the best part: the reunions. The pressure of those hugs, that tangle of arms. The intensity of relationships for the first few days back home: Lisa and Henry running through to me in their pajamas each morning to check if I am still home, to check if I am still real. The four of us eating tea and toast in bed together, crumbs everywhere. That simple joy. I have tremendous guilt and have noticed some vicious scowls from other mums at the school gates, but Steve has always supported my career choices.

As I leave Spock to retreat back to my bunk I say, "Their ages?"

He looks at the photo in front of him and smiles. "Two, four, seven, ten."

"Almost half a football team," I say.

"Two of them play football."

"Lovely kids."

"Their mum's not well. Anxiety. We're in a rough spot and she won't see a doctor."

I consider sitting down opposite him but I fear he'd close up again. Gently, so not to startle, I ask, "Does she have someone else to talk with? A vicar or family friend?"

He shakes his head.

"She's a good mum," he says, chewing the inside of his lip. And then, turning away from me, he mutters, "Good mum."

"Perhaps if—"

"Not now," he says. "I shouldn't have raised it. More of a *dryland only* thing."

I nod and turn and climb into bed and pull the curtain as quietly as I can manage. Maybe that was a breakthrough of sorts. A start. I'll suggest we go out for a coffee or a beer when we're onshore. *Dryland only or onshore only* is a code we all use for any subject too emotionally fraught or complex to deal with in this confined space.

It's not easy being the partner left behind.

I understand this only too well.

Decompression slows down time: no opportunity to stretch your legs or work up a sweat. That drag is exacerbated when there has been an accident or a near miss. I was in deco one time off Nigeria in my early days working in blackwater, zero visibility, with a man from Lisbon, an experienced ex-Comex diver, who lost his mind. He didn't hurt himself, or anyone else, not like the guy who removed his helmet at depth, but he lost control. Fortunately Dive Control were on top of it and authorized me to sedate him against his will. We keep very powerful narcotics on board for such eventualities. You have to make pragmatic decisions sometimes to save lives. It was the same yesterday with the so-called remote autopsy procedure, or pre-autopsy procedure, taking fluids and samples. That wouldn't be permitted onshore but out here, with pressure that would boil your bodily fluids in a fraction of a second, it is vital to adjust, improvise, and overcome.

A long, disconcerting creak from above.

Metal, adapting.

We are still in rough waters, I can sense it. My ears: the delicate vestibular system. Even though I am locked inside this chamber, the level of fluid endolymph in my labyrinths, the complex tubing of my inner ears, keeps me informed of sea conditions. I know this anatomical detail because I am well trained. We all know a lot about ears. The storm intensifies. Imagine lying awake at night and your bed starts to tip as if to propel you forward, and then it rolls and leans back so your feet are almost over your head.

Guilt, again. Shades and layers of it. I try not to give in, especially when I am working. I forcibly purge my mind of guilt and panic and claustrophobia just like I purged my helmet when it flooded on the seabed. I purge over and over again because I have no other option. The guys feel guilt, too, I know they do, but perhaps it is tougher for women. It shouldn't be, of course, but it is. The lads are seen as heroes and providers working out here for a month at a time with only a sporadic text message or letter home. Whereas I know full well that many reasonable people offshore and onshore alike see me as an absentee, a parent who has regularly abandoned her beloved children, a woman somehow lacking the maternal instinct we prize so highly. The harshest critic, of course, is myself.

I had a career break awhile back, and it was hearing about the legendary Marni Zabarsky that made me realize I could still do this. Hearing that Marni even existed, a woman who works as a successful saturation diver in the GOM, a woman respected by her peers, a diver who is proficient and well paid and admired. She smashed through whatever glass ceiling there was in her area, and what I respect her for most is that not only is she matter-of-fact practical about her job, like all the best divers are, but she also credits other women who worked offshore in GOM before her. Maybe they didn't quite make it to Sat like she did, but they were excellent commercial air divers, worked as deckhands, worked on the Bridge. She credits them all, and hearing stories about her stellar career made me realize I could still do this.

Four a.m. This should be when André and I are woken up via the speaker. Breakfast menu. Ablutions. Preparing for the day's dive. We should be emerging from our bunks and ordering sausage sandwiches and containers of baked beans and scrambled eggs. Plus bran. We should be rubbing our eyes and preparing ourselves mentally for the descent. Dive plans and war stories. But that won't happen today. The gauge on the wall says 280 feet of depth, together with the corresponding pressure rating and temperature reading. A slow, gradual return to normalcy.

Except for Tea-Bag.

I read *Rachel's Holiday,* a book gifted to me by Gilly, for a full hour, and think on and off about what Spock told me. With four young children it is normal for his wife to struggle. Completely normal. Then, when I hear someone stirring, I resolve to wake up earlier tomorrow and do some stretching and air squats in the Wet Pot before breakfast. We have to stay strong and we have to stay flexible.

André and Jumbo are sitting at the breakfast table. The tallest and the shortest. We have no fresh newspapers because of the storm, no chance of resupply anytime soon, but the Bettys have brought through new magazines, together with two pots of hot. The corner of the chamber consists of three racks of condiments. Hot sauces, including Tea-Bag's unopened bottle: Hillbilly Hooch. It's a decent sauce, I've had it a few times. Mike's is Pappy's XXX White Lightnin' and Spock has Pain Is Good Jamaican Hot Sauce. I haven't tried that one yet. Salt, pepper, ketchup, mustard, mayonnaise. Honey, sugar, sweetener, maple syrup, soy sauce. All kept steady in rough seas thanks to mesh and wires.

The next three days will consist of sleeping, reading, chatting, and listening to music through the headphone sockets in our bunks. Also: updating resumes and coming up with plans to find the next job. We are not employed, we are contractors. We each have to chase work. The coming days will creep along and our nerves will end up fraying like they always do. Perhaps because André sounds like a mule eating an apple through railings every time he enjoys a meal, or because Spock doesn't ever get angry or sad or frustrated, which can be strangely infuriating. Maybe Mike takes up too much bench with his shoulders, or Jumbo's jet-black gallows humor cuts a little too close to the bone, even for us.

I sit down opposite André and Jumbo.

"Sleep all right?" asks André.

"On and off," I say. "You?"

"Off, mainly," he says. "Jumbo reckons he didn't get a wink thanks to his abstinence."

"You abstaining, Jumbo?" I say. "Not like you."

"Out of respect," he says.

"Can you keep that respect going for another three days, do you reckon?" I ask.

"I'm not Superman," he says.

Breakfast comes through for the three of us. Mike and Spock keep on sleeping.

Sitting on the benches is comfortable with this few people. It's like being in Sat when a pair of lads are down diving. Feels almost spacious, almost manageable.

Jumbo lowers his voice. "You two notice Mike messing about with the hatch in the middle of the night?"

André says, "With the hatch?"

Jumbo nods. "He was checking it, I think." And then he says, "I hope."

"Nothing wrong with checking it," I say.

André nods. "Typical Mike. Squared away. Big on maintenance and contingency plans."

Jumbo says, "You're probably right."

"You think he was trying to open it?" I say.

Jumbo takes a deep breath through his nose and shakes his head.

André finishes his bacon sandwich and says, "There was a black gull on deck when we left port."

Jumbo says, "What?"

"Dead gull," repeats André the Giant. "Wings splayed, neck snapped, head hanging off to one side. Deck lad threw it overboard."

I nod and Jumbo nods. Neither of us believes too much in the spiritual side of maritime tradition, but personally, I'd rather not tempt fate.

I start with an aluminum container of overcooked porridge with golden syrup and my heart yearns for my children in this moment. We would usually have breakfast overlooking our patio, views out over Gibbet Hill to the north. On a good day, Steve would head out for a long run by the River Nidd, or to repair a watch in his workshop, and the kids and I would laze around with comics, coloring books, Game Boys, newspapers, croissants, and porridge cooked slow on the Aga. I used to call it oatmeal but I guess I'm half British now. Took me years to understand how to cook on the Aga, but Gilly has one and she insisted I try it. I wish I could be checking their porridge this morning, making sure it isn't too hot, adding a little sea salt, resisting their pleas for more sugar and syrup. I wish I could be back with them right this instant.

We finish breakfast, send the clear garbage bags and used containers back through the Medlock, and then wipe down thoroughly. *Leave it how you found it.*

André and Jumbo play chess on a small magnetic board and I take a shower.

When I emerge from the Wet Pot in my towel Mike starts yelling at the top of his voice as André tries desperately to show something to an LST through the porthole. Hand signs and men shouting over each other in helium voices.

I take another step deeper inside our chamber.

It's Spock.

24

"GUYS," SAYS MIKE, looking right into the camera on the wall. "We're going to need the medic down here immediately."

André and Jumbo lift Spock's limp body off his bunk and lay him down on the floor.

The ambient hum intensifies, and I am paralyzed for a moment.

It is happening again.

Fear in André's eyes.

"Brooke," says Mike, urgently. "Brooke, listen to me."

I visited the Wet Pot again and then when I returned to this chamber another man dies? What happens when I am not here?

"Brooke," Mike says, his hand firmly on my shoulder. "Look at me. Med kit."

I snap out of it and collect the medical kit from the wall.

With three men talking over each other in helium voices it is difficult to understand any one instruction or question.

"No pulse," says André. "Starting CPR."

He places his large palms down on Spock's chest and pushes down so hard it's like he is trying to push him through the metal base of the chamber. I worked with a diver once in the Red Sea who had six ribs broken by one of his colleagues when a dive went wrong and he was left without gas for too long. That man never dove again. He told me his broken ribs and cracked sternum were more difficult to recover from than his heart stopping.

Gonzales appears at our porthole, her hair damp, and the expression on her face says it all.

"Adrenaline coming through Medlock," she says, assertively. "Stand by."

Cycles of compressions and then Jumbo checks for a pulse. While he does this Mike shines a pen torch into Spock's eyes and then looks at me.

I look back.

André resumes chest compressions.

"What else can we do, Doc?" asks Mike. "Tell us. What more?"

She's not a doctor, I don't think; she's a paramedic or senior nurse.

"Use the foot suction pump. Clear his airway. Lube the oral pharyngeal. Maintain compressions."

Jumbo does as she asks. He is meticulous and organized.

"Brooke, can you prepare and insert an ante orbital cannula, please."

I look at her.

"His arm."

I know what *ante orbital* means but I cannot comprehend that this is happening again. Is this a gas problem? An airborne pathogen? A virus we are unable to flee from?

Mike gives an adrenaline shot and then I insert the cannula.

He was worried about his wife, about her state of mind.

Additional cycles of CPR. Jumbo takes over from André. André helps me to rig up an IV bag of sodium chloride solution even though his hands are red and sore. He has to remove a small towel, Spock's small towel, from a bunk hook, in order to hang up the translucent bag.

"Still no pulse," says Mike, his tone even.

Gonzales guides us through applying the gas valve mask, which she calls the *Laerdal* mask, and attaching it to our BIBS system.

Leo Babic, *Spock*, father of four little girls, has had a shot of adrenaline and his airways are clear. He is receiving an IV and he's getting CPR.

"What else can we do, Doc?" says Mike, again, a little frustration in his voice now. "We need to do more for him."

I know there is no defibrillator. Many pieces of medical equipment won't survive Medlock pressurization. A stethoscope, for example, will not work well under pressure. Anything with gaseous spaces or venting will malfunction or prove unreliable. Additionally, we have to be constantly vigilant of any gear that could start a fire.

André takes over from Jumbo. "Come on, Spock, you handsome bastard. Stay with us, mate. Come on. They're waiting for you at home."

The veins in André's arms are standing out, as is the prominent one in his forehead. He looks like he may pass out any second himself.

We work as a team. Valve mask, pulse, compressions, IV, more adrenaline.

Forty minutes go by.

"You should stop now, lads," says Halvor over the speaker. "You did all you could for him."

Again, we do not stop.

We go on.

Four kids and a wife back home.

It is a golden rule of deep-sea diving that you always do as you are told. If you are working at depth and you are told to take a break, you take a break, no questions asked. If you are told to drop your tools and return to the Bell you do so without delay. If you are told to blow down the Bell, as we were yesterday, you blow down the Bell. And yet, in this circumstance and this circumstance only, we defy Halvor's command and we keep on trying to revive our brother.

When we finally stop we fall about like petals from a wilting flower.

We sit panting, syringe wrappers all around us, BIBS tubing and IV tubes tangling, Spock's chest red and beaten from all the pressure.

There are numerous invisible threats we accept in this line of work. Factors we cannot see or smell, but which can end us in myriad ways: pressure; gas mixes; Gram-negative bacteria with names like *Klebsiella*, *Proteus*, and *E. coli*.

Mike looks at the camera, and, holding its gaze, slowly stands up.

"What in God's name is going on here?"

25

I HAVE NEVER seen Mike or Jumbo lose their cool. Not once. I witnessed the stress in André's eyes when the Bell started to rapidly decompress, and I noticed a look in Spock's eyes at four this morning. Was that fear? Was his gut telling him he would never see his children again?

Halvor's voice through the intercom. "I am very sorry. I know this is tough for all of you. We are doing everything we can from outside. Deco is progressing as fast as we can safely go."

If the Super had said those words, or an LST, or someone external, we might have scoffed. But Halvor has lived through more than any of us. At depth, he has witnessed far more than his fair share of tragedy.

Two of us?

I fight to slow my pulse, to slow my breathing.

"We are doubling up testing, sampling, and cleaning protocols. We will purge the chamber and freshen up the gas. The storm has changed course so we are heading directly to Aberdeen at full steam and we will have some answers for you soon. Hang tight."

What else can we do?

As a first mate or an engineer you always have the option of a break. A walk out on deck to let rainfall soak your face, to feel the stinging wrath of nature, to be alone with your private thoughts for five minutes. Here, we have nowhere to turn. No breaks. The only answer is to look inward, to be introspective, to face the darkest space of them all: the chamber within.

"One of the strongest lads I ever worked with," says Jumbo, pushing his shoulders back. "He loosened a bolt once I couldn't get to budge. Gave it everything and couldn't shift it. Spock sorted it for me and didn't say a word after. No banter. Nothing."

Mike nods and then looks out the porthole. He says to Gonzales, "If you think we're going to prod him with needles and take fluid samples you can think again."

"Listen up, lads," says the Super. "We've got the Procurator Fiscal on the line again. Before we start working through any protocols why don't you all take turns to have a minute or two in the Wet Pot. Splash cold water over your faces, wash your hands, then we'll see about what comes next, eh?"

Mike hangs his head.

Jumbo goes first.

Four of us in the chamber now. One dead on the floor. Another in the lifeboat a few yards above our heads. My mouth is dry. There is something seriously wrong with this vessel.

Mike takes his moment in the Wet Pot and I can hear him smack something metallic, and then I hear him yell something unintelligible. A guttural scream of despair and exhaustion: more animal than human. André goes next, and then it is my turn. I ask for the water to be turned on. I take a fresh towel. I wash my face and wet my hair. Then I emerge into the living chamber and place my used towel with the others in the Medlock. We are hardwired to dispose of items we have soiled or had physical contact with. The towels need laundering, boiling more like, and I have a sudden and not entirely irrational urge to wipe down all the surfaces in this chamber. To disinfect and insulate. What hurt these two young, healthy men?

It is discombobulating to see unshakable divers flustered. If a man who went into battle, who ran willingly into the direction of gunfire, defused ordnance in an active war zone, begins to lose his cool, then what hope do I have?

Hot, still gas all around us.

A constant droning.

No weather, no natural light, no indication of time passing.

"There won't be a lifeboat for Leo," says André, as if talking to himself. "Not while it's decompressing. He will have to stay with us in here." He turns to the camera on the wall, an unblinking eye, constantly watching. "Are we supposed to keep him here? We haven't the space. We can't sleep next to him." And then he turns to me. "Not with the humidity in here. He's going to start breaking down."

"Lads, please," says Halvor. "Take a breath, will you. DCI MacDuff is on the line. He would like to speak directly to all of you. Stand by."

26

PIERCING SQUEALS OF electronic feedback through the speaker.

I cover my ears with my hands.

"This is DCI MacDuff of Grampian Police. I spoke to each of you yesterday. Your management has filled me in on the status of Leo Babic, your colleague. I know this is a distressing situation but I ask that you all remain calm. I understand mild sedatives are available via the ship's medic if required. I want you to know that if I could get you out of that chamber right now I would. But we're not dealing with the world as we'd like it to be, we're dealing with the world as it is. For now, I'm going to hand you over to the pathologist. Do as she asks and we'll have answers for you as soon as possible to explain exactly what happened to your fellow divers."

Fellow divers. I prefer that term to *colleagues*. *Brother* also works. I don't mind being called a brother just as I don't mind being called a lad. Relationships between brothers are usually complicated and close and dynamic.

We are no different.

Same pathologist as before. Edinburgh accent. Clear diction. She talks André through the saliva, blood, urine, hair, and nail scrape samples. Mike, wearing a fresh Pantera T-shirt, takes the lead role this time in organizing, bagging, and tagging, and then

Jumbo and I make sure they are sent back through the Medlock to Gonzales on the other side.

The process takes over an hour. A pathologist talking to a medic directing us while being remotely monitored by Grampian Police and, possibly, the Procurator Fiscal. We are all gloved and masked. At the end we are told there is a body bag in the equipment lock in the Wet Pot. It won't fit through our Medlock; it is different from the one we used for Tea-Bag. This bag is dark blue and heavy-duty. We move Spock like pallbearers at a burial. We take his weight and we lift him, our tendons straining, hips and elbows scraping walls, and we place him as gently as we can in the thick synthetic bag.

Our friend in a bag.

Concealed and locked away.

And, appallingly, we have nowhere to put him.

There is some conversation back and forth about whether we leave Leo on his bunk or transfer him to the Wet Pot. Two miserable alternatives. We choose his bunk. It seems more humane, although this makes no rational sense. Perhaps none of us want to be alone with a corpse in the Wet Pot when we take a shower or brush our teeth before bed.

We leave Spock on the floor for now; no, I can't call him that anymore. We leave *Leo* on the floor while we strip his bed. All his sheets and blankets are bagged before being sent though the Medlock. The charade is appalling in every way, including the ungainly stance I am forced to maintain to remove the family photos from his section of wall without trampling his torso. I can't catch my breath when I look at the images, removing each magnet carefully. Four girls all in navy-blue school uniforms except for the youngest. An attractive redheaded wife in jeans and a T-shirt. The family dog by her side.

Two divers? I spot Jumbo's right eye twitching.

After Spock's bunk is stripped we disinfect it with wipes, which are then dispatched immediately through the Medlock, and then we leave Leo, bagged, in his resting place. Mike says, "Anybody want to say anything?"

We look down at the floor.

After a long time Mike says "strong diver" and closes the bunk curtain.

27

FOR THE REST of the day we are questioned in turn. Like before, we are invited into the Wet Pot to speak with DCI MacDuff in Aberdeen via Dive Control and their unscrambler. The detective does not sound comfortable at all with the fact that another man died and he still hasn't been able to visit the crime scene, because, have no doubt, this is either murder, manslaughter, corporate manslaughter, or gross negligence.

I ask the DCI what safeguards they are putting in place to keep the rest of us alive until decompression is complete. He assures me he is in constant communication with the Captain and the Superintendent. He then asks me a series of questions about our interactions with the Life Support Technicians and their assistants, the people Mike and I call Bettys. He asks about Halvor, about the Super and the Night Super, about whether we had any issues with the cleaners or kitchen staff on the voyage out to the oil fields. DCI MacDuff has a capacity to sound concerned, accusatorial, and almost priestlike, all at the same time. He has the tone of a serious yet benevolent headmaster.

I am tired so I sit on the floor of the Wet Pot cross-legged and then he asks me to stand because he can't hear my answers clearly. He grills me about my family, about the mortgage, my mental health, my filming project with the camcorder, about a lawsuit I settled years ago with the now-defunct dive outfit Halvor was a founder of. Then, with some brief hesitation, he asks me more personal questions about Javad and Leo. Whether they got on. If they had any issues on board the ship. Whether it was true that both men had partaken in a high-stakes card game the night before they went into saturation. I said I wasn't present at any card game; I had an early night before we were blown down. I did not tell him I had heard there was a card game that got out of hand or that an assistant on the gas team went to bed in the early hours with a black eye. I am not a snitch. None of us are.

As I answer further questions about the way we treated both victims, I focus on the pressure gauge on the wall. The *Caisson* gauge, to give it its proper name. There is one in our living chamber, one here by the shower, one in the Bell, another in the lifeboat where Tea-Bag lies simultaneously decomposing and decompressing. DCI MacDuff asks me about the medic, Gonzales, and our interactions at the medical checks before we went into the bin. He asks me if I had noticed any animosity between her and the other divers, and if I am aware of any rumors circulating of her relationship with a diver. I tell him it was all standard procedure and I know of no such rumor. I tell him we wanted to start work as soon as we could. In some ways, we probably still wish the same thing.

When I emerge into the chamber André is reading a Thomas Harris novel, his flip-flops hanging off his long, bony toes. Mike and Jumbo are in their bunks. Mike jumps down and passes me without comment as he takes a fresh towel and heads into the Wet Pot. I sit down and pour myself a glass of water. He starts to do push-ups in there, the hatch open. We share no words.

"Menus in the Medlock," says the Life Support Technician.

André retrieves them.

I go to bring my Styrofoam cup of water to my lips and then I hesitate.

"What is it?" says André, watching me closely.

Our feet are almost touching.

"I don't know." I sit completely still, staring at the tension across the surface of the water.

"Tell me. It could be important. What are you thinking?"

Jumbo pulls his bunk curtain open but stays in his bed.

"It's probably nothing," I mumble.

Jumbo jumps down from his bed. "Did the copper tell you something?"

I shake my head again.

"Mikey," says Jumbo.

Mike appears at the hatch, panting.

I grab my Nokia from my bunk, careful not to touch the curtain concealing Leo's body bag, and they watch me as I step back to the table.

"Look," I urge, as I begin to type a message on my phone. "Look what I'm saying."

Mike chews gum.

They are very close to me. We are breathing over each other. The heat of them.

One might be an accident, I write. *Two is a crime.*

28

"NAH," SAYS JUMBO. "Someone screwed up. Same as it ever was."

I shake my head and point to my phone.

Police asking about lads outside. Bettys. You've heard about those nurses . . .

"Wait a minute," says André. "Slow down. I didn't have time to read the last bit. Go back."

I don't go back. I keep writing. *You know how sometimes nurses kill their patients, even children. Care, reversed. Maybe to feel powerful, or so they can try to revive them. What if that's happening to us?*

The three men glance at each other.

Mike opens his mouth as he chews and I see his gum in the back of his mouth, molded to his molars. Then he closes his mouth again without speaking.

André says, "*Present fears are less than horrible imaginings.*"

Jumbo frowns at him and says, "Don't start with your quotes. Not now." Then he turns to me and says, "Can I borrow that, Brooke?"

I hand him my Nokia.

He types something and then says, "It keeps changing my words, writing for itself."

"Predictive text," I say. "Keep writing."

His forehead creases with concentration. He places the phone down on the steel table and turns it to us.

2.5 days.

As long as it's not the gas then we can make it.

All four of us.

Mike says, "Roger that."

André looks confused.

Jumbo writes on.

Panic kills quicker than anything.

Even in here.

Don't get ahead of your hat.

He's right. Jumbo has seen more than the rest of us put together. If we watch out for each other, maybe keep one person on sentry duty, the four of us can make it out alive.

André takes the phone and his long fingers look like crab legs as he types awkwardly. He writes, *We all breathe the same gas. But could they pump something out to us individually? To the bunks? Via BIBS?*

Mike and Jumbo both shake their heads.

And then I realize the Life Support Technicians and Halvor and the Super have been our constant conduit while talking with police. We can only talk *through* the very people who might be harming us.

I take the phone.

They are watching us.

All the time.

Camera and portholes.

From now on we need to start watching THEM.

29

WE CONVENE AT the bunks, bunched together next to Spock's closed curtain.

Me, André, Mike, Jumbo. The four most experienced divers. All qualified medics. All afraid because the nature of whatever happened here is unknown to us.

"The two Bettys," says Mike, his voice low, his hand in front of his mouth. "The longhaired one's dad is an executive at the client's company."

He says something else but we can't hear him.

"I said the skinny one has ambitions to be a diver one day."

"They seem like decent lads," says Jumbo. "I've had no bother from either of them."

"I'm just saying they're both relatively new to the game," says Mike. "Unlike Halvor and the Super and the LSTs."

"Halvor, I'd trust with my life," says André.

"We all would," I say. "We all *do*."

"I can vouch for the Super, I reckon," says André. "Don't know the Night Super much; he used to work a lot in your part of the world." He looks at me and Mike.

"I've had him on a few jobs," says Mike. Squeezing his nose to equalize. "But I don't know the dude well. There was that thing in Norway in the eighties."

"Early nineties," I say.

"Tea-Bag and Spock both died on his shift," says Jumbo. "Both died in their bunks sometime between midnight and midmorning. Night Super was the man in charge both times."

"Lads," says Duncan, through the speaker on the wall. "Make sure one of you is in front of the main camera in the living quarters at all times, would you? So we can know you're all right."

We move back to the main part of the chamber. A journey of four feet or so.

André takes his journal and moves to the back pages. He takes his pen from the elastic loop that holds it secure, and he begins writing.

We need to be more careful talking openly.

He looks at us to make sure we have read his words.

We shouldn't sleep at the same time.

I nod. We all nod.

At least one stays awake to keep watch. Bunk curtains open?

Mike takes the journal from him.

Staggered shifts through the night. Four of us on two-hour shifts.

We all nod again.

Jumbo takes the journal, dropping the pen on the floor. He looks around and picks it up.

Could this be coincidence? Both had health problems, maybe? Are we being paranoid?

I look out the porthole and see the face of the life support assistant, the longhaired one. He moves away as soon as our eyes lock.

Jumbo goes on writing.

What did Leo eat last night?

André takes the journal, rotating it on the gleaming table. His hand is shaking. He pauses to steady it but then carries on regardless, his scrawl like that of a child.

Pork. Only one of us who ordered it.

We all look at each other. I have some pressure in my sinuses so I equalize.

André keeps on writing.

We can't eat their food. We can't drink their water. Must be a dozen people involved in the prepping, cooking, serving to us. We need to fast.

Mike laughs. "Fuck that."

Jumbo takes the journal.

We ask for sealed food. Whatever it is. Packets of potato chips, chocolate bars, pineapple chunks, granola bars, sealed milk. If they burst in the Medlock we'll deal with the mess. If not, we inspect the seals. We only drink bottled water from now on, no jugs.

Mike and André nod.

We are trapped.

I take the journal.

Trapped like cave divers.

No water for teeth-brushing. Use bottles. Could be something in the water they don't know about.

Mike squeezes the bill of his cap to maintain the curve.

"Just checking all is well," says the Supervisor.

We breathe their gas.

We are locked in.

Contained.

"All well, boss," says Jumbo, giving a thumbs-up to the camera.

All is not well.

It is as far from *well* as I dare to imagine.

30

"GENTS, WE NEED to talk right now," says Jumbo, looking straight into the camera lens.

"Roger that," says the Super. "Go ahead."

"We'd like prepackaged food from now on. Sealed. Water bottles rather than jugs. We're concerned locked in this thing that some of the food might have been contaminated by a virus, bacteria, or some kind of toxin. We need to know the food we're eating is completely safe."

A long pause.

Silence.

"We can do that. Just so you know nobody out here has been taken ill and we all eat the same food you do. But I totally understand. Sealed food for the rest of decompression period. Ignore the menus. I'll get a list drawn up of what the kitchens can do and we'll send it through ASAP. Over."

Relief.

"Could also be the hot sauce," says Mike, frowning. "Did they share the same sauce? Did Leo have it with his pork?"

"I don't know," I say.

"I think Tea-Bag borrowed Jumbo's hot sauce on the first night," says André.

Jumbo says into the microphone, "Boss, humor us. Can you

check the tapes to see if Javad and Leo had the same hot sauce with their food?"

"Roger, Roger. Will get back to you."

Two of us on either side of the chamber. The steel table, folded so it's barely a handwidth across, separates us. When we eat later we will be dining in the same space, a capsule as large as an SUV, with a dead body still inside it.

Not a healthy setup.

For mind or body.

Jumbo wipes sweat from his brow. "Midnineties, it was. We were off the coast of Libya, one of the deepest dives I have ever done. Over six hundred feet. Had a nine-day deco. Bastard of a job fixing a wellhead. Decent visibility but an old system. Bell had issues, bloody assistants gave us damp suits."

"The most heinous crime of all," says Mike.

"Nine days in a system in need of an upgrade. Blinker McGee acted like he was in charge of us all, bossing us around, giving it the big one."

"*Blinker McGee?*" I say.

"He used to blink a lot," says Jumbo. "Five days into deco, all of us half-crazed with boredom, the whole ship came down with food poisoning. Both our Bettys disappeared, so we knew something was up." He goes to pour himself water from the jug and André pushes it away and hands him a sealed bottle instead. "They had to explain the Bettys being off. People we didn't even know bringing us dinner and towels, taking away our dirty laundry. South African Super called Fruity explaining it to us. I've never felt more vulnerable being so dependent on relative strangers."

"You telling us all this to raise our spirits?" asks Mike, removing his baseball cap for the first time since attending to Leo earlier.

"I'm telling you this," says Jumbo, his expression turning serious, "because we can't let anything slip through the cracks here. It's hard to relax with the lads outside looking after us, but it'll be even tougher with new guys we've never met. Four of us left. This, whatever it is, makes food poisoning look like a walk in the park. We're four now. And we need to be four when the hatch pops open."

31

"I NEED TO find a new career," says André. "I'm too old for this."

Following several other accounts of food poisoning in the Caspian Sea, we start wiping and scrubbing vigorously, careful not to nudge Leo's feet in his bunk or his shoulder as we pass him.

"Pot of hot, please, fellas," says Jumbo, who looks deflated all of a sudden. It is when the stories end that we are forced to live with our new reality.

"No," says André, shaking his head. "No pot of hot, Jumbo. Remember what we said?"

No unsealed water.

Everything from bottles.

Sterile and safe.

"Are you telling me no more coffee?" says Mike, his voice low.

"It's only a few days," I say.

Mike grits his teeth and takes a long, hard breath in through his nose.

No coffee, no tea, no hot sauce, no proper cooked food. At home this wouldn't be a significant imposition, but in a chamber the size of a domestic sauna, any minor infraction on our expected experience: a problem with the toilet or heating regulation, never mind two deaths, will mess with your head in unimaginable and disproportionate ways. When the living conditions are already trying, any deviation from our regular standards takes a heavy toll.

"Lads," says the Superintendent. "I've been told we can get telemedicine to you individually, in terms of professional counseling, via the Wet Pot, for anyone who needs it."

We don't say anything.

"No stigma, no banter," he says. "Just a chat with someone who'll listen. It's not the nineteen fifties. I know I would take up the offer if I were still in your boots."

Again, we don't say anything.

Our team of four feels stronger than ever. Perhaps because of what we have lived through together these past few days. The storm, the valve malfunction, the two sessions of CPR, the police questions, the transfer of Tea-Bag to the lifeboat. Now that we are taking extra precautions with food and water, now that we have retaken control, we will survive this experience and it will be added to the long list of diving anecdotes we all tell in the pub after a few drinks.

Most diving stories start with *You'll never believe this* or *No shit, lads, this happened last year* or *Big Scottish will back me up here, it happened off the coast of Malaysia, right, and . . .*

We turn to our old memories because we survived those times.

However harrowing, our near misses are also, somewhat perversely, reassuring.

Creaks from the bolts and rivets holding this tin can together.

The familiar drone goes on and on, and the walls seem to be creeping in around me. The gray-green walls appear unclean and grimy even though I know they are no such thing. The curve of the walls is also untrustworthy: you associate this shape with an execution chamber or a septic tank. The lights are mustard-colored and they flicker. I wipe down the floors over and over again, and then I see an eye at the porthole. The size of the windows never felt uncomfortable before. I have watched cup finals and Super Bowls on TV through these tiny portholes, but now, considering the danger outside, from either negligence or malice, they feel like peepholes directed at us.

32

WHEN YOU CANNOT escape from the door you came in through, and you don't have much headspace time on your own, you must travel in a different way. Virtually, through time and space. We reminiscence about Australia in the early nineties, and the excellent and revolting food we have been served on Norwegian DSVs.

André says, "It's all right for you three. The only places I can stretch out properly is on the seabed or in my bunk." He stands up to show us how his bald patch meets the chamber ceiling. "Now I only have my bunk and I don't like being so close." He gestures to the closed curtain of Leo's bunk.

"Cans of pop coming through, lads. Chocolate bars too."

Jumbo opens the Medlock and brings out the cans. A Fanta, two Cokes, and then a Sprite for Mike. André shakes his violently in his hand and then opens it.

Not so much as a hiss.

We work through the jobs and courses where we first met each other, and the Diving Bells we have shared. We don't eat the Cadbury Dairy Milk or Mars bars until we have checked each one for puncture marks. I miss the Hershey's of my childhood right now. When the chocolate came through the Medlock the wrappers were shrink-wrapped onto the bars like they had been vacuum-sealed for freshness.

Our career histories are entangled.

Jumbo saved Mike and André their jobs a few years back. Both guys had missed the chopper flight out to the rig. It took the dive company eight hours to hire replacement divers, and God knows what extra incentives they offered them to do it. Jumbo explained to that particular Super how Mike and André had been in a car accident. He told them they were shaken but unhurt. The truth is they had flown to London to attend a party of one of Mike's old navy buddies and, afterward, they'd hit a casino. Even after all that, they managed to be on time for their return flight to Aberdeen. Divers tend to be punctual that way.

The only problem is their flight was canceled.

Mike is the reason I am here in the first place. I had done more than enough air diving time, enough challenging jobs. I had also worked the decks like a trooper and completed all the certifications needed. I was a qualified scuba, air, mixed gas, rescue diver, the whole caboodle, at great personal expense. But to work your way into Sat you need to have a solid reputation. Veteran divers must like you enough to want to give you a chance. There was no way I was getting a chance at Sat in the North Sea or GOM back then, but Mike got me a Red Sea gig, persuading the boss to give me a try. He vouched for me and probably exaggerated my credentials. I worked well on that first job. It was only ten days in total, and I was terrified of the confined spaces—I had to calm myself with mantras to handle the claustrophobia—plus my joints ached terribly from the saturation. My standard of work was reasonable, but I didn't have enough muscle back then to force nuts and I didn't have enough confidence to use my boot to finish the job. Mike's voice, a voice he doesn't really use very often, carries a lot of weight in the deep-sea community. Without him I would never have progressed to this life.

This is why we do not suspect each other of foul play. We rely on each other. We trust each other implicitly, and we need each other.

Any alternative is unthinkable.

André has saved me on more than one occasion, and I am not even talking about his quick thinking in the Bell when he shut off the valve I had inadvertently knocked. There was one time in north Norwegian waters back in ninety-seven, when the gas turned bad. At depth I blacked out and he came out of the Bell to rescue me. I have no memory of what went wrong or how he managed to bring me back, but without his strength, ascending the umbilical carrying me with him, I would have left Steve a widower and Henry and Lisa motherless.

A heavy feeling in my stomach.

I miss them in a way I cannot put words to.

The last time I saw Steve we had a disagreement. I wouldn't count it as an argument; it was simply us getting on each other's nerves. I interrupted him when he was repairing a particularly complicated vintage split-second chronograph, apparently a watch at the very limits of his watchmaker abilities. This friction is not uncommon before I go offshore because that's a lot to deal with, for both parties. I wish I'd have grabbed hold of him that day and kissed him with all my love.

I wish to God I hadn't wasted that chance.

"OK, lads, some better news," says the Super through the speaker. "We're making decent progress back to Aberdeen now that the easterly's moved on. It's now 4:00 p.m., which means you've done half your deco, only two days left. Hang in there, all of you."

Within this capsule—a metal chamber the size of a diner banquette or an Apollo space reentry module—we have ultimate, mutual trust. Four veteran divers, who have watched each other's backs a dozen times, helped each other, saved each other.

Alas, the same cannot be said for the people outside our walls.

33

IT STRIKES ME as I sit drinking my second soda in as many hours that we are sharing stories about Leo, and periodically glancing over at his bunk, at his body concealed behind a curtain, and yet we have all but forgotten about young Javad. It is partly a question of proximity. He is in the hyperbaric lifeboat: out of sight, out of mind. We cannot smell him or sense him from down here. He is sealed away like corpses should be. But it is also the fact that he was relatively new to our world. We don't have any stories that involve him. We hardly knew the man.

Mike opens a Milky Way and inspects it for signs of contamination. His eyes are bloodshot and he looks twitchy, like an alcoholic on day two of cold turkey.

"You remember Craggy?" says Jumbo. "I saw him at a funeral last month."

André smiles. "The man, the myth, the legend."

"How did he look?" asks Mike.

"Craggy turned up in his Rolls-Royce Silver Shadow," says Jumbo. "I was surprised it could still make it up the street. Personalized license plate still there, helped along with some strategically placed duct tape. You guys know he used to head down to London after each decompression?"

"I went with him one time," says André.

"I didn't know that," says Jumbo.

"Early days, for me anyway." André smiles at the memory. "We drove down from the Newcastle docks and when we arrived at the Savoy, no less, unwashed, with bleary eyes, he handed the keys for the Rolls to the lad out front all dressed up in livery, and we took two junior suites. He paid for both, of course. After a swim in the pool and a dirty martini or two in the American Bar he took me across the road to Rules for dinner."

"And he still doesn't own his own place," says Jumbo. "I asked him about it. His brother's got a house from the council, nice little town in Kent, and they live there together. No stress. Craggy told me he used to buy certain people I won't name a new watch each year to keep them sweet and to ensure he had enough days in Sat to satisfy his lust for luxury. Gave two of them a Sea-Dweller one year."

This low-key bribery still goes on to this day. I know it does because I gifted two Omega Seamasters the year I came back from my break.

"Whose funeral was it?" says André.

"Halvor's old business partner, Smithy. From their company back in the day, the one that went under."

André and Mike look at me. They both know about the lawsuit.

"Lads, time for a BIBS drill. Go to your masks. Over."

We run through the drill, breathing auxiliary air, checking masks, training for what we would resort to if the gas went foul or if there was suddenly a fire in the chamber.

"Drill complete. Just to let you know DCI MacDuff is en route by helicopter now that the weather allows it. And the samples taken from Javad and Leo will be returning to Scotland on the same chopper."

"Can we watch some news on TV?" asks Jumbo.

"Not at present. Ship-wide issue."

"Radio through our headphones?" I ask. "We'd like to keep up with the news."

"Working on it."

We look at each other: a quartet of survivors. Every Sat diver half expects some traumatic accident or at-depth casualty at some point in their career. You also understand how that diver might well be *you*. But you do not expect it in the chamber system, with no obvious cause, no access to reliable information from land, and you certainly don't expect it to happen twice in so many days.

34

I TAKE SOME time in the Wet Pot, alone. Creaking noises from the pressure change. I stare at the hatch leading up to the hyperbaric lifeboat. Tea-Bag up there in his body bag, completely alone, on the floor by the portside seats. They will take him away soon.

"Can I have a flush, please, boys?"

The incongruity of asking life support assistants, Bettys, for a flush, that most base and private of human needs, when it might just be them who are hurting us.

Valves are opened and closed in order. A guttural noise as the water is sucked from the toilet. I use the hose to wash down. *Leave it as you find it.*

I wash my hands and in this strange artificial light I see red on my fingertips and nail beds. Looks like I've cut myself but I know I haven't. I scrub and scrub. Then I wipe the sink.

When I slide through to access our living chamber I check the gauge on the wall. The needle is falling. We are making it closer and closer to freedom. And, hopefully, to answers.

The alarm on my G-Shock watch beeps and I return to my bunk like I try to do every night at this moment. Bedtime for Lisa and Henry. I climb up and look at their photos. I breathe them in through their stacked pillowcases. Lisa looks older than she really is; wise and knowing for her years. Along with Steve, she and Henry are undoubtedly the best things that have ever happened to me.

"Menus in the Medlock, lads."

We congregate around the steel table, curious to see what they have managed to put together for us. An improvised menu as important for morale as for nutrition.

It is laughable.

Chocolate bars, factory-made cakes wrapped in plastic, spicy Peperami sausages, again, individually wrapped. We tick boxes on the grid of four and place the menu sheet back in the Medlock.

"This whole ship is designed to keep us safe," says André, reflective. "*Diver Support Vessel*. Almost a hundred crew to make sure we can reach the seabed and do the work. Not this time."

"Never have I ever craved my vitamins like I do now," says Mike, holding up his bottle. "After twenty-eight days I usually feel like a pale wreck, but this time it's worse. Need some Miami sunshine in my veins." He throws his vitamin bottle away in the clear trash bag.

"I might request a fresh, sealed bottle," says André.

"Screw vitamins," says Jumbo, his voice suddenly sour. His eyelid is twitching again and he looks mean in a way I have never seen before. "It's one and a half days. I'm not taking anything I don't absolutely need to take."

"Like a Pepsi and a Babybel?" says Mike, smiling.

"Essential life support," replies Jumbo, flatly.

Mike's reading some book about the HBO show *The Sopranos*. I haven't watched it yet. Jumbo's reading André's copy of *Rich Dad Poor Dad*. André's reading Jumbo's biography of Tiger Woods.

"Lads, the heli arrived and left. Detective's having a debrief and then he will be down to visit the system. Hide your girlie mags, eh? The samples have left the ship. I'll keep you updated. Over."

We look at each other.

"Hundred quid says the detective is seasick within eight hours," says Mike.

"I'll take the other side of that," says André. "Copper's an Oil and Energy specialist, isn't that what the Super said? Part of the Liaison Unit. He'll be on rigs every other month."

Mike reaches out his right hand, thumb missing from the first knuckle, and André shakes it.

"You lose that in the SEAL Teams or in Sat?" asks André.

Mike scratches his jaw. "Trapped it in a clamp off the coast of Brazil."

Jumbo shows us his left hand, two fingers missing. "Iran. Had to fly me into Israel to operate."

Mike says, "Members of an elite club of idiots."

André asks him, "What happened in the SEALs, Mike? You can tell us."

"Oh, I can tell you?"

"Quit being shy."

Mike looks up from under the rim of his cap.

"If I give you a dive tale instead, will that satisfy you?"

André says, "Depends. We might have heard it already. Might even be one I made up myself."

"Nineteen eighty-nine, Gulf of Mexico." Mike takes a deep breath. "I was working for an outfit out of Mississippi. There was a dude on the ship called Murphy. Irish name but he was half Hispanic, I think. Irish face but dark hair. Real ladies' man. So, he's a decent enough diver, can hold his own, teaches me a thing or two as I haven't had my ticket long. We do a twenty-six-day stint and then he tells me he has two women waiting for us in a bar off I-fifty-five. He says they're second cousins and they want to hang out and party for a few days. Now, I neglected to tell you that Murphy is married with three rug rats at this time. Third marriage, I think it was. Three different mothers. The math is complicated. Classic multi-alimony deep-sea diver cliché. Every time he gets back from a long job he gives himself a weekend to adjust, calls it the *double decompression method*. I don't know if his wife was complicit or what, but he did it every single time." Mike flinches suddenly. "What was that?"

We look around.

"Just a creak," I say. "Carry on."

Mike scowls at the walls and bites his lip. "So him and me drive out to Winona in his piece of crap Mustang, tangerine paint job, and he drives like a maniac the whole way there. Drive shaft collapsed outside Senatobia and he refused to let anybody else fix it, so he welded it back together himself. Did a decent job. In Memphis we collected the women, they were about my age, and rented two Harley Fat Boys from a place near Emilio's Grocery. He pays for all this in cash. We rode out into the desert as the sun set and he bought mushrooms from a Cuban dude who wore a cowboy hat a couple sizes too big. Three days and three nights drinking in rodeo bars, sleeping outside with the bikes, getting into dumb fistfights, and enjoying the company of two stoned country girls. He taught me to seek vengeance for those who have wronged me, but to take my time about it. No spontaneous brawls or rash decisions. Plan it, wait, wait some more, then execute. He taught me that to let disrespect go unpunished was to be weak. Like the old guy you were talking about, Murph never owned his own home or had anything pinning him down to any particular location, except for his collection of kids, I guess. He settled scores even if it took him years to do it. He lived life on his own terms. Car he always dreamed of, plenty of Benjamin Franklins in his back pocket, a network of dealers, and no plans whatsoever to reach pension age."

"Good for him," says André. "Now tell us about the SEALs."

35

MIKE INSISTS IT is a nonstory.

Jumbo tries to change the subject. "Your mate in the Gulf. Murphy? Never flagged up on the blood tests for narcotics? Neither of you picked up?"

"He only ever took mushrooms," says Mike. "Reckoned they were undetectable. Not sure if that's true or sat rat myth. I think on the whole they were more worried about liquor than anything else."

"Can we get some spirits in here?" says André, pointing at the camera on the wall, miming drinking from a glass. And then he mumbles, "I'd like to self-medicate, please."

My mind starts racing. *Spirits*. Ghouls. Two souls unable to make it out of this sealed, pressurized system. Tea-Bag and Leo. Spirits, entombed.

"We were given red wine one time," I say out loud, forcing myself to move on. "My second Christmas in Sat. I had to work hard to get that dive too. One small glass of red wine each with our turkey in a foil container. Couldn't even taste it was wine."

"You get a buzz, though?" asks Jumbo.

I scratch my itchy scalp. "Sure did."

André looks at the camera again. "One drink, please? Small one?"

152

"Negative, Joe," says the Night Super.

André turns back to Mike. "I heard you were a SEAL. You don't have to tell us if you don't want to."

"André, mate," says Jumbo. "Let it go."

We all stop what we're doing. Electricity in the air like before a thunderstorm. An eye appears at the porthole.

"I'm just yanking your chain," says André.

"I ever *say* I was a SEAL?" asks Mike.

"No," replies André. "Which might be typical SEAL behavior."

"Iraq," utters Mike, resigned, weary. "First wave. *Before* the first wave. 1991."

We fall quiet. Like children who have managed to remain unseen in the TV room past their bedtime, we quit shuffling and let the man speak, keen to escape our current situation for a few minutes.

"My third deployment. I was a few years out of BUD/S. Felt like I was finally earning my trident. My first two deployments were training: Guam and Bahrain. Then Bush and Cheney decided to come to the aid of Kuwait, so my team was sent in to conduct a mission from the USS *Nicholas*. Night vision wasn't all that sophisticated back then, in fact it was next to useless compared to what they have now, so we went in from the water at first light. The majority of us had never seen combat. We were physically capable and well trained; we'd been taught by the last of the Vietnam veterans. Brave men. The sun was rising over the ocean." He glances over at Leo's empty bunk and swallows hard. "Already the heat was causing a shimmer off the *Ad-Dawrah* oil fields. My chief led us to a location on the oil platform and we were ready for a firefight, or as ready as you can ever be." He pauses, removes his ball cap, scratches his head, places it back on. "I thought I was a real badass. We ran up ladders and cleared section after section of platform and received no hostile fire. Took a few Iraqi prisoners who offered little resistance and it was eerie how easy it all was. There was a distant shotgun blast, that unmistakable noise, as reinforced doors were breached, but we saw nobody fighting back. I was hot as hell, my jacket was already soaked with sweat, and I was getting dehydrated. We cleared a control room with three technicians who, again, offered no resistance. The sound of yelling in the distance. We continued running up and down metal staircases clearing rooms, and then we reached the one section of the platform reinforced with Iraqi Marines." He looks at Jumbo and Jumbo looks down at the floor. "These guys were trained and they'd fought a hot war with the Iranians. They knew what they were doing. We came under real pressure. The guy ahead of me had a frag grenade out and he was ready to use it. Anyway, only God knows why, but I froze. Voices all around me, the team moving like we had trained, smooth and slow, and I was worse than useless. My Master Chief yelled in my face and one of my brothers tried to shake me back to life, but I was frozen solid. They dragged me to the rear and told me to watch their six. The look of disgust on my brothers' faces. We were operators, trained for years, and I didn't cut it when I saw real combat. We weren't even taking fire, that was the worst of it. The other men did what they were trained to do. They moved and they communicated. Reps and sets. All with me standing still like an idiot. After the mission—we were lucky to come out with no serious injuries—I was sent off to work on the ships. Big navy. Two sailors decided to talk shit about my experience on the teams, both behind my back. One of our guys, and one from an Allied force. They'd never even met me. I taught one of them a lesson he'll not forget. It took me eight years to track him down and right that wrong. I lost my fingers in Brazil but my honor in Iraq. Failing my unit in the heat of the moment is the single biggest disgrace of my life, and I will bear the shame of it until the day I die."

36

"NO JUDGMENT, MATE," says Jumbo. "Wasn't even you, it was your sympathetic nervous system. No fault, no blame."

"Tell that to the men I failed. The men who could have been killed because I failed them."

Jumbo nods. It is clear André and I have nothing to bring to this conversation so we stay quiet. "Not your scene, mate," says Jumbo. "Not everyone's built to go downrange. Like I said: no judgment. Most would never even try it."

A long silence.

"That's why I never call myself a retired or ex-SEAL," says Mike. "I don't talk about Hell Week at BUD/S or swimming off Coronado or my training deployments or antics with operators from Allied forces. I don't deserve the few stories I got."

We say nothing.

Mike lowers his voice even more than usual. "I used to worry that if I had kids of my own one day, they'd turn out to be cowards like their old man. Dumb thought lodged in the back of my brain for years and years, festering and growing. Then, when I found Emily and she was foolish enough to move in with me, she eventually talked me into the idea." He scratches his Adam's apple. "She said our children would turn out just fine if we raised them right." He purses his lips. "The doctors told us it wasn't ever likely to happen. Issues with both of us. Doc said it was a non-starter. So I guess I failed on both counts."

"I never knew about any of that," says André. "And I don't know much, as you know. But I *do* know you're a world-class Sat diver."

"That I am," says Mike, nodding. "That I fucking am."

"Lads, we've got DCI MacDuff making his way down to you. You've already spoken to him over comms. He'll be with you by midnight."

I check the time on the wall next to the pressure gauge. The needle is falling but the pressure feels like it's building again. Five minutes to midnight. Again, we have no real sense of time inside this chamber. No space, either. We live an inch from the real world, from *your* world, from a world where the usual laws and rules apply, and yet we exist in another realm altogether. Grampian Police and the Procurator Fiscal and the HSE claim authority over us, they claim jurisdiction, but that is mostly delusional. For our time under pressure we are at once untouchable and completely vulnerable.

"One other thing, for you, Brooke," says Halvor. "Your camera batteries have been recharged, they will be coming through the Medlock now, but the DCI has asked for you not to delete any existing footage and also not to record anything new unless approved by him personally. Over."

I frown. "Roger that."

I retrieve the batteries from the Medlock and install them in my camcorder. Twenty-seven minutes' recording capacity left on the tape.

The new towels lie stacked on the bench in the exact position where Leo liked to sit as he ate eggs or played solitaire or wrote in the back of his books.

"Are these safe?" I say, gesturing to them.

"Towels?" says André.

I shrug.

Jumbo says, "I reckon they must be. Didn't the Super say we'd get post from the helicopter? Are we due post?"

Mike says, "He didn't mention mail. He said the fluid and tissue samples will go back with the chopper."

"He said magazines and newspapers, I think," says André. "Fresh reading material for you Luddites."

"Look who swallowed a dictionary," says Jumbo.

"I need the fiber," replies André.

We all smile. It feels safe when we're making inappropriate comments. It seems normal. Like we might make it out of this metal sarcophagus alive.

Mike rests on his bunk.

I begin writing a letter to Steve and the kids.

37

IF WE HAD no working clocks or watches we would still glean that it is nighttime. Not because we can see the world. The light levels do not adapt for us. There is little change in the number or frequency of visits from Bettys, because offshore workers are always on shift. It is so expensive to operate a DSV since it must operate twenty-four hours a day. I should be asleep right now to be woken at four in order to be prepped and in the Bell by five. Instead, I am lying in my bunk close to a dead, bagged man, trying to detect the scent of my children from their pillowcases. No, the only real indication of time comes from the reduction in deck noise. We are close to the open deck of the *Deep Topaz* by design. We need to descend via the Bell through the ship's moon pool, and we need to be supplied with equipment, hardware, and tools from the crane and riggers on deck. In daylight hours we can hear bangs and we can often feel the vibrations they create. The equipment tends to be heavy and industrial because it needs to be capable of withstanding the forces ever-present at the bottom of the sea: currents, and the corrosive power of salt water. We operate in a murky realm that we are not remotely welcome in.

Occasional low-level noises from deck. There are men and women working out there and their jobs are as dangerous as ours, only it is a different flavor of risk. They work in ungainly wet-weather gear and boots, life vests, hard hats, on a slippery open deck, in all weather, waves splashing up from the sea, muscling awkward gear onto hooks and into nets. I used to be one of them, and I will always have the utmost respect for what they manage to do on a fraction of our wage.

Mike is sitting in the living quarters writing something in his leather-bound book.

I move a little closer.

Is that a diagram? It looks like hand-drawn schematics or blueprints. And a list.

He notices me looking and closes the book.

"Brooke?" asks the Night Super.

"Still here."

"André?"

"I'm breathing."

"Jumbo?"

No response.

38

"JUMBO?" YELLS MIKE. "Gary, you lazy Brit bastard. You still with us, buddy?"

Again, no response.

Sweat at the back of my neck.

The chamber hums.

Mike leaps up and rips Jumbo's curtain open.

I can see it all from my top bunk.

Front row ticket.

A single bead of perspiration makes its way down my spine.

Jumbo's eyes snap open. "What?" he says.

"You alive, dipshit?"

"Am I *alive*?" he says, horrified, instinctively checking his neck for a pulse. "I think so. Of course I'm fucking alive. Fuck's sake, Mike, you can give a man a heart attack, you know. Am I bloody alive?"

"Copy that," says Mike, smiling out of relief, retreating to his bench.

Jumbo fixes his curtain and then drags it shut again, cursing under his breath, and I can't help but smile. Two fellow divers dead and we still view new safety measures and checks as inconveniences. Shock quickly turns to frustration and impatience. Maybe Mike and Jumbo talk to each other that way because of how they were trained years ago. They have slept in the jungle and the desert with no proper shelter at all. They get on with the job at hand. They sleep when and where they have the chance to do so.

The DCI asked me so many questions earlier tonight and I can't help going over them again and again in my head as I lie here, my socked foot touching the curtain. He asked about our relationships with the other crew, with the life support team, with Halvor. He doesn't look like he sounds, meaning he is not quite what I expected. MacDuff has a thick moustache, darker than what is left of his hair. He went through my previous Sat jobs in great detail, trying to piece together who had worked with whom in the recent past. It is clear he has access to *all* the logs. He asked me a lot about Steve and the kids, and about our mortgage, and about a complaint that's on record with Yorkshire Police. It's only a citation related to speeding but he drilled me about it nonetheless.

I hold my nose and equalize.

Four a.m.

A full day and a half until we can open the hatch.

Thirty-six more hours of purgatory.

DCI MacDuff and the Super checked if we would mind living with an additional camera once we reach Aberdeen. They asked whether we would protest to our sleep quarters being recorded. We all said we wouldn't mind.

I, for one, would welcome it.

The yellowish lights flicker on the wall.

Are the others looking over their shoulders like I am? I keep finding myself on edge, keeping watch out of the corner of my eye, head on a swivel. At the same time I know I can, and should, trust these three men. They have earned it. But I watch them nonetheless, partly because I have noticed them begin to watch me.

I would pay twenty bucks for a hot chocolate right now. Or one of those malty, oaty drinks Mom used to enjoy before bed. She would read a Stephen King novel or a Danielle Steel, horror or romance, her two favorite genres, and then she would sip from her favorite *I Heart Maine* mug while she turned the pages. All we have now is sealed bottles of orange juice, flat soda, and water.

The sound of Mike turning another page in his notebook. I'm not sure if it's a journal or a diary or a poem book, or all three. He might be designing a new piece of dive equipment by the look of the page I glimpsed. Divers sometimes do that. They identify an opportunity, keep the idea close to their chest, take it to a patent attorney, then, potentially, create their retirement fund when the prototype is bought. Mike is the kind of guy you would never expect to write prose or verse, or design a new flange system, but he is also exactly the kind of guy who constantly surprises you. Like how he studies biochemistry for kicks, and he has a half-poodle at home named Samantha.

We are all contradictions. Jumbo listens to thrash metal but he also enjoys cello concertos. André acts like he's barely literate yet he can recite Shakespeare and Yeats, and sometimes does, much to the annoyance of his fellow divers. He delivered a full soliloquy from *Hamlet* in a Bell one time and his fellow diver, an Irishman named O'Malley, asked never to work with him again.

The pressure gauge moves. I swear I see the needle shift a little. Last day and a half. The slowest part. I would consider sacrificing a kidney if it meant I could get back home.

And then I realize I forgot to ask DCI MacDuff what I planned to ask him.

Is it just us being questioned? Or are the crew being interrogated too?

39

WE TAKE IT in shifts to have short naps. I thought we would be able to push through, to avoid food and water completely, and to stay awake. But it turns out your body will not allow it. I saw once on a documentary how guilty suspects routinely fall fast asleep in police interview rooms while waiting for detectives to question them. They call this phenomenon *the perp sleep* and it is the body's coping mechanism for dealing with extreme stress. You shut down and take a catnap. For the four of us, it is the trauma of what we have already endured combined with simply surviving at this much pressure, going through a four-day deco, in a storm, with no clue what, or who, attacked our fellow divers.

Two nap on their bunks and two more sit on the benches pulling sentry duty. I never thought it would come to this. You half expect a flange to fail or a valve to leak at some point in your career, for outdated equipment combined with human error to cause a catastrophic failure. But never this.

Trust is built over many years.

And yet it can be destroyed in minutes.

Mike and I sit facing each other, and we are both on camera. Jumbo and André aren't really sleeping, they are enjoying what Mike calls *tactical naps*. I'm not really reading either, my eyes are too sore. We listen and we watch each other and we wait. Mike has put down the nonfiction book he borrowed from André. We each sport an expression of exhausted resignation.

"You gonna stare at us like this for the next thirty-four hours?" Mike says, his tone more grunt than speech, looking into the Betty's eyes through the porthole. The glass itself is who-knows-how-thick and it is circled by six bolts. I count them and then I count them again, clockwise, then counterclockwise. It is a coping technique; one of many. When I have intrusive thoughts, dark thoughts, unhealthy thoughts, I look for something reliable and quantifiable in my environment and then I count and re-count as if to confirm that reality, and truth, can be reliable in some circumstances. I have never been professionally advised to do this, but I read about it once in a book in Harrogate Library on Victoria Avenue.

The life support assistant does not shift position.

One thought keeps forcing the others away: What if it's one of us? A diver? But it cannot be possible. We have saved each other countless times. If I let my mind wander down that path it will lead to madness, to sedation against my will, to complete powerlessness.

The Betty watches us watch him. I sweat and I take short, raspy breaths of the oppressive gas this chamber is filled with.

A Mexican standoff, but at multiple atmospheres of pressure.

Mike turns to face me. "You look like shit."

"You look how I feel," I say.

He clenches his teeth, stands up, and starts to flex. He can't stretch his arms up, they'll hit the ceiling. He can't stretch them out, they'll hit the curved walls that encase us, or else he'll hit my face, or the lifeless feet of Leo. Mike has developed a routine over the years. He can run through a series of movements: hamstring, quad, shoulder, and back stretches while not taking up much more space than he usually would standing still. He opens the

Wet Pot hatch and with a smooth movement projects himself through to it. Leaving the door open he begins his daily regimen of push-ups and crunches.

I start filming him with my camcorder, narrating about the importance of healthy routines, of exercise, strength, good sleep. It's less than a minute. MacDuff won't mind if my project helps me stay on the level. Mike scowls back so I turn the thing off.

"Two pots of hot in the lock. Breakfast coming in a few minutes," says life support.

I frown. Then I open the hatch. Then I close it again with a bang.

Mike reemerges.

"No unsealed food or drink," I say, angrily. "As much as I'd kill for a coffee right now, can you bring bottles of water instead? This is important. And bring us some granola bars or something."

André staggers over, his eyes bloodshot. "We might risk it for a decent coffee, surely?" His voice is hoarse and it is low. "Not sure I can make it through the day without a hot beverage, Brooke."

"Suck it up, you lanky bastard."

He yawns and his breath is foul.

As Mike moves his arm I notice the writing in the back of his notebook. Looks like Bible verses. I can't make it out clearly so I fake a stretch and inch closer.

If your enemy is hungry, feed him.

I wasn't expecting that.

I wait for Mike to focus on the bunks for a moment and then I take another look. Block capital handwriting. Clear and large.

The Lord is a God who avenges.

Avenges? Is that in the Bible? I arch my neck and take another look.

They slay the widow and the foreigner; they murder the fatherless.

Mike turns his head back, so I sit down abruptly and clear my throat.

"You need some chow in you, André," says Mike, still staring at me. "Bony bastard. Only man I know who can take a shower and not get wet."

"Hit me with another," says the tall man. "I can take it."

"Sealed breakfasts coming through presently, lads," says the Night Super. "Apologies for the mix-up before. Shifts, you know. Over."

André looks unimpressed.

The biblical quotes reverberate in my head. I have no idea what they mean to Mike, but they must mean something for him to set them down in ink.

"I'm told Javad will be released from the hyperbaric lifeboat very soon," says the Night Super. "It'll take time to supervise, prep, for the police team to oversee transit, but then we'll blow it down again ready to accept Leo. Over."

"Understood," I say through clenched teeth.

We receive bottles of orange juice, apple juice, iced tea, and Mars drinks. Chocolate bars, cereal bars, sealed packs of chopped fruit, and an assortment of sealed, wrapped donuts.

"A novel way to slay us all, is it?" says Mike, eyeing a donut, its wrapping sucked tight to its glazed skin. "This isn't food."

Jumbo smiles.

"What?" says Mike. "Something funny?"

I do not appreciate this change in atmosphere.

"No, you're right," says Jumbo, on the back foot. "This isn't real food. I was just thinking about my uncle. His memories from World War Two. Ration packs. Logistical delays. He always said he considered himself half-starved, losing his strength and his mind, ribs poking out." Jumbo shakes his head. "He complained of having to make extra holes on his belt using his pocketknife.

Then him and his pals in Eleventh Armored Division liberated Belsen camp. He told me he would never complain of being hungry ever again after witnessing that."

Mike grinds his teeth, and then, after a long period of reflection, says, "Copy that."

The tension in the chamber stabilizes, at least temporarily.

Rivulets of sweat run down my back at what feels like regular intervals.

"My grandpa Leif," says Mike, "was on the USS *Indianapolis*."

Jumbo shakes his head. Mike takes that as a signal to continue.

"His ship was torpedoed off the coast of the Philippines."

"Is this more of an onshore-only subject?" I say.

Mike ignores me. He has already opened up more than he usually does onshore, and he appears to be half in a trance. "Grandpa said it was something that God should never have allowed. He said God must not have seen their plight. All I know is what Grandpa Leif told me and my brother when we were driving across Iowa. The truck was shaking and rattling and his words sank deep into our bones and they never left."

"I remember the speech in *Jaws*," says André.

"Never seen it," replies Mike.

"*Never seen it?*" says André, surprised.

"Let me tell you why." Mike narrows his eyes and takes another long pause. "After the ship went down my grandpa and his Marine brothers were in the water, covered in oil, many of them already injured. No lifeboats were deployed. The ship went down too quickly. It wasn't long before fins started appearing all around them. Hundreds of fins, if not thousands. Grandpa said the screams were unthinkable. Men floating just a few dozen feet from you, torn into pieces, a frenzy, and you're there waiting, seeing it, smelling it, hearing the groans, waiting your turn. Sometimes the men would survive for a while but everything under the waterline would be gone. They prayed and they prayed. They prayed as loud as they could to drown out the screaming all around them, the young sailors crying out for their mothers and their sweethearts."

The chamber creaks so loud we all look around, probing for leaks or alarms.

I know what Mike is doing. Even the most gruesome story is a distraction. We cannot be left to face our stark reality. It would be too much.

Mike goes on. "He made it through the night only to be greeted by boiling, relentless sun the next morning. No respite, no shade, no water to drink. Some of the boys drank seawater and then they lost their minds. Hundreds waiting for rain, even waiting for fins. Grandpa had buddies who pleaded to be killed. Brave men begged to be drowned." He takes a deep breath. "Days of drifting, of madness. Sailors with blank eyes who couldn't pray out loud anymore because of their thirst. Grandpa told us there were no atheists in the water. Not one. He had a buddy from Texas and he had to watch the man give up his spirit and die. Shadows everywhere, circling, never stopping. Life vests, stained, bobbing up and down in the distance. Then the planes arrived. They heard them before they spotted them. The men cried in among the bodies, with the sharks still writhing and thrashing, taking one after the other. No defense. One plane came down and landed. Three hundred and change survivors from a crew of twelve hundred. He told us about it one time. That's all it took."

There is no response from us.

"Grandpa taught me to live life. No regrets. Do what your gut tells you."

After a quiet stretch, we receive a stack of magazines: *Men's Health, GQ, Gardeners' World, Reader's Digest.*

"*Reader's* fucking *Digest*?" says Jumbo, cutting the atmosphere as he emerges from his bunk. He picks up the magazine. "Am I that old?"

"You actually are, Jum," says André, relief in his voice. "You're a genuine fossil."

"I am, aren't I?"

We go through the stack and select three each. They have also included a *Cosmopolitan* and a *Vogue*, both of which André takes because I'm not interested.

"Feels like I've been under for a month already," says Mike. "What I want is *news*: *The Sun*. *The Times*. *The Wall Street Journal*. Something to take me away from this ship."

"Not happening," says Jumbo, running his tongue over his teeth.

André frowns. Gestures for him to elaborate.

"You're it, baby," says Jumbo. "The *news*. I have figured it out. We're all it, you see. They're not going to send through analysis and reports on what happened to Tea-Bag and Spocky, now are they? No radio news either, remember? *Technical malfunction*. Yeah, right. *Affects the whole ship*. Of course it does. No news for us, lads. Best way to make us lose our minds, that would be. This way they have complete control of our information."

40

THE ATMOSPHERE INSIDE the chamber is not dissimilar to a student kitchen the morning after an all-night house party. We are not messy or filthy, that's been drilled into us all a dozen different ways, military and civilian, but we are tired and vague. We are not hungover and yet we are: by the constant hum of this place, by the lack of air, by the helium saturated into our soft tissues, by the pressure gauge needle taunting us with its glacial progress.

We eat because we know we will soon need the energy to drag Leo's body off his bunk, through the tight chamber, via the hatch tunnel, into the Wet Pot, up through the hatch in the ceiling, into the trunking, following the bend, into the hyperbaric lifeboat itself. Diet is vital for divers. Sure, we can eat like pigs from time to time, but if you want a long career in Sat you need to be able to call upon your body to complete strenuous tasks whenever required.

On advice from Dive Control we check each other's vitals: body temperature, pulse rate, breathing, blood pressure.

No updates on the lifeboat. We might be able to hear them open the hatch and remove the body. We might be able to sense it because we are all connected.

"Pinochle or Spades," asks Jumbo.

"Spades," says André.

"Bourré," says Mike.

"No," say Jumbo and André together. Mike always wins at Bourré.

We wipe down the central table and the benches and then we place trash bags into the Medlock and wipe down the lock and the hooks.

André deals cards, his legs taking up too much space around the table.

"What happened in the big game, first night, steaming out, when we came over to the table?" asks André.

"No factor," says Mike, bringing his cards close.

"Come on," urges Jumbo.

"What?" says Mike. "They wanted a game so I gave them one. Was all over in less than an hour. Like I said: no factor."

"Who is *they*?" asks André.

Mike lifts his chin. I can now see his eyes under the peak of his cap. "One of the Bettys, the skinny one who wants to work on this side of the hatch. And one of the kitchen hands, looks like Bigfoot's uglier, older brother. And one of the crane dudes. Four players."

André finishes dealing the cards. "And?"

"What do you think?"

"You won."

"Yes," says Mike. "I did."

"And?" says André again.

"Are we playing cards or aren't we?"

Jumbo says, "Bourré is a dangerous game."

"It was that night," says Mike, unsmilingly.

"I wish I could go for a walk," I say.

They all laugh.

"Ain't that the goddamn truth," says Mike.

I look at him.

"We played a game," he says again, adjusting his cap. "Things got a little . . . heated. Usual bullshit. I took some cash off the kitchen fella. Nothing serious. Took a set of keys off the crane operator, ex-navy guy. Again, no big deal."

André frowns. "When you say *keys*, you mean you took his car or his house?"

"Bike," says Mike. "Honda, five hundred cc. I didn't take it, I *won* it. I'll see what I got when I leave the bin. Probably a heap of rust, knowing my luck."

"And the other guy, the Betty tasked with actually keeping us alive?" asks André.

"He'll be good for it."

"How much does he owe you, Mike?" I ask.

"Some."

I let out a big sigh. "How much?"

"Fifteen grand."

41

I SIT, BLEARY-eyed, staring out the porthole as numerous uniformed people in hard hats with ear pro dangling from their necks walk past on their way to and from the deck. We are approaching Aberdeen. These lads have enjoyed a good night's sleep, and now they will head home, whereas we have to stay locked in for another day and a quarter.

"Exhausted," says André.

"Quit complaining," says Jumbo. "We survived the night. Mike?"

"What is it?" says a gruff voice from the bunks.

"We all survived the night."

"Big deal."

"So now we know it's someone out there with a grudge," says Jumbo. "Someone either messing with our food and water, or else teaming up with his mate in the kitchen."

"All this inconvenience over a game of Bourré?" says André.

He is not being callous. I mean, he is; to a nondiver his comments would seem outrageous. But down here our humor is about as black as the oil we help extract from the seabed. André once told me: *We laugh at absolutely everything. And we fix absolutely everything. Whatever it is, we sort it out ourselves.*

"I want a bacon sandwich with red sauce," says Jumbo. "Crispy bacon, butter, cheap white bread. I am prepared to risk it."

He is kidding.

I think.

We all look terrible. Decaying. Physical exertion is one thing, but this variety of mental torture, of time slowing down, of having no confidence in the people outside whose job it is to keep you alive, saps the energy from you.

Jumbo scratches his ankle down by his Sonic tattoo and complains he cannot remember his PIN code, his daughter's birthday, or his new cell phone number. This is what we call *bubble brain*. Too many Sat hours affect our minds in some strange and undocumented ways.

We clean the surfaces and wipe down. Jumbo disinfects rails and handholds, André does the floors, I focus on the table. Lisa once told me, and she can't have been older than seven at the time, that I wasn't a real human for the first two days home after finishing a twenty-eight-day contract offshore. She'd say I was an alien for two days because I wouldn't stop repeatedly scrubbing the table and the kitchen countertops.

André looks exhausted all of a sudden. A meanness in his eyes. A strange defensiveness.

You OK? I mouth to him.

He looks conspiratorially at Jumbo and Mike as if a thought has come to him. A theory or a deduction. Then he nods to me and looks down at the floor.

"In the old days," says Jumbo, absentmindedly flicking through a copy of *Reader's Digest*, "it was more peaceful in here. Sat was a time to escape, in the chamber, I mean. We read way more books back then. There were no fancy Nokia phones or Sony Ericssons with Snake games, no digital MP3 players or anything of the sort. You came in and you spent some time with yourself. Tackled your demons or else buried them so deep you'd never, ever dig them up again."

42

I ACCIDENTALLY FALL asleep sitting upright on the bench. *Catnap*. We've all taken a few in the past hours and we don't look or feel any more rested after waking.

I saw a lot of Bourré troubles in the Gulf of Mexico. Mixed memories of those days. I worked with some of the best people I have ever come across, learning a lot, taking home decent money for the first time in my life, being independent, laughing so much my sides hurt. The water is warmer and clearer than it is here in the North Sea. But the safety and comfort levels were lower, and I saw too many divers lose it out there.

We had one crane operator, a young half Haitian man from Mauriceville, who was accused by a Sat diver of sleeping with his wife. The diver, who I will not name, was a huge bald man with hands like shovels, and he was on his fourth marriage. He had heard rumors that the handsome young crane operator had been spotted in the same mall parking lot as his new bride. He heard these rumors as he was stepping into Sat. He heard more about them when he was blown down to depth. There were twelve of us in that system and most of us wanted out immediately. The big man, a true veteran of the industry, a legend, a name uttered with equal amounts of awe and fear, worked himself up into a fury. We didn't know if he would turn on one of us, or if he would try to open a hatch and destroy us all in the process. He would pace the chamber, maybe three paces, over and over again, fuming. It was like being locked in a pressurized caravan with an incensed bull. That was one of the longest Sat experiences of my life. Luckily, as it was a larger, more elaborate system, we could decompress in an extra chamber designed for the task. We got him out after a few days. He went through deco with one other diver, as is the custom, and was sent onshore. Three weeks later he shot the crane operator between the eyes with a .45 outside a steak house in Lafayette.

Bourré was the source of the problem in that case too. The half Haitian man, a complete innocent, had won a significant sum from a diver I will call Mo. Mo, instead of facing up to his debt, started the rumor about the wife of the bull. He made the bull pay for *his* problems, eradicating the owner of the debt. He manipulated the situation to make the bull, and the crane operator, pay the price for his own failings.

Love, money, vengeance.

André sits next to me. "Sharks."

I look at him as if half drunk.

He says, "Go, Brooke."

I frown.

"I said: *go*."

I am not in the mood. If I'm to survive this chamber I need to keep my wits about me and keep my eyes on my fellow divers and the crew outside.

There is no time for this.

"Not now," I say.

"Mike. Any shark attacks?" asks Jumbo.

No reply.

"Mike," says André. "Sharks."

Again, no response.

"Mike. Sharks. Go," I say, my voice breaking.

Still nothing.

"Lazy good-for-nothing," says André, smacking Mike's foot with his own from the bench. "Sharks. You told me something one time about doing combat sidestroke off the shore of San Diego."

Nothing.

Jumbo sits up.

I stand.

"Is everything OK?" asks Dive Control through the speaker.

I step over to Mike's bunk.

43

"PUT HIM ON the floor," I say. "Take his feet."

Fluid leaks from Mike's lips. He is facing the curved wall of the chamber. This former special operator is in the fetal position. We move him. More vomit from the corner of his mouth.

I look at him, aghast.

André says, "One, two, three," and we swing him down onto the ground.

Jumbo dashes over to the porthole window and bangs on the wall in frustration. "Medic. Mike's unresponsive."

We should never have gone back to the bunks.

Bad things happen there.

"Medic's on her way right now," says the Super.

I scoop vomit from his mouth with my fingers, and try to clear his airway.

"I've got a pulse," says André, triumphant. "Faint pulse."

The medic does not appear at the porthole but Halvor does. He looks haunted, rubbing his hands up and down his face.

"We need help in here," says André, panic suddenly in his voice. "We need you to help us right now. He's got a pulse, boss."

"IV," says Halvor. "Stabilize him. The medic's on her way."

Could *she* be behind all this? Gonzales has access to the medication, to the specialized equipment, to the food. Is Gonzales tampering with the adrenaline shots she's passing us through the Medlock?

DCI MacDuff arrives on the scene and tries to give us emergency medical instructions, but he soon realizes we are far more qualified in this regard than he is. André puts a line expertly into Mike's limp arm, piercing a trident tattoo later transformed into an anchor and chain. An IV bag is passed through the Medlock by Gonzales, and Jumbo stands over Mike holding the bag.

"I can't find that pulse," I say. "André, you try."

He pushes his fingers to Mike's neck and listens to his chest, his ear in direct contact with Mike's skin.

"No pulse," he says. "Start compressions."

Jumbo hands me the IV bag and begins CPR. He is better at it than I am. We have never talked about this fact but we both know it instinctively, and we both understand we must give Mike the best chance possible.

I stagger back a pace in disbelief.

Nobody is helping us.

André knocks his head hard on a bunk as Jumbo pushes his palms deep into Mike's chest, thrusting with his whole bodyweight, cycles of five. This never worked for the others, why would it work now? It might work. Mike is stronger than the others. He has been through more and he has survived more.

"Come on, lad, where's your bottle?" says Jumbo, spittle flying from his lips. "You've got more than this, haven't you? Mike? You hear me, brother? You're harder than this, aren't you?"

Liquid drains from Mike's mouth. The vision of it is appalling. Hopeless.

"What are we supposed to do?" asks André, wide eyed, as he turns to the portholes for answers.

Gonzales passes through adrenaline shots. André administers them. She instructs us to use the mask attached to BIBS. We do it. We try everything. We do not give up on our friend.

"Who's going to lift the boats?" says Jumbo, tears in his eyes. "Or the logs? Who's going to lift the damn boats, Mike? And the logs?"

He's talking about BUD/S training. Mike has told us onshore how he had to complete selection partly by running with his teammates carrying heavy boats, their legs chafing with wet sand, and running with wet logs in the middle of the night. He was in the Smurf crew, consisting of the shortest hopefuls. He told us men would follow them around with a bell on wheels for them to ring whenever they wished to quit and for the pain to end.

"Don't ring that bell, Mike," I say, my voice quivering. "Stay with us, buddy."

André takes over compressions and I hold the IV bag.

Jumbo steps over to the porthole and presses his face up to the reinforced glass, pushing his nose into it. "Don't just stand there for God's sake. Help us."

44

SEVENTY MINUTES OF CPR.

No words exchanged beyond the minimum necessary to take shifts performing compressions, giving additional shots of adrenaline, following instructions from Gonzales, administering further interventions.

But we all know it.

We keep on fighting because it is Mike but we have seen too much of this. The drifting away of life from this place.

"I'll call it," says Gonzales.

"The fuck you will," says Jumbo, loudly, jumping up, taking over from me pumping Mike's lifeless chest. Pushing down with all his might. One, two, three, four, five. After a few minutes he breaks down, weeps, and then he thumps Mike in the breastbone. He thumps him again with a hammer punch. Then he checks for a pulse.

There is none to be found.

"Get us," he growls, "the fuck out of here right now."

Halvor replaces DCI MacDuff in the window. "Soon, Gary. Very soon. If I decompress too quickly you'll all get bent, you know you will. I wish I could change the physics."

Jumbo stands up. Then he reaches down and closes Mike's

eyelids gently with his fingertips and crosses his chest. I have never before seen Jumbo give any sign he was a man of faith.

"I'm not taking samples from him," says Jumbo, out of breath, standing at the porthole. "We came up together, do you understand?"

Halvor is replaced by DCI MacDuff. His moustache. His tired eyes.

"You don't have to do it," says the DCI. "The others can help."

Jumbo thumps the metal wall of the chamber. "Do your damn job, Inspector. We're down to three. Do you have any idea what it's like to be locked in here right now with your dead mates? Do you?"

DCI MacDuff looks down for a moment and then says, "We'll be in Aberdeen later this morning. We'll bring in a fresh team and boost supervision. We'll also have results back from forensics today. I'm sorry for your loss."

Gonzales replaces him. She looks shaky. "I'm passing through the instruments for the tissue and serological samples. I wish I could remove this burden from you. I wish I could take the samples myself."

In a state of disbelief combined with brutal acceptance, I take swab samples of vomit, saliva, and nail scrapings. We are becoming numb to this ugly protocol. Piercing the leg artery of a lost friend. Sealing blood samples. Pulling out clumps of his cap-flattened hair. Passing it all through the Medlock in order.

"Send through a body bag," says André.

"We can't," says Halvor. "We have run out."

45

JUMBO SHROUDS MIKE'S body in a fresh pale blue bedsheet.

"Don't touch him in any way," says Gonzales. "I'm being told now we shouldn't cover him."

"There is no *we*," utters André. "And he's already covered. We can't live in here with him uncovered."

His voice is calm but firm.

"OK," says Halvor. "Roger that."

André mutters, "You should have more body bags on board."

Three of us left on the benches now.

Half.

Tea-Bag was a new diver. We didn't know him well. Leo lived up to his nickname but we respected him and we'd all dived with him multiple times. But now *Mike* is gone? Mike is a kind of father figure to many. He was a slow-talking elder of the community. I once overheard a supervisor say, *Mike always plays with a straight bat.*

And yet we cannot grieve his loss. Because we are still present in this waking nightmare, but also because we are being watched by the camera and through the portholes. Eyeballs observe the three of us as we sit here in disbelief. They *claim* they are protecting us. Is the news really unavailable or is it being withheld intentionally?

Jumbo rubs his eye.

"What is this?" says André, to no one in particular. "What did we do to deserve this? *Who* is doing this?"

"We did nothing, mate," says Jumbo, under his breath. "We need to lay low and then get clear of here. This is my last Sat job. I know I've blurted that out before but I am serious this time. I'm done being in the bin."

Neither of us say anything in response.

The hum intensifies.

"Listen." I take a breath. "We can't drink any more water. Eat any more food. Nothing at all, not a single drop, no more risks. We insulate ourselves from the outside world completely, except for gas. Cut ourselves off. Twenty-six hours left on the clock. We can't sleep in the bunks, either. Lads go to sleep there and they don't wake up."

"How *could* we sleep on them?" says André, gesturing to Mike on the floor, his socked feet protruding from the base of the bedsheet. "They all died there."

Jumbo lets out something between a stunted laugh and a cough. "No food or water. No sleep. Screw this." Then he says something unintelligible.

"What?" I say.

"*Three hots and a cot*, Brooke." He pronounces my surname with such a strong Liverpool accent I can sense it even through the helium. "We'd say that in the military. Life taken care of for you so you can get on with the job at hand. Three decent meals and a bed to sleep in. They also say it in prison."

I nod.

I know the phrase.

"Life is simple when you're provided with three hot meals and a cot," Jumbo goes on. "Serves a certain kind of person well, that does. You can focus on your work. Mates of a similar mindset included free of charge into the bargain. Now, thanks to these thoughtless bastards"—he gestures to the bunk where Leo lies in his body bag, and the floor where Mike rests under his sheet—"we've lost our basic privileges."

DCI MacDuff's face appears at the porthole. His moustache whiskers press up against the glass.

"We're arriving into Aberdeen docks soon. I've just been up and seen bottlenose dolphins."

André pushes his face to our side of the glass and snarls. "Are you telling us *that* after we just lost our mate?"

"I saw Pocra Quay," MacDuff goes on, seemingly unfazed, no retreating. "I wanted to remind you that the teams will be swapped out. New kitchen staff, new life support, new assistants, new gas man."

"But we're keeping Halvor for the rest of deco, right?" says Jumbo, sitting up straight.

I pat Jumbo on the arm and whisper, "Do you really think that's wise?"

46

WE REQUEST TWO minutes of privacy from the portholes and camera, but DCI MacDuff says that's not possible at the moment.

I write down on my paper, *Halvor should move off as well, surely? No matter how much we all trust him.*

Jumbo utters, "Bullshit," and then writes on the pad. *I've dived with Halvor more than any other man outside the Royal Navy. He would sooner die himself than any of us come to harm.*

André says, "I agree."

I think back to the lawsuit, the financial and reputational implications, the subsequent HSE investigation into their unorthodox shift protocols. But Halvor and I made our peace immediately afterward. He was a gentleman about the whole thing, unlike his business partners.

"We'll keep Halvor," I say to the eye at the porthole. Despite everything I trust him more than anyone else outside this chamber. "But I think there should be supervision of all the supervisors, if you know what I mean."

"Already arranged," says DCI MacDuff. "We're putting in place a series of extra precautionary safeguards for the three of you, just as soon as we reach shore. Could one of you pass the camcorder back through the Medlock."

I do as he asks.

"Once we have docked we will have more surveillance equipment to feed through to you for your safety."

"Bottlenose dolphins," mutters Jumbo when the Detective Chief Inspector has left the area outside the dive system. "What planet is he on?"

"He's trying to let us think of something else," says André, nodding to himself. "Allowing us to escape the chamber in our minds, even for just a few moments. He knows we could crack if we don't have a better outside world to cling to."

Jumbo looks like he'll come back with a biting retort but then he swallows it. He starts to break down but then disguises it with a cough. André and I pat him gently on the back. Three of us left, reassuring each other without saying as much.

Ten minutes go by.

"I owe Mike fifty quid," says André, somberly. "Bet from Easter. He never asked for it and now I'll never be able to repay him."

"Pay it to his girlfriend," says Jumbo. "Give it to Emily."

I close my eyes. His girlfriend, Emily, whom I have only met once. His parents back in California. Leo's wife and four daughters. Tea-Bag's family and friends. So many points of grief. They will deal with this news in their own ways: disbelief, fury, exhaustion, despair, recklessness, insomnia, blame. Some may grow while others wither.

Did I do anything inadvertently to facilitate this? Was there a safety step missed, like in the Bell? Have I been negligent? There is a part of me, a shadowy, illogical part deep down inside my brain, that tells me I might have. It is like the recurring dream where I find myself digging in the wet sand of a deserted beach. It is always squally and twilight in that dream, that nightmare. I am digging with my bare hands in the rain, shoveling sand out of the way as the hole I am creating fills with gray salt water. There is a sense that someone is approaching in the far distance.

A line of people. The rain intensifies and the skies darken further still. My fingertips are bloodied. My nails begin to split and blacken. Lightning illuminates the horizon, forks of it lighting up the sky. As I dig and dig I uncover a finger, then a hand, and then I remember, with breathless panic, in the very final moments before waking, that I buried the body myself weeks before.

47

THE SHIP DOCKS into Aberdeen.

We can't see it happen; we are merely informed that it *is* happening. Once again, we are forced to trust the information we are fed. There is banging on deck. I can feel the DSV move differently in the water, thrusters being used to edge us closer, and there is commotion outside. Men in hard hats walk in the distance. Are there news vans out there? Tabloid photographers with telephoto lenses? I watch two deckhands through our dollhouse-scale window. Orange overalls, beards, radios on lapels. Are they as afraid as we are?

No.

They are not.

Twenty minutes later people arrive outside our chamber.

The Superintendent informs us he's staying, along with Halvor and one of the life support supervisors. The rest are moving onshore. The Super tells us everything they do is being logged like always, but it is also being filmed and independently supervised by a specialist team from Grampian Police. He says Assistant Chief Inspector Siward and Procurator Fiscal Fiona Caithness are currently conducting a tour of the ship, and will pass by the chamber, but they will not be stopping to talk.

"Too important to listen to us sat rats," says Jumbo.

"Not at all," says the Super, his Argyll accent shining through. "I'm told it's routine. You'll be pleased to hear fresh supplies are making their way into the galleys and that whole process is also being supervised and recorded for your security."

"We're not eating," says André. "Not a single bite. We're not drinking or sleeping, either."

Another voice comes over the intercom. A new Life Support Technician. "We've discussed the matter and we've decided you need to eat and drink," he says. "In case of an emergency you must have sufficient energy to help yourselves and your colleagues."

We look at each other.

Three pairs of bloodshot, anxious eyes.

We do not verbally protest, but I know for sure that we will not eat their food.

DCI MacDuff asks us to don gloves and masks to package up Mike's belongings, including the water bottle in his bunk, and pass them through to be bagged and tagged. It is a laborious process and we have to be mindful not to step on him as we retrieve objects. Sat divers can be bulky oafs, but we develop some degree of balletic ability over the years. It is rare that we bump into one another or spill a drink. Every movement is calculated. We tend to have well-developed spatial awareness.

"He seemed invincible," says Jumbo, looking down at the sheet, at the protuberance of Mike's nose pushing up from below. He clenches his teeth. "Was sure he'd outlive me."

"Will we have Wi-Fi now we're in dock?" I ask, knowing that Jumbo has his laptop here. "People are keen to email relatives, you know."

A long pause. "We're still working on that. Will keep you updated. Over."

André shakes his head. "They don't want us reading stuff, do they?" His voice is not much more than a whisper. "Not texts, not photos, not pics of the *Daily Mail*. They don't want us finding out the truth."

Jumbo sits down on the bench and keeps his voice low. "I'm not sure I want to know. What can I do about it inside here? I miss the old days when we weren't downloading ringtones and irritating each other with them. The old days were quiet. We'd sleep more. It felt like a simple life, like being a teenager again."

"Lads," says the Super. "Body bag coming through the equipment lock now. Stand by."

48

ANDRÉ AND I retrieve the body bag package from the Wet Pot equipment lock. It is the same color as the one Leo is zipped inside of. We slide through the hatch and find Jumbo all alone, kneeling, uttering something to his old mate.

We stop.

We do not proceed.

In a place like this, with no personal space, we recognize this for what it is. We choose not to impinge on Jumbo's moment.

"I wish they'd turn the cap," says André. "I'd rather be bent than spend another night in here."

He means he'd rather risk decompressing in a rapid and unsafe manner. Safety is relative I guess. André describes accelerated deco as *turning the cap* because he sees us as living inside a shaken up Coca-Cola bottle. Dive Control twists the cap a tiny fraction at a time, easing out a little pressurized gas, then closes it again. The process is controlled and steady, and if done correctly, no drop of Coca-Cola, or in our case, hemoglobin, will be spilled.

Jumbo takes the bag from us and shakes it loose. We place it by Mike but there is little room so most of it rests on top of the bedsheet. Dive Control asks us to keep the sheet in place and I am not sure if they are suggesting this to protect us from seeing Mike with livor mortis, or to preserve potentially criminal evidence. Jumbo holds the bag at the head end. We are at the feet, by the folded-away table and the benches. There is no room to work. As gracefully and carefully as we can, we lift Mike's limp, heavy body and place it inside. The transfer is not as smooth as we would have hoped. Mike was a big man. Jumbo sweats from his nose and his forehead, and finally, after much manhandling, we zip him securely inside.

As we wait for stretchers capable of transferring these two to the now unoccupied hyperbaric lifeboat, Jumbo tells us a story about him and Mike diving off the coast of India. He says they were air diving, but that it was borderline too deep and it probably should have been a Sat job. He says their aim was to bounce down to depth and get the flanges finished as quickly as possible, then resurface and spend a little time decompressing in a surface chamber before taking the rest of the day off. You shouldn't sunbathe after a dive like that, it's against regulations, but you could relax in a bar and chat to locals. Jumbo laughs. "Mike and I got a taste for narcosis, like the wankers we were."

"Past tense?" says André.

"In his case it's true," says Jumbo, gesturing to the body bag.

I can't help but laugh. Lord, forgive me.

"We were becoming drunk from all the nitrogen. Coming up half bent, giggling, not knowing what day it was. We had it down to a fine art in the end. One of the best jobs I ever did in India, that was."

"Stretchers coming through into the TUP now."

I retrieve them from the equipment lock.

As I pass through into the main chamber my head is light. I am numb and dizzy at the same time. Exhausted and hungry and lost in a space with no fixed point to tether to.

Floating.

"You OK, Brooke?" asks André.

"I will be."

We place the body bag onto one of the orange lightweight flexible stretchers, and since Jumbo still hasn't zipped up the end we can see the pale blue bedsheet covering Mike's face. It is as if Jum is leaving him some space to breathe.

We stand. André and me at the feet again. Jumbo by the head.

"He only had a few more bin runs in him," says Jumbo. "Would have made a half-decent supervisor, I reckon. A Night Super, in time."

"I could have seen that," says André.

Jumbo takes the zip in his good hand, and, with his voice cracking, asks us, "Anybody have anything they want to say?"

André crosses his hands over his groin and looks down at his feet.

I shake my head.

Jumbo coughs, bites his upper lip, clears his throat, sets his jaw, and answers his own question. "Strong diver." Then he zips up the body bag.

49

"CAN CONFIRM THE hyperbaric lifeboat has been cleared, sanitized, sealed, and blown down. It is ready to accept the two stretchers when you are. Over."

We stare at each other.

Jumbo laughs.

André frowns.

"Sorry," says Jumbo. "This is ridiculous, you have to admit it. I've done a war halfway around the world, over twenty years in and out of Sat, some pretty hairy dives and close calls, and then this happens."

"Nobody can say it's a boring career choice," I say.

"Ready in five minutes, lads?"

I look at the other two and reply, "Copy that."

We are not ready. We are emotionally unprepared and physically wrecked. Not by manual labor at sea—that is a walk in the park for us, relatively speaking—but by the constant pressure, and droning, and humidity, and enduring against an invisible enemy. Three shipwrecked divers locked inside. Our threat is external, it must be.

Anything else would he unthinkable.

"We can do this," says Jumbo. "Let's get to it."

We stand.

I trust Jumbo and André.

"Leo first," says André.

Am I being naive, though?

You cannot trust them.

Oh, no, not now. Deep breaths.

You're crazy to trust either one of them.

I bite down hard on my lip to make it stop.

My shirt is sticking to my back, to my neck. I open the hatch to the Wet Pot and then the hatch to the trunking. I venture up the ladder and squeeze up the tight, enclosed space, no natural light, toward the lifeboat. This one should probably be renamed. I open the hatch and take a deep breath. Ridiculous notion. I expect fresh air in this new space but there is no air. Just our stale, recycled helium breaths. Ten bucks a sigh. Twelve for a scream.

If I suspect either of them I will lose my cool.

I must stay focused.

Stay calm.

I rig up the Maasdam rope on the winch and double-check the fastenings. Then I call out, "Rope in place, ready here."

"Roger that," says the Superintendent. "Lads, bring up the first when you're ready."

I wait.

They are lifting Leo's day-old corpse onto one of the stretchers, awkwardly carrying the deadweight over and around Mike's still-warm body so they don't drop one on top of the other. The abhorrent charade of this. They are bringing him through to the hatch. Protocol and training kicks in. We have drilled this a hundred times. They take a small cloth that is designed to minimize friction, and they place it on the connecting trunking between the living chamber and the Wet Pot, and then one will slither through, and the stretcher will be pushed, and then the other diver will follow. All this and Jumbo hasn't even been wet on this trip.

"Rope coming down now," I say.

I lower the rope and watch as Jumbo takes it, the whites of his eyes shining up at me in this fetid, murky trunking, and he clips it to the head end of the stretcher. I watch as Jumbo climbs the ladder—his tattooed knuckles protruding—and maneuvers the stretcher to avoid it hitting rungs. A blockage or fall here could be a major problem. André operates from below. The rope takes the strain but it needs working. Constant adjustments. Leo's body rises up vertically—as if a prelude to some spiritual ascent—and after twenty minutes of finessing, we manage to bring him into the lifeboat. The mood is somber. Panting from exertion, we place his stretcher down by the portside seat, exactly where Tea-Bag once was.

Removing our lost brothers one by one.

"Make sure you create enough space for Mike," says the Super.

We do not respond to that.

Of course we will leave enough space for Mike.

André clips on the climber's carabiner to the head end of the second stretcher and Jum says, "steady." Panting, sweat falling off our faces, we bring Mike up. Jumbo has a prominent vein in his forehead and it is pulsing and throbbing from exertion.

"Too many pies, mate," he whispers to his fallen friend, stifling a sob and a smile.

We bring him up as smoothly as we can, cautious not to knock any of the rigid plastic seats that line the tight lifeboat.

None of us can stand up straight in here, not even close.

Two bodies.

We come together, hunched, our T-shirts drenched, and we have no words.

The forbidden scent of death lingers all around us.

We disconnect the Maasdam rope.

"Close the hatch on your way out, please," says the Super.

"Hatch secure," I say. "Over."

We climb down.

Standing in the Wet Pot, the three of us wipe perspiration from our faces and then we step back into the living chamber. Cables, gray-green walls, fire extinguishers, painted metal.

Jumbo positions himself close to the porthole window.

"That's enough now," he says, smiling through gritted teeth. "Nobody else gets hurt, you understand me. You're life support. Do your fucking jobs."

50

OUR METAL CHAMBER creaks as the pressure continues to adjust. A tin balloon being pumped up and let down. The integrity of each and every individual rivet vital.

The gauge on the wall edges counterclockwise as slowly as anything has ever moved. With every drop in atmospheric pressure we seem to lose a life. Some cruel escapology game, corrupted. *If you can survive until the pressure equalizes with the outside world you may have a chance to walk out.*

I am faint. My eyelids are heavy and my breathing labored.

André looks like he might pass out any second. "They watch us take showers, watch us eat dinner together." His voice isn't much more than a wheeze. "And yet they cannot work out what or who is hurting us?"

A Life Support Technician comes over the comms. "Lads, we have movies for you if you want to watch something. Take your mind of it. I'm told we have the new Jodie Foster film."

"What's it called?" I ask.

The Life Support Technician glances at the DVD cover. "*Panic Room*."

André and Jumbo exchange looks.

"I'm kidding," says the LST. "I'm just kidding. We've got *Fast and Furious*."

We do not appreciate him including himself in our dark humor club. It doesn't work like that, especially not on this job. He has no right. He hasn't earned membership.

Gonzales's voice. "I've been speaking to the team at Edinburgh University and we'd like to put you all on a course of broad-spectrum antibiotics immediately, just to be prudent. There's no indication bacterial infection caused any of this, but it is a preventative measure."

André stands up. "I'm only speaking for myself, but you can stick your prudent measures where the sun don't shine. I can't trust anything that's sent through that Medlock."

Jumbo nods. "We're sitting this out, Doc, thanks, nothing personal. Don't fancy getting accidentally poisoned in here, you know what I mean?"

A loud creak.

We all stare at the hatch, at the handle.

I wipe the back of my neck and say, "Twenty-four hours to go." Then I take a deep breath. "Feels like we can do this."

We are not brothers in the same way as soldiers are. We are merely divers working contracts, desperate for the next job, competing, worried about underwater drones taking our careers in the years to come, and yet I feel the same urge to comfort Leo's family as I would if we had fought together in Mogadishu or Vietnam.

"New camera coming through, lads," says the Super. "Set it up same as the last one, please. Make sure the whole chamber is in shot. Every corner."

There are no corners.

I take the camera from the Medlock and switch it on. Then I position it on the wall.

So many recording devices and so few answers. The lack of information degrades our spirits. We have too little autonomy.

"Antibiotics?" grunts André, rolling his eyes. "When we were working in Russia for you know who. Big Frank was the dive supervisor, deep Sat, too deep for our team if you ask me." Jumbo looks defeated as he watches André tell his story. "Young lad, navy lad, no names, he had a pimple on his chest. Wasn't picked up in med checks. Just a small one, it was. But after a day under pressure it grew into a boil, then a cyst. Anyway, our medic didn't seem overly worried but he gave the man antibiotics. Lad decided to mess around with it one night after his dive. Squeezed it or nudged it, I don't know which. It burst. Probably something to do with the ultradeep Sat pressure. Luckily for him the rest of his mates were asleep and I was busy in the Wet Pot. When I came through he was wiping down the walls and blood was trickling down his shirt. The air smelled rotten. I asked him what had happened and he told me it just ruptured. We used enough bleach that day to kill a small whale, cleaned him up, sterilized everything we could, wiped down again with alcohol, fresh set of wipes, clean dressing on his chest, further cleanup, then sent everything out through the lock double-wrapped in bags."

"Is this supposed to cheer us up?" says Jumbo, flatly.

André doesn't answer him. "He had a staph infection. That pimple turned into something far more sinister. Maybe we missed a droplet of puss on the wall or maybe there were some in the air, the gas, I don't know. Went through us like wildfire. Eight-day deco."

Jumbo, cringing, scratches at his wrists.

"That's enough," I say.

André ignores me. "We were all on strong antibiotics but we still became sick. Very sick indeed. Super called a meeting and decided to deco all of us immediately just like this. Bosses were furious. They must have lost millions on that one job. Anyway, most of us had flu symptoms, which is bad enough in the bin, but one lad, a Scot, suffered something else."

"Go on," I say, eager for him to finish, my throat rasping for lack of water.

André scratches the area between his upper lip and his nose and says, "Got a rash on his foot, then one on his face. We were about six days from the hatch opening and he was in agony, poor lad. We gave him all the pain meds we could. Ketamine, morphine, the good stuff. But the infection was slowly eating him alive. *Necrosis*. We had to sit around and watch him, listen to his moans and pleas each night, try to comfort him without getting too close."

"André," says Jumbo. "That's enough, mate."

"Lost half his jaw before the chamber opened," he says. "We could see his teeth roots through the holes in his gums."

51

SIX BEDS. THREE bunks in a U-shape.

Three of those beds unoccupied.

In the early days, before our modern safety protocols, divers used to hot-bunk like submariners. They would finish a long dive, shower in the Wet Pot, eat wearing a towel, then have to sleep in someone else's warmth. Protocols and standards are generally only ever improved after a disaster. Trauma breeds innovation. I wonder what improvements will be made in the coming months to ensure nothing like this, whatever *this* is, ever happens again.

Jumbo is doing push-ups in the Wet Pot. The hatch is open. He is taking long rests between sets because despite being a wiry, naturally fit man, he is almost out of gas.

I hear him start sobbing.

He closes the Wet Pot hatch.

"I need to lie in my bunk, Brooke," says André, chewing his lip. "I can't stand up straight in here. I need to lie down. I have to."

"Keep your curtain open at all times if you do," I say.

"Can you . . . don't worry, it's stupid. What's wrong with me?"

"Go on."

He cringes. "Can you check on me every once in a while?"

My heart almost stops. I can't reply to him so I just nod. Can I *check* on him? Henry used to request this when I went away

203

offshore to work for a month at a time. When he was four or so he would ask me to check in on him in his room when I returned, even if that was at 3:00 a.m.—like I could ever resist checking in on him and Lisa, to kiss their cheeks, their foreheads, to watch them dream, to smell them—to make sure he was OK. Henry's night-light is in the shape of a glowworm and he forbids me to tell his school friends about it.

I open my eyes wide so not to cry.

I cough. "I'll check on you, bud."

He doesn't say anything but gives me a thumbs-up as he approaches his bunk.

I sit, *almost* alone, on the bench, and bring out my notebook.

André returns from his bunk in seconds.

He shakes his head, defeated, and folds himself up onto the bench opposite.

Using a pen I stole from Steve, one he was sent by a watch retailer, I write to my beloveds. Not a poem, exactly, I couldn't know how to write a proper poem, and not a letter either, as that would feel too fatalistic right now. I will not name what this is. I just start.

I don't miss you three.

Miss isn't the right word.

Right now, in this place, I am hungry for you. For your laughter, for the way you wrestle together on the living room carpet, for bedtime stories that descend into giggle fits, for quiet time after baths with mugs of hot milk and Oreos.

I do not miss you.

My stomach growls with longing. For silly things. Watching you feed the ducks. Dropping you off at the bus stop, helping you with a homework question and then realizing I can't help you because I don't understand the question myself, nagging you to tidy your room. I miss nagging you! I miss your cheeky responses and outlandish excuses.

I don't miss you.

Miss?

I ache for you. I go on, hour after hour, for you.

You three.

I try to taste you on the tip of my tongue, I try to smell your hairlines, I try to remember the softness of your T-shirts when I hang them up outside on the line to dry.

I don't miss you, Steve.

Your arms around me when I arrive back home. Rock solid. A pot of Yorkshire tea on the kitchen table, half of which is covered with books and felt pens and charging cables, Lisa and Henry tucked up safely in bed. The house quiet and clean and low-lit. The feel of your hands on mine. You and me together again and the kids sound asleep.

A family.

Whole.

I don't miss you.

I break open inside for you.

I long for you all and I go on for you.

52

THE HOUR HAND drags itself around the clock face on the wall, countering the pressure gauge needle.

We are questioned by police once again.

I can barely keep my eyes open.

André recounts his old days of drinking and gambling, again.

My ears itch. I cannot listen to his words. I am losing the ability to focus.

We try to play Spades, again.

The insanity of it all. I should be down on the seabed working away in peace; the only noise my own breathing, calm, measured, and the rhythmic beat of my heart in my ears: *thub-um, thub-um, thub-um*. From confinement to ultimate freedom, casket to outer space: nobody else evident for miles around.

An ocean to myself.

"I need to push my resume out to a few people," says André. "Running out of time. Schedule's out of whack now." He looks unhinged. Manic. "I must find my next job."

He's right, in a way. I do not judge him. On the last day of deco we usually scurry around to find the next contract. The next bit of work is never guaranteed, and rest assured we all need to hustle to secure those limited spots on rigs and DSVs. *You eat what you kill* is what Jumbo once told me. If you are not liked by dive supervisors or clients or supers, you won't have opportunities. If you make mistakes or are unreliable, you won't be offered jobs. If you are a liability and freak out when there is trouble, you won't find work. And when you have spent as much as we have on courses, refresher courses, tickets, you have to make darn sure you get that next contract.

The chamber walls make unreal noises. Not creaks, more like low groans. The metal flexing. Pressure levels adjusting incrementally.

Is it awful I'm glad they're gone? Tea-Bag, Leo, and Mike. Gone. I am not glad they're dead, I'm not that coldhearted. I will miss them all, especially Mike, but there's noticeably more space in here now. That notion is unforgivable, isn't it? I am a monster. I'm not glad they're gone, of course I am not. But I am, though. I can breathe again. The benches seem larger. My shoulder isn't always pressing into a man's shoulder, my hips aren't being squeezed as we sit together.

Jumbo shakes his head, wearily. "It's my dinnertime. At home I'd go out in the Land Rover and buy fish and chips—cod, large chips, salt and vinegar, scraps, buttered roll—and eat them at Thurstaston Beach overlooking the water. What I wouldn't give for fish and chips right now. I would order them wrapped, obviously, sealed, so they wouldn't poison me."

André snorts.

"This bloody job," says Jumbo. "I should have gotten out the bin years ago."

"Now's your chance," I say. "You'd be a good supervisor, Jum. Few years watching over air divers, then some onshore Sat supervising, then come watch over us."

"You reckon?" he says.

In truth, Halvor has suggested I consider the same thing. He thinks I would make a decent supervisor over time. It's a lot of responsibility and, personally, I'm not sure I am ready. *Time to move up in the world, Brooke*, he keeps saying.

"I'd be happy with you out there, mate," says André. "You've seen most of it."

"Are you both saying I smell or something?" He sniffs his underarm. "Am I stinking?"

"Yeah," says André, his focus returning to his book, his eyelids almost closing. "That's what we're saying."

I am so thirsty. At this time we'd usually be enjoying dinner, the table extended, a Tetris muddle of aluminum containers. We would be laughing and relaxed, bored, ready to leave. We would be sharing old tales but mostly we'd be looking forward to seeing our families again. You are always a bit odd after a bin run. A bit *off*. Achy joints are a given. I mean psychologically. I am usually a little different for a few days as I complete the home part of decompression. Learning to talk normally and let the banter go. Dampening down the bleakest of gallows humor. Softening. Divers often make plans for how they'll spend their Sat money. I am the responsible exception, paying down the mortgage, setting money aside for the next tax bill. Some of them run out and spend the lot in a matter of days. It is even more apparent when we're in the Middle East or Australia. We have cash and we're a bit wired and excitable, and there are always industrious, and attractive, locals, highly skilled in the multifarious methods of relieving us of that cash. If I think back to previous jobs, I was often planning theme park trips with the kids, writing lists of back-to-school gear and new uniforms to buy, pencil cases and gym pumps, while my fellow divers were lining up nightclubs, escorts, high-stakes poker games, and rekindling casual relationships via text message.

"I want a sleeping pill," says Jumbo.

"No," I say. "You don't. You wouldn't even need one. Look at the state of you."

There is no mirror in here, but he knows how he looks because he can see it in our faces just the same. Tiredness mixed with fear. Unanswered questions. The sensation of having lived through too much.

We are questioned again by DCI MacDuff.

Ten p.m.

We swap out the camera for a new one. How many did they buy or scavenge? I have visions of some junior detective running up and down Union Street buying up every available battery-operated camcorder.

Eleven p.m.

The three of us play cards—gin rummy—and we can hardly keep up with the game.

"Boss?" says Jumbo.

"What can I do for you, Gary?" asks the Night Super.

"If one of us falls asleep sitting up, would you do us a favor and wake us up with a call through?"

"Of course," says the Night Super. "You can count on me."

53

THE EARLY HOURS of our last morning.

We are alive.

One ex-navy diver and two civilians. Jumbo never had to pay for his tickets, whereas we did.

I sense André has been watching me closely. Observing my movements.

Or perhaps I am completely losing my grip on reality.

Two a.m.

I keep hearing dogs barking. Dogs *could* be barking outside on the dock. But surely I wouldn't be able to hear them inside here.

I am not sure if I slept for a few minutes or if I hallucinated. We smell terrible now. Too humid. We are washing: the Life Support Technicians remind us if we forget; they tell us to brush our teeth, which we refuse to because we'd need water; and they remind us to wipe down, as if we need to be told. But the gas we breathe seems stale. I had a nightmare. It might have been a dream or a daydream. A lucid dream? I was quite sure I was running down a long gray pier, a beautiful Victorian metalwork structure, only this one extended itself with each breathless mile. I sprinted, my mouth exaggeratedly open, gulping down fresh air and raindrops, and I never managed to reach the end.

The hatch will pop open today at 4:00 p.m.

That is when we will have to deal with what happened in this place. Back with our relatives, with our friends, having to answer their questions even though they will never fully understand our answers. Years in the future, in the black of the night, we will each have to face our demons one by one.

It ends at 4:00 p.m.

We have fourteen hours left in Sat. The needle is twitching counterclockwise. Two friends are in the hyperbaric lifeboat enduring their own deco, even more cramped than our own.

André sticks his tongue out a little and bites down on it.

I watch as he does it.

"You OK?" I ask.

He stares at me like a man with shell shock from the Great War, the war to end all wars.

"You want anything?" I ask.

"I can't have anything," he says. "Nothing. If you don't eat or drink it's natural to lie down and sleep. To kill that time. We can't even do that."

Jumbo sits up straighter and looks at him. "You look terrible, André. I've seen Egyptian mummies with more life in them."

André grins. Even in these yellowish lights his teeth gleam white.

We have each developed a peculiar variety of thick skin. You cannot get into a fight in Sat. You shouldn't even hold a grudge or lose your temper. A few have done in the past, even inside the Bell, even on the seabed. But most learn to swallow it down and deal with it outside the chamber afterward. Otherwise they know they might never work again.

"Tell us about the Sea Darts, Jumbo," says André.

"I'll pass, thanks."

"Come on."

"Ancient history, mate. I can't even remember half of it."

"You do remember," I suggest.

Jumbo looks at me, takes a deep breath, and slumps a little. "I guess I do."

I should tell him he doesn't need to share with us if he doesn't feel comfortable with it, but I resist. Some selfish, malevolent side of my character wants to be taken away from our grim reality again for a few minutes. I will lose all semblance of rationality if I sit here and endure fourteen more hours of nothingness, us watching each other, the outsiders watching us. I need his story. I crave it.

"You've heard it before," says Jumbo.

"I haven't heard it," I say.

"Come on," says André. "I've got no appointments in the diary today."

Jumbo smiles ruefully. "I was just a kid."

André and I exchange glances but we don't say a word.

"Eighty-two. I was just a spotty little lad who wanted to leave home and get out of school. We were British kids fighting Argie kids on the other side of the world. I'd never even heard of the Falkland Islands." He looks at the eye looking back at us through the porthole window. "I was an average clearance diver, to tell you the truth. Nothing special, believe me."

"I believe it," mutters André.

Jumbo frowns. "Thought we'd be picking up whatever bits and pieces the navy dropped in the water. We thought we'd be the cleanup squad. Never thought we'd see danger." He swallows. "Argies were using Exocet missiles, see. Proper weapon, the Exocet is, especially back then. Capable, like a cross between a torpedo and a missile. Flies just above the sea's surface and then boom." He glances up at us both for a split second. "We had a countdown one time on our ship, I'll never forget the dread. Fighter planes don't hang about, so the countdown was quick. *Fifteen miles away. Fourteen miles away to the west. Thirteen miles. Twelve miles. Eleven miles.* That's how quick it was flying. *Four miles. Three miles. Brace, brace, brace.*" Jumbo's staring at the unmoving eye of whoever is outside, a life support guy or detective, we're not sure which, and he clenches his fists into tight balls. "*One mile to the east. Two miles. Three miles.* We all sighed with relief. That's how close we came. The planes flew on toward another ship in the fleet, and I shouldn't have felt relieved about that but I did. Pointless war." He wipes the sweat from his forehead with his arm. "They're all fucking pointless. The enemy's big bombs weren't exploding because they were dropping them from low altitude to avoid our defenses. Our job was to deal with *anything that could go boom but didn't.* We had to fix it. There was a bomb on the HMS *Antelope*, see. Unexploded ordnance that the Royal Engineers were dealing with. Good lads, they were. Strong divers, no messing around. Bomb went off and killed one of our men." He pauses. Rubs one hand with the other, and I notice he is stifling a shake. His hand is trembling. "We heard it and we felt it too. Next day we had to work on the HMS *Argonaut*. Two bombs, this time. Thousand-pounders. The day after the lethal incident on the *Antelope*. Had to do our jobs, didn't we? Just like this, really. If we didn't do it then somebody else would have to, so we got on with it. I only played a small role, truth be told. The other lads were better than I was, more experienced. Took us five days to defuse the bomb we were working on." He scratches his chin and tilts his head. "Still drink with a few of the lads from Goose Green, from Bluff Cove. Brave men, compared to me. Strange thing is nobody else talks about the Falklands anymore, do they? It's a forgotten conflict. Like us locked away inside here. Forgotten about. We were kids fighting kids, and for what? Fella in my pub was a junior medic in the Welsh Guards. We never really talk about it with family and friends, just to each other, and even then this medic doesn't say much until he's drunk a few pints. Like us, you know, nobody else really understands. He treated a wounded Argentinian lad on the battlefield. Did what he could for him. Enemy combatant but my friend gave him his morphine, patched him up as well as he could, treated his injuries like he would have done for one of our own. The man spoke a little English, and that was the worst part of it. My mate says the Argentine told him, *We not enemies. Not enemies.* One kid saying that to another in the South Atlantic. And then the injured soldier died in his arms."

54

WE DON'T TALK for a long time.

It is engraved on our faces. The pressure, the loss, the hunger, the suspicion, the incomprehension of what Jumbo shared with us.

I ponder for a moment what that kind of trauma can do to a man. Trauma mixed with the effects of years of saturation diving. It would almost be understandable to lose your mind after all that. Almost understandable to commit heinous crimes. I am not sure a court of law would even find you culpable.

I stare at Jumbo.

Just how traumatized are you?

"All right, divers," says the Night Super loudly through the speaker, making me jump. His tone is that of a father or a priest. "Checking you three are OK, physically. I can get the medic if you need anything monitored or looked at between now and 4:00 p.m. Over."

André rubs his eyes. "I'm OK, boss."

"I'm OK," I say.

"We're sound," says Jumbo, looking anything but. "No need to wake Gonzales up. It's nice and quiet in here."

I suspect Gonzales has already been replaced.

"Keep your chins up," he says. "Big team out here now looking after you. Not long to go."

Jumbo nods. "Last day. Let's keep upright and operational, lads."

I feel guilt for questioning Jumbo's state of mind.

If anyone needs more therapy it's probably me.

"I don't know if I can keep my eyes open anymore," says André. "I'm tired just thinking about how tired I am."

"Bullshit," says Jumbo. "I've had nights out with you later than this. Tell us about that habitat place you lived in off the coast of Florida with the scientists."

André shakes his head. "I'm too tired, mate."

"Gold," I say, looking at Jumbo, trying to see beyond his brown eyes. "You've never really told us about the gold."

"I have," says Jumbo.

"Not to me."

He looks surprised. Then resigned. "Not sure my jet-lagged bubble brain is up to it. We're talking ancient history again."

"Don't be a pansy," says André, but he sounds more vulnerable now. "We need the distraction, mate."

Jumbo takes a deep breath. "The HMS *Edinburgh* was on a mission to bring gold bullion back from the USSR, from the Arctic coast, back to England. The commies needed to pay for some of the military hardware we were sending over. This was forty-two, if I remember right. Mission going fine, small escort, but then the U-boats found them. Torpedoes, I can't remember how many, and the ship had to turn back to whichever Soviet port it had sailed out from. Only the Germans didn't let it go. Not sure if they knew how precious the cargo was, but they tracked it eventually and sank her in about eight hundred feet of water."

André and I suck air through our teeth at the exact same time on hearing that depth, knowing instantly what it means, and Jumbo points to us and says, "Yeah."

"When was this?" says André, his eyelids barely open.

"Forty-two, mate. Keep up. You need a coffee?"

The yellowish chamber lights flicker on and off.

They stabilize.

Jumbo wouldn't hurt Mike. He couldn't. It's someone on the outside. I need to stop questioning him or I'll start spiraling.

"Ship sat down on the seabed for decades," says Jumbo. "The Ministry of Defense designated it a war grave so nobody would mess with it. In eighty-one a consortium was put together. Our MOD, the commies, a few diving firms. What a strange club that was. I wasn't involved in this, I was still in the navy, but they managed to dive to what was a record depth back then and burn an aperture in the side of the ship. No smash-and-grab jobs because it was a grave, like I said. Anyway, the lads took out four hundred and thirty-one bars."

"Not a bad payday," says André.

"There's video of it, apparently. Bosses told the lads going into Sat: *don't leave any behind*. There were Soviet ships lurking nearby; this was the height of the Cold War. Rossier found the gold. You know John Rossier?"

We both shake our heads.

"They left thirty-four bars down there. They were in the bomb room, surrounded by old munitions. Now, fast-forward to eighty-six, me and a group of lads were asked to go back in and bring the bars up."

"Nice work if you can get it," I say.

Jumbo rubs his eye and says, "Not really. We managed twenty-nine bars. The lads in eighty-one got all the glory. We were just doing a routine job compared to them. And the ship was eerie, you know. It was a ghost ship. We trained on the HMS *Belfast* on the Thames."

"I've been on there with the kids," says André.

"Sister ships." Jumbo squeezes his nose to equalize. "Almost identical. We had private tours to inspect the bomb room and take measurements. And then when we got all the way down to the wreck it looked exactly the same as what we saw on the *Belfast* in central London. Unreal. I never liked working on the *Edinburgh*. It was like a perfect vessel, from what I could see, frozen in time."

"You sneak a bar out?" asks André.

"I remember Dive Control telling us not to go back to the Bell until the last ingot had been loaded into the metal basket. That was the deepest we'd ever dived and they were more worried about their gold than the welfare of us divers. Now it's oil instead of gold, but it's the same old principle. We are expendable when it comes down to it, lads. That's clear from this job, isn't it? They treat us like wrenches."

55

ANDRÉ AND JUMBO play cards, but André keeps dropping his to the floor.

"André," says a Life Support Technician. "*Joe*, are you all right? You falling asleep? Over."

André gives him a weak, unsmiling thumbs-up.

I use a pen and the back pages of my notebook to sketch the bunk section of our living quarters. The outline is reasonable, although the sense of depth is perhaps a little exaggerated. We have no depth, not that kind, anyway. I begin crosshatching. It is strange not hanging out in my bed. I can reach all six if I stretch and yet I have no wish to venture past the threshold. Divers perish there. I sketch the curved walls, mediocre shading to hint at the roundness. I use heavier pen strokes to define the three double bunks, each one bare, stripped of all bedding, partly at the request of Dive Control, partly because we don't want to be tempted. I *am* tempted. Exhaustion in here isn't like exhaustion outside. Outside, sleep deprivation is manageable, especially with caffeine and TV and walks outdoors. Here, with nothing at all to eat or drink, with this humidity and boredom, and the constant pressure, breathing thick gas, exhaustion is life-threatening in and of itself. I usually spend ten or twelve hours a day sleeping in my bunk. Being in the bin requires it. The work wears you out and just surviving in these conditions pushes the body to its limits. The light on the wall seems almost greenish now, and it picks out the photos I have next to my bed, their edges starting to curl. Three magnets: two round and one square. Magnets from our fridge that should be holding up school photos and shopping lists back home, not stuck to the wall in this tank.

I turn my head a fraction and catch Jumbo sneaking a look at my notebook.

"You can sell that to the press," he says. "*Daily Telegraph* will pay a pretty penny for that sketch, Brooke."

André has a retort lined up but he lets it fade into the heliox ether. His eyelids keep on closing and he knows our tolerance for the usual to and fro is diminished. *We* are diminished.

They continue their game of cards.

"I'll play you at chess after Jum takes your money, André."

"I can't play chess, mate," says André. "I'm too sleepy. I can't think in a straight line."

"I'm not taking his money," says Jumbo. "We're playing for the best bunk on the next dive."

"You're joking," I say.

"What?" says Jumbo. "I'm dead serious."

"Periodic welfare check, lads," says the Night Super, coming to the end session of his shift. "Anything we can get for you?"

We all groan in unison.

"No thanks," I say.

"Water? Hot drinks? Sealed snacks?"

Jumbo looks sternly at the camera. "We said *no*."

"Roger, Roger. I'm told the DCI is on his way to speak to you. Another twenty minutes or so until he gets here. Hopefully we won't have to wake you."

"You won't," says André.

"Developments outside," says the Night Super.

We all sit up straighter, alert. "What kind of developments?" snaps André. We are hungry for news, for information. "Do you know what's happening to us, boss? Tell us. Come on, bloody hell. Tell us right now. Have they caught anyone?"

"I don't know anything," he says. "I know nothing, I swear. It's a police matter."

"Tell us what you know," says Jumbo, his nose curled into a snarl. "You can't leave us hanging like this. You have a duty."

"I shouldn't have mentioned it," he says. "The DCI will be here soon. I merely wanted you to know everyone outside is working around the clock on this. Their focus is to get you out safe and sound, and work out what happened in there."

Thoughts flash through my mind. Awful thoughts. I blink them away. Notions of rapid decompression, of fires, of . . . stabbings. Mike's biblical quotes about vengeance and murdering the fatherless. Images of my hands, wet, caked with something crimson and dry, crusted fingernails, old blood set like concrete, scrubbing at them, rubbing them raw, making them bleed again. I take slower breaths and shun the thoughts. They return immediately. Images of accidents, fights, eye-gouging, vomiting, bile . . .

"How much longer before he gets here," I blurt out, urgently.

"Twenty minutes or less," he says.

I nod, sweat beading at my hairline.

They are out there. Normal people a stone's throw from the ship walking along the docks before catching a film at the cinema or going out for a fish supper. No, wait, this is early morning. They'll be staggering home after a night out, enjoying some sea air before a fried breakfast in a café, passing us, completely oblivious to our plight.

"You missed the eighties, then," Jumbo says, dealing a card to André.

"We're not all as old as you, Jum."

"You missed Piper, I mean. The *Herald of Free Enterprise*. Byford Dolphin. You managed to avoid all the big ones."

André shakes his head.

"No?" says Jumbo.

"No, mate."

"What?"

"I didn't miss them."

"Come on, then," says Jumbo, agitated now, twitching. "You pushed me to share my history. Wanted all the details. Come on, fair's fair."

"I don't have any history."

Jumbo's frown intensifies. His hackles are up. "We've got twelve hours to go in here. It's almost four o'clock in the morning and each minute feels like three fucking hours. If not now, then when?"

André smiles a forced, exaggerated smile, and folds his hand of cards. "I wasn't supposed to be on the job."

Jumbo sits back. "Right. Go on."

André shakes his head. "I'm not talking about it. I can't talk about it, to tell you the truth. I don't want to, mate, and I can't even remember the details. It was nineteen ninety-four when she sunk. I thought I knew it all. Cash burning a hole in my pocket. I'd already bought a Toyota Supra and I was driving around like a prick."

"Nothing's changed," I say.

André closes his eyes and keeps them closed. "We were told that the *Estonia* had gone down in the Baltic." His skin looks gray and loose. "But we didn't reach the wreck until several weeks later. It wasn't a military war grave or anything like your dive, Jum. It was families with kids." His voice cracks. "A lot of families with their little kiddies. This is onshore-only. I don't want to talk about it, all right?"

"You don't have to," I say.

"You do," says Jumbo, angrily, snarling. "We're your brothers. Nobody else will understand like we will. Talk. It'll help you. If we don't understand then who will?"

"Ask her. Get her to talk."

"No," says Jumbo. "I'm getting you to talk. It's good for you."

André wrings his hands together as if squeezing water from a rag. "Two hundred and fifty feet down. We went . . . we went in to collect logbooks from the Bridge. There were bodies. They were in a bad state. Horrible. The fish, I don't know how to describe it. Awful. Dante's version of hell. If I'd been diving scuba I'd have blown through my tanks in minutes. Supervisors kept on telling us to keep calm and breathe slow, usual stuff, but you can't, can you? All them families. Over eight hundred died on that ship. I'm sorry, that's enough." He covers his mouth with his hand. "I don't like seeing the pictures in my head. I can't stand it."

I nudge his foot with my own and say, "No need to say more, André, mate."

He nods.

"Bet lost," says Jumbo, frostily, collecting up the cards. "You owe me that bottom bunk on our next dive. I won't forget."

56

AT THIS POINT through a decompression, usually twenty-seven or twenty-eight days into the job, I would have my teeth on edge with annoyance at the sounds of my fellow divers chewing, swallowing, snoring . . . and worse. By now you would be able to recognize who is eating by the noises they make. I would lie in my bunk—the blue sheet pulled up to my neck—and guess who is doing what. Nine times out of ten I would be correct. Sometimes I can even predict precisely what they are eating and in which position on the benches they are sitting. Not today. I miss those sounds. It is not easy to get across how irritating the smacking of lips and picking of teeth is when you are confined for a month at a time. Men who sigh in an exaggerated manner after they drink soda, or scrape their cutlery down across the base of the foil containers. And yet I would give anything to hear those noises today, and to be making those same noises myself.

Jumbo is in the Wet Pot most likely requesting a flush. He has started to eye us both distrustfully. I never, ever expected that from him. I find myself staying in front of him and acting *honest*, if that makes sense, not hiding my notebook or using my phone. Almost like I want to reassure him that he is safe with me.

André is sitting opposite, hunched over onto himself, like a prisoner of war who has finally given up his spirit. His body lives on but his eyes have lost their light.

"Heads up, you three," says the Night Super. "Detective on his way down."

Jumbo opens the Wet Pot hatch and slides himself through to us. He looks bony. A day in here with no food or water is like a week on the outside. We are not thriving in this pressurized tin can, we are barely hanging on.

Jumbo wipes his hands on his shorts and DCI MacDuff's face appears at the porthole circled by six industrial bolts.

"Ellen, Gary, Joe. I hear you're not taking in any food or drink?"

"How can we?" says Jumbo.

"Can I personally bring bottles of sealed water to you? I can watch it pass through the little hatch here." He gestures to the Medlock.

"Not happening," says André, licking his cracked lips. "We've only got about eleven hours to go, Chief. We'll manage. We have three bottles here in case anyone passes out. No unnecessary risks. Like I said, we can manage."

"I don't want to see any of you passing out," says MacDuff.

"Better than the alternative," I utter.

He looks morose through the thick glass. The police must have their own flavor of dark humor, something to help them through tough times, just like paramedics and nurses and soldiers and doctors and firefighters have theirs. Each variety is subtly different.

"The pathologists are working on your colleagues," he says, through the speaker. "We don't have forensic toxicology results back yet but, on first impression, there is a strong suspicion of poisoning."

"I told you," says Jumbo, suddenly bolt upright, looking to us both in turn.

"What kind of poison?" says André, eager for details.

"Sorry, repeat that, please?" says MacDuff. "I didn't catch it."

"What kind of poison?" he says again. "Poisoned gas, or . . . ?"

"We don't know yet," says MacDuff. "We'll have more information in the next hour or two. There has been a crisis meeting of the Oil and Energy Liaison Unit along with specialists from the University of Glasgow Department of Forensic Medicine and Aberdeen Royal Infirmary. As a safety precaution we've decided to bring activated charcoal into the Diving Bell."

"Do you mean the chamber?" says Jumbo.

"Sorry?" says DCI MacDuff, frowning. "Repeat that, please."

Jumbo sighs. Each word is a Herculean effort. "The chamber, not the Diving Bell."

"That's right. Sorry. The medic will talk you through how to administer charcoal in case it is needed."

"It'll make the poison harmless?" asks André.

"I don't know the full details, but I believe it will help counter a wide variety of toxic substances. Here she is now. I'll pass over the microphone. Keep your spirits up."

Gonzales comes into view flanked by a paramedic in uniform. She looks almost as frazzled as we do.

"Activated charcoal tablets coming through the Medlock," she says. "Swallow them if you suspect you've been poisoned. Tight chest, burning sensation in your throat, urge to vomit, dizziness. If you suspect your colleague has been affected, administer the tablets orally to them. They are a simple intervention with few side effects."

Jumbo waits a few moments and then opens the Medlock suspiciously. Normally we'd receive hot water for tea at this time of day. Foil trays full of scrambled eggs, crispy bacon, sausages, charred toast, real Irish butter with salt in it.

All we have is dry charcoal.

"Thanks, Doc," says Jumbo. "And you, too, MacDuff."

We sit back down, the black tablets on the table between us flanked by a Nicci French novel and a book called *The Kite Runner*.

André's eyes close slowly. I nudge Jumbo.

Jumbo yells, "Wake up, André, you lazy knobhead. Keep your eyes open, son."

He slurs. "Let me sleep a little bit." He closes his eyes again.

Jumbo says, "I said, open your eyes, mate. Last memory from me. Listen up. Piper Alpha."

André's eyes open wide.

57

I STARE AT the activated charcoal tablets.

"Not sure I have the energy to do this," says Jumbo.

"I knew it," says André.

Jumbo pinches his nose to equalize.

The needle drags around the dial.

"Eighty-eight," says Jumbo, closing his eyes for a few seconds before looking at me. "Brooke, were you in Sat back then?"

I shake my head. "Air. Gulf of Mexico."

Jumbo nods. "Stop me if I'm rehashing things I've told you before. Brain isn't what it used to be. You know a lot of this, I'm sure."

"I don't," I say. "Nobody talks about that night."

Jumbo wipes his face and neck with a wet wipe and places it in a clear garbage bag.

"Everything changed after Piper Alpha," says André.

Jumbo runs his tongue over his teeth. "I was working in Nigeria at the time of the explosion. Piper Alpha was the biggest rig in the world at the time, supposedly, or the most productive rig. Over two hundred crew. Human error, couple of paperwork issues, bit of equipment failed. One hundred and sixty-seven men died."

André frowns.

Jumbo says, "I heard about it from Samuelsson. You guys know Samuelsson?"

We both nod.

"He said it was like the devil came up that night. Even the sea was on fire. Men threw themselves off the rig. Forty stories. When they reached the water they found that was also on fire. Brave lads went out on rescue boats trying to pick up survivors. Some of them were killed by debris and secondary explosions."

André says, "I was five miles away on a DSV that night. Standby diver."

"I never knew that," says Jumbo, taken aback. "I wouldn't have talked about it if I'd have known that, mate."

André shakes his head. "I have no tale to tell. We saw the fire in the distance. We heard the boom. But we were no help to those lads."

"You were in Nigeria, Jumbo?" I ask.

"I was working on a clamp installation. The Piper job came in later. We had to go down and search through the accommodation module." He swallows, scratches his arm, leaves a trail of white nail marks. "The module had gone down after the fire. Came to rest upside down on the seabed and we had to go in so we could bring it up and put it on a barge at the surface."

"Why didn't we try harder in school, eh?" says André, smiling a sad smile. "Avoid all this."

"I did try," says Jumbo. His voice quietens. "We went in and the module was full of debris. All upside down, us walking on the ceiling. Lads never stood a chance in that place. I remember trying to slow my breathing, trying to keep it together, while walking around them all, between them all, keeping track of my umbilical. There were too many bodies. Too many lost futures, you know. It gave me bad dreams, I'm not too big to admit it, like we were strolling around on graves down there, graves that hadn't been filled in. Felt sacrilegious."

Jumbo's head lolls to one side.

"Are you OK, Jum?" I say, my voice raised. "Gary, you OK? Medic?"

"No," he says, waking up. "I'm just tired. No medic needed. Gonzales, stand down."

He rubs his eyes.

"You sure you're all right?" says André. "You look like—"

A voice cuts him off.

DCI MacDuff is outside the chamber. I hadn't noticed him arrive.

"We have confirmation from forensics," he says breathlessly. "We now believe all three of your colleagues succumbed from cyanide poisoning."

He looks satisfied with this discovery. How can he look satisfied?

"Cyanide?" asks Jumbo.

"*Cyanide*?" yells André, looking at us all in turn. "Poison?"

"There is some better news," says MacDuff. "For you three, I mean. We have located an antidote kit and it's being biked to the docks as we speak. It will arrive presently. I am told cyanide can come in solid, liquid, or gaseous form. It can be a by-product of various industrial processes, or a result, for example, of fire damage. Whatever is causing this is unknown but we will soon have an answer for it. I hope this brings you some comfort."

58

JUMBO SHUFFLES HIS deck of cards.

André mutters, "Cyanide? That's poison gas, isn't it?"

For me, the word conjures up images of Eva Braun and other Nazi elites in Berlin. They each had a cyanide pill so they could exit before the Allies arrived. I associate cyanide with cowardice.

"It's what they used in the gas chambers. Auschwitz?" says Jumbo. He reaches out to touch the walls of our own chamber. Seems smaller than ever. "Either somebody out there hates us or else there's going to be one hell of a health and safety executive inquiry once we're let out."

How could cyanide gas affect only half of us, when we're all breathing the same mix?

I am too exhausted and too hungry to make any sense of it.

"Spies took cyanide," mumbles André, barely awake. "I read about it in a book one time. Think I read about it in the Bell, actually, working off the coast of Malaysia. Or saw something on TV. Maybe I was in Indonesia."

"Spies?" says Jumbo.

"Soviet-era operatives," says André. "They had cyanide pills in their back molar teeth, didn't they? Not sure if that was fact or a myth. Pretty sure it was in that book."

I watch the pressure gauge on the wall.

We are ten and a half hours from freedom.

"The vitamin pills," I suggest, pointing to the rack. "We had so many pots and blister packs. Vitamin D, C, riboflavin, iron, multivitamins. Mike had his own supplements from the US. Leo had some he'd bought in France, I think, from his Comex days. Could there have been a mix-up?"

"All I know," says André, still slumped, "is we made it through last night. We had nothing to eat or drink or take from outside. No pills or medicines. We avoided the bunks and the three of us are still conscious." He turns to me. "I need another distraction. *The night is long that never finds the day*. You got any war stories, Brooke?"

I shake my head.

"You can talk if you want to, you know," says Jumbo. "You never talk much about old dives, or . . . you know, life outside."

"I was never in the military," I say, standing up and moving over toward my bunk, shielding them with my back. The temptation to crawl in and pull a blanket over my head and sleep is overwhelming. I crave the softness of the mattress, the privacy, the concealment.

"You are among friends," says André.

I pick up the pillowcase and hold it to my face and breathe in. One case inside the other. I inhale through my nose and try with all my might to detect them.

"Talking helps, mate," urges Jumbo, softly. "I know you asked us not to bring it up offshore, that it's a strictly *dryland-only* topic, but talking does help."

It doesn't.

Nothing helps.

Nothing will ever bring them back.

59

I CAN'T DO this in here. It's not the right place to talk about it.

Open the hatch.

I stare at it. At the handle.

Get out while you still can. What are you waiting for?

I clear my throat and shake the thought away, and then I gather my feet up onto the bench. I have never sat like this before because there is no room usually, and because it is not done. I try to be as much like the guys as possible.

I will not talk about it.

I can't.

If the others ingested cyanide it either came from outside or inside. Them or us. It was either accidental or it was intended. Tablets or gases or powder or liquid? My bubble brain cannot cope with this. I want to talk about this with the lads. This, and nothing else.

"Checking you're all feeling physically OK?" says the Night Super. "I'll be handing back over to Duncan soon."

I give a thumbs-up to the camera and André does the same. Jumbo says, "See you on the other side, boss."

"Four p.m.," he says. "I'll set my alarm to check you out of your accommodation."

I prepare myself. I do not want to talk about it with them. Especially not in here.

Tell them what really happened.

I cough.

They're staring at me.

Waiting.

"You both know the basics?"

They nod.

I nod back. The words don't come easily. I keep fumbling over them. "Three and a half years ago. Feels like three weeks ago and thirty years ago. It changed my sense of time and everything else."

I stare at my feet. I can't look them in the eye.

"Steve was running late, bless him." Deep sigh. "I was three weeks into a job on the Schielhallion oil field when I found out. I understood there was a problem as soon as I heard the Super's voice over the speaker. I knew my life would never be the same again. He told me there had been a . . ." I trail off, gathering my knees up close to my chest. "A serious car accident. Told me I was to decompress immediately in the other chamber with Fred Knuckles. Fred was very kind to me. Five-day deco, so worse than this."

"Christ," says Jumbo. "Five days with that news."

"I went a little crazy, I'll be honest. In a quiet way, I lost my mind. I wasn't punching the walls or trying to open the hatch or anything like that. But I lost it in that tiny chamber. Knuckles had to keep talking me down, soothing me. He kept on saying how I needed to keep myself together for the struggles that come next."

"Good lad, is Knuckles," says André. "Worked with him out in Saudi."

"He's kind." I swallow hard. "They gave me tablets to get me through deco, and then when I came out there was a counselor there, and an officer, and someone from the company, and they told me Steve and Lisa had been killed by a drunk van driver at

8:40 a.m. on the road outside town. Steve was often late, which I blame myself for, not easy doing it all on your own when your wife's offshore for a month at a time, is it?"

"Same for all the partners," says Jumbo.

"Yes," I say. "I suppose."

It's not.

You were a bad mother.

Open the hatch, go on.

To drown out the voice, I blurt out, louder than before, "On the drive down to the hospital I kept thinking, *I can do it, keep going, don't swerve into a bridge*, because I had to be strong for Henry. He would need me to be his mum and his dad and his sister from then on. I knew I'd focus on helping him through the many layers of grief, getting him back to school, through his teenage years. I had to be strong for my son." My voice cracks.

The guilt was unbearable.

In deco, and in the drive down there.

And right now.

The appalling, smothering, festering shame weighs down on me. My heart is still in pieces.

Their hearts are in pieces.

Go into the Wet Pot and open the hatch there.

"No," I say, through gritted teeth.

"Your boy was lucky to have you for a mum," says André.

I look at him and shake my head. "Got to the hospital and Henry was in ICU. I wanted to hold him, to take him into my arms, to shield him, to rip out the cannulas and tubes and take care of my boy. But I couldn't. He was hooked up to so many machines and I couldn't cuddle him properly." I wipe my eyes, but more tears come in their place. "I wanted to be his mum and I wanted to take him back to our house and care for him there. Keep him safe."

"Cretin in the van was to blame, not you," says Jumbo.

"I know that," I say, nodding. "I was hanging on. But then Henry died the day after I arrived there. Massive internal injuries. He never regained consciousness, but I want to believe he knew I was with him in his final hours." The eye in the porthole disappears for a moment. "The nurses were angels. They let me stay overnight and they brought me tea. But it was over. My life was essentially done. Gilly, my sister-in-law, drove me out to my house and I was completely numb. I kept thinking, *I have to live tomorrow? I have to go through all this again tomorrow? And every day to come?* She didn't want to leave me at the house but I insisted. My family flew over from the States and I went full steam into oganizing the funeral." The taste of blood in my mouth. Stomach acid. "I wouldn't let anyone do a thing. I made every single decision and ran it like a mission: spreadsheets and schedules. I probably upset a lot of relatives who wanted to provide their input. I feel bad about that. I needed it to be perfect, to do it well for them; it's the only thing I could give them."

"I'm sorry," says André, rubbing his own eyes.

"I remember asking Gilly, *Was I a good mother*? She broke down when I asked her. It was the day before the funeral and I had never seen her lose her composure like that. She was the rock for the rest of the family. She had cried, but she was still in control until I asked her that question." I take a deep breath. "The funeral passed as a blur. I can't remember much but I know the church was full and people were lined up outside in the rain. Dozens out there, if not hundreds. Speakers were put up. Three holes in the churchyard. Three holes slowly filling up with water."

60

I FELT SUCH resentment against the world. Such burning anger. I never understood how to process those feelings. You can't lose a child, it is unimaginable, but you really can't lose your whole family in one accident. I was not able to visit the hospital right away to be with my boy. Five days' decompression. What kind of cruel trick is that?

What are you struggling on for, then?

Weak. Open the hatch. End this.

I bite down hard on my tongue to push away the image.

"When I heard you wanted to come back in the bin I was a bit shocked, I admit it," says Jumbo. "We didn't know what to think."

I take a deep breath.

"That was brave," says André.

I shake my head. "The opposite. You know what you were saying about *three hots and a cot*? That's what I needed. Simple days of hard, tiring work, and actual sleep, and having everything provided for me. Friends I could rely on. That pitch-black humor people on the outside don't understand. I couldn't stand being home walking past their rooms, driving past their school, checking on Steve's immaculate watchmaker bench with its tools and loupes, sleeping next to where he should be each night. I

237

needed Sat to escape reality. But even then I had to fight hard to get back offshore."

"Lots of people were strongly against it," says Jumbo.

"I was one of them," says André, apologetically. "Nothing personal, Brooke. I thought you needed more time, lots of us thought it."

"That's why I worked Asia again. For less pay. Back to the beginning, at least for a few jobs, to prove I could still do it. Then they accepted me coming into the office for a chat. Said I wasn't ready. I kept on working around the world and I kept coming back into the office when I was home. They could see I was serious and ready, and maybe Halvor felt contrition after the lawsuit years ago, all the stress it caused me. Management knew me well and they talked to the guys I'd worked with in Asia, checked on the tapes, asked around to make sure I was still reliable. Two years out of Sat was like a torture."

"Glutton for punishment," says André, swallowing with clear difficulty.

My thirst matches his.

I can't stop thinking about cyanide. Gas entering through vents, a hand slipping droplets of liquid into our aluminum food containers as they leave the kitchen.

"I used to drive by their school gates in the mornings. Used to park and watch the other kids go in, their heavy backpacks on their shoulders, their laces undone, and I never understood why Lisa and Henry weren't among them. They were innocent children. They had never hurt anyone."

Jumbo rubs his eyes and equalizes.

"Nothing helped. Talking to family didn't help. Talking with counselors didn't help. Meds didn't touch it. Then I went to a local grief group in St. Mark's Church on Leeds Road and something clicked. Nobody else understood, the professionals couldn't relate, but these people could. Some of them had lost loved ones to suicide, and the pain on their faces was the most heartbreaking thing I had ever seen. I started to be able to laugh again, as horrific as that sounds. After my first laugh I felt guilty for days. What kind of mom laughs when her children are gone? But the group helped. They were completely broken like I was. We shared. The pain comes in waves, mine did anyway. At first the waves are all together, tight, overwhelming, no chance to catch your breath; you're knocked under time and time again. Then the waves spread out a little and you *can* catch your breath. Then the gaps become wider and wider. You start to look after yourself again. I know now that I need to be alone with my grief sometimes. I need to sit with it and let it happen, let the wave crash over me and wreak its havoc. That is what I do on the seabed when I'm waiting for tools from the surface. Heavy, limp, I sit with my grief with my hat light off. Same thing when I'm Bellman. Six hours to sit with it. To live with it."

"I never thought of it like that," says André. "The Bell, I mean. I just read a book in there."

I wipe my eyes.

They both pat my arm awkwardly.

"When I'm diving with new people and they ask me if I'm married I usually say: I am. I told Tea-Bag that. If they ask if I have kids I tell them: two. They ask their ages and I tell them their ages when they left me. It feels true to me. It is my truth. I cannot bring myself to answer anything else."

"How much time inside did that driver get?" asks Jumbo.

"Fourteen years. I want to forgive him, I know I have to, for my own sake, for my own sanity, but I haven't managed it yet. I know what's best for me, it'll be healing to forgive. I know all the logical reasoning, and I want to do it, but I can't. I'm not strong enough."

"You're one of the strongest divers I know," says Jumbo.

"Steady on," says André.

I laugh.

"I'm pulling your leg," says André. "He's right. You get the job done, Brooke."

61

I MISS HALVOR'S wake-up calls, and I even miss eating breakfast knowing I will need to go to the bathroom before the dive. I miss Bell checks and pulling my heavy, uncomfortable helmet up into the Bell from the Wet Pot. I miss climbing into my hot water suit. I miss the anticipation as we descend to depth. I miss the leap of faith as the hatch is opened, my hat is secured, and the final checks are made before I drop down through the water onto the clump weight. I miss the silence down there, the sense of space, of eternity, of escaping. I miss the undocumented creatures and the beauty. I miss doing backflips and aquanaut jumps, and climbing back up my umbilical at the end of a successful shift. I even miss the yellow boots.

"You all sure you don't want any sealed food for breakfast? We can open up the sealed multipacks outside the chamber so you can watch it happen, and then pass them through the Medlock."

We all shake our heads.

Not with cyanide around.

I can't help thinking of bacon and then my mouth pools with saliva. Crispy bacon and eggs, sunny-side up. Whole wheat toast with real butter. Good coffee and hot sauce on my eggs.

"I just realized," says Jumbo. "They put Mike and Spocky in the hyperbaric lifeboat. But they would have decompressed with us in the same time if they'd left them here with us. Saved us the bother of hauling them both up on stretchers."

"They're trying to keep us occupied so we don't lose our minds," says André as he licks his lips again. Mine are bleeding like his. Neither of us wants to risk lip balm and we are breaking down, cell by cell, in this humid, unsanitary tin can. "Besides, humans are programmed to freak out around the scent of death," he says. "It's hardwired into us. We smell a fatality and we head the other way. It's the most primal thing. They couldn't leave the bodies with us because we have nowhere to run."

Jumbo and I think about that for a long time. Then Jumbo asks, "Boss?"

The Super comes over the speaker. "Yes, Gary."

"When is this cyanide antidote kit coming? Any updates?"

"It's on a bike now," says the Super. "I'm told it's inbound and won't be long. We're still trying to locate additional kits. Will keep you updated. Over."

The three of us sit hunched, watching each other.

We are becoming more vigilant, probing for signs.

Could someone have left a compound inside the chamber before we arrived here? I find it difficult to believe one of us brought a poisonous substance onto the ship.

This Super, the new one, the man working with Duncan, checking each other's decisions, is half Italian. Short man with broad shoulders. He was a pioneer in the late seventies, one of the early boys back when there weren't many safety standards or fail-safes. The thing about speaking Italian and English fluently, like a native, is he could work more Sat jobs than most of his peers. Deep-sea divers team up in accordance with language, mostly. Italian teams work together. Norwegian teams work together. Indian teams work together. There are overlaps sometimes, but generally it's not nationality that is relevant, it's language.

Mainly because it's hard enough to understand each other breathing gas as it is.

Jumbo starts scribbling in his diary.

The pressure gauge quivers behind its glass.

He pushes the pad to us. His handwriting isn't clear but he has written in block capitals.

Only one person has been with us up close, interfered with us, helped us, and has access to toxic substances. It's the one person who is supposed to keep us healthy.

André's eyes widen behind his reading glasses.

I take the pen from Jum and write.

And she pushes meds through the lock. We don't know what those shots contain, or if they've been interfered with. The IV bags too. We don't know what she is giving us when we get sick.

"Boss?" says Jumbo, loudly.

"Go ahead," says the Super.

"We need to talk right now. On the phone. You and me."

62

JUMBO STEPS TO the bunk area and picks up the receiver.

He speaks but guards the mouthpiece with his other hand so his words aren't detectable on the microphone in the chamber, or via the latest camera on the wall.

Bent at the hip, Jumbo looks vulnerable. Older than before. He is wearing white flip-flops, hiking shorts, and a freebie blue T-shirt with a helmet manufacturer logo.

Jumbo steps back to us.

"So?" I say.

"Changing shifts. New medic on the job now. Supervised."

"What does that mean?" says André.

I shrug. "What does any of it mean? We do drills for everything, drills coming out of our ears, but we could never drill for losing half a team like this."

My ear itches. I know what this is. I am coming down with otitis externa. Bacterial ear rot. I'm not going to mention it and I'm not taking antibiotics until I am well clear of here.

Jumbo starts to shuffle his deck of cards but then puts them down. "You guys feel OK? I'm dizzy. My bubble brain's not working like normal."

"Doesn't work well when you're on dry land," says André.

"Don't," replies Jumbo. "Don't bring that up again. We've talked about that."

André stands up in shock because we do not talk to each other like this in the chamber. Not under any circumstances. We mock each other, we take the piss, we laugh at our own expense, but we never shut someone down in that manner.

André opens the hatch into the Wet Pot and disappears inside.

"You want me to check your vitals, Jum?" I ask, soothingly. "You OK?"

He shakes his head and mumbles something unintelligible.

"Let me just check you over real quick."

He sighs and then he relents. "André thinks I'm too old for the job."

I check his pupils, saying nothing, shining a pen torch into each eye. His whites are bloodshot and he has some kind of discharge coming from his tear duct but his pupils are reacting to the light as they should. Dilation, contraction. I check his pulse, my fingers to his wrist, watching the clock, the seconds hand. Normal. I check his blood pressure. A little high but within normal range. Understandable. I check his breathing. We can't use a stethoscope in here but I place my ear to his chest. Nothing out of the ordinary.

I used to lie with my ear on Steve's chest before we'd go to sleep. I sleep in pajamas at home, but he was a hot person and usually slept in his boxers. I would rest my head on him and breathe him in. He'd read a little or we'd lie like that and chat. Thoughts on the day, on how Henry was getting on with his classmates now that the class bully had been confronted, on how Lisa was enjoying, or not, her cello lessons. It was the perfect conclusion to each onshore day. Tuck in the kids, usually two or three times in the case of Henry, and then we'd have a little time to ourselves.

"You'll live," I tell Jumbo.

"Thanks, Doc."

I wipe down the table and benches and place the wipes in a clear garbage bag and then push all that through the Medlock. The mere act of it makes me feel unsteady on my feet. And then I question if I should even be touching the wet wipes. Could they contaminate us through our skin? The skin is the body's largest organ. I start to panic, wiping my hands on my trousers, cursing André for taking so long. I need to wash my hands with *water*. Clean water. I need to rinse them. Dry them. Wash them again. But is that water safe?

A noise behind me.

I turn to see Jumbo crumple to his knees.

The strong man, the veteran, the fell-runner.

He folds in on himself.

63

I YELL, "ANDRÉ!"

Jumbo didn't fall with a crash, he went down on the spot.

I say, "Jumbo. Gary. Can you hear me?"

His eyes are closed. He is unconscious but his airway is clear. I have a pulse.

André behind me, his eyes wide. "Let's lay him out flat. He's trying to tell us something."

We try to put him in the recovery position but it is not easy between cramped bunks.

"Medic. *Now*," says André.

"What is it, Jumbo? Say it again."

A groan. No discernible words.

He goes limp.

I lift Jumbo's eyelid and use a pen torch just like I did ten minutes ago.

"Can you get the charcoal?" asks André, as he prepares the BIBS mask.

I move back to the folded table to take the black tablets from their blister pack.

"Oh, easy, buddy," says André. I turn and Jumbo is vomiting, his eyes have snapped open, and his hands are stretched out like claws.

His chest begins to convulse.

"Medic!" I yell.

"Tablets," shouts André. "Right now. Hand them to me."

We place two activated charcoal capsules in Jumbo's mouth and massage his throat so they go down. The risk of poisoning outweighs the risk of choking at this moment. One tablet comes back up.

I check for a pulse.

"I still have a pulse," I say.

Jumbo splutters.

André kneels and clears his airway with the foot-operated pump.

"Stay with us, Gary, mate, please."

A seizure.

The repeated hopelessness of all this.

His body ripples and thrusts.

The new medic is giving us instructions. CPR. Chest compressions. Epinephrine. The same again. We follow her commands.

No pulse.

Nothing.

André completes compressions and I take my turn with the mask hooked up to the BIBS.

Five cycles.

My ears buzz.

Still no pulse.

Is this cyanide?

I take over compressions as I can tell André is completely exhausted. I push down as hard as I can, crushing Jumbo's chest, and images flash into my head. My nightmare. I force them away. The body on the beach reappears, though. Figures walking toward me through the rain, the sound of waves crashing over pebbles. I shut my eyes and push my palms down hard.

"André, stay with me," I say, catching sight of him looking unsteady as I open my eyes. "Don't pass out. I need you here."

He nods. Then kneels down beside me, a syringe in his hand.

For the first time I feel uneasy with him being so close.

One shot of adrenaline. Awhile later the medic tells us to administer another. Then another.

One of Gary's flip-flops hangs off his tattooed foot.

He is gone.

64

ANDRÉ SLUMPS TO the floor by the chamber table.

He lets out a primal cry.

The Super gives further instructions but we are both too depleted to understand them. They are of no consequence. We cannot bring him back.

"Jumbo, now?" André says to me, his eyes crazed. "What the hell happened when I was in the Wet Pot, Brooke?"

I shake my head. "Nothing happened. He collapsed. He took a step to the bunks and went down where he stood."

"Nothing else happened?"

André starts coughing, then retching.

"Are you OK?" I grab the charcoal tablets.

He holds his chest and calms his breathing.

"Jum didn't say anything at the end," I say. "He didn't complain."

"What is it about that sleeping area? You didn't give him anything when I was in there?"

He edges away from me.

I stand at the threshold, rubbing my eyes in disbelief. The entire chamber is fifteen feet long and six feet wide. Half of the chamber is the table and benches, half the bunks. We sit down opposite each other and stare at Jumbo as if he is in a different realm than the pair of us.

"Two minutes more for the antidote kit to arrive," says the Super. "The bike has already entered the dock."

I stand up and look at André, trying to read him.

Who is this man? Who is he *really*, behind the offshore façade we all present when working. We each have an onshore version of ourselves, and a saturated version.

There's a fire extinguisher on the wall.

Crack his skull with it.

Save yourself.

"Stop. I mean, listen," I say, frantic, edging away from the extinguisher. "Can we still give the antidote to Jumbo?"

"Get it to us now," roars André to the microphone on the wall. "Go get it yourself!"

We step to the Medlock and the new medic briefs us about what the kit will look like and what it will consist of. Has Gonzales been taken away for questioning? Her replacement speaks slowly and clearly. The kit will consist of three elements. First, amyl nitrate. We will have to break the seal and hold it to his nostrils. Then sodium nitrate. We have never trained with this. Then the sodium thiosulfate. She asks if we understand.

"Yes," I say. "But will it work after he's had no pulse for this long?"

She looks pensive through the porthole window. "Just try your best. I'm right here behind you."

Fresh commotion outside.

Halvor brings the kit to the medic and she places it into the Medlock.

It is the size and shape of my Henry's lunch box.

After the pressure has equalized I open the hatch and retrieve the kit.

A terrible thought crosses my mind, a thought I am ashamed to acknowledge.

We only have one of these.

Should we use it on an unresponsive man?

Or should we hold it back for ourselves?

65

ANDRÉ OPENS THE box and we spread out the kit's components on the steel table.

"Amyl nitrate," says the medic, clearly, watching us eye the glass container.

I lift up the tiny bottle, break it open, hand it to André. "Amyl nitrate."

He holds the bottle to Jumbo's nose. "Come on, mate. Come on. Come back, Gary."

Nothing happens.

"Should we try CPR again?" André shouts.

We run through the rest of the protocol and multiple rounds of chest compressions, but it is clear nothing is working. We were too late. Because of an accident, or a criminal act, or an unfortunate series of red traffic lights, our friend lies unmoving on the floor of the chamber and we have no kit left with which to treat ourselves if we suffer the same fate.

The medic is talking with a doctor. The doctor, dressed in jeans and a sport jacket, calls time of death and leaves.

I back away from André.

DCI MacDuff's face appears at the other porthole window.

"I'm sorry," he says. "The crime scene manager will oversee what happens next. I'm told by the pathology team there is no need for you to perform any tests or retrieve samples as your decompression will conclude later today. I'm also told it would be best if you could leave Gary where he lies, please. My colleagues will be passing through a sterile sheet and you can use that to cover him. You've been through a lot and I'm sorry for that."

"Eight hours," says André, blinking away tears. "He only needed to make it eight more hours and he'd have walked out of this. Eight hours is nothing, it's one shift. I don't understand what is happening. Did he die from cyanide poisoning?"

I am so thirsty I can hardly talk. My peripheral vision is blurry. Bubble brain and a parched throat. "They don't know what's happening, either," I blurt out. "Don't you see? With all their expertise and science, with their surveillance and blood samples. How did Jumbo ingest cyanide? If they don't know, then how on earth could we?"

66

WE ARE QUESTIONED separately, me from the Wet Pot, André from our living quarters.

Could André be behind all this? To what end? How could he have hurt Tea-Bag and Jumbo from the Wet Pot?

I can tell from the DCI and his tone that, despite his seniority and experience, he is rattled by what we are living through. He must feel as frustrated and powerless as we do. I suppose, in a way, he will also have to answer for this. There will be enormous scrutiny, from his superiors, the press, the HSE. He will need to present the evidence he and his team have collected, to the Procurator Fiscal. There may even be a judicial inquiry, or a House of Commons Select Committee meeting. He asks me about how Jumbo looked when he collapsed. If he had eaten or drunk anything. He asks in-depth questions about his dizziness in the past hours. His vitals. He asks about Jumbo using the disinfectant wipes to clean down the chamber table and then I snap and say, "You can all see what we did. What we *do*. We're not doing *anything* for goodness' sake. We are dying one by one from poisoning and you're asking about cleaning protocols?"

"I apologize if my question was insensitive," he says.

I pace around the Wet Pot shaking my head, scratching my itchy unwashed scalp, and say, "No, I'm sorry. You didn't deserve that. It's the not knowing. It's driving me insane. Have you seen André do anything strange?"

"How do you mean?"

"Nothing. I feel faint. I need to sit down."

By the time I open the hatch and slide back into the living quarters, André is sitting and drinking a cup of tea.

"No," I say, holding out my palms. "No!"

He shrugs and points to Gary's covered body between the bunks. "He had nothing and he still died, Brooke." His voice is desperate. "Look, we have four cyanide antidote kits in total now. They arrived when you were in the Wet Pot. There might be even more outside. We're ready if one of us shows even the slightest symptoms. I need sustenance, I don't know about you. I'm two sips into this tea and I'm already thinking clearer. You want a brew?"

I shake my head.

"I think you need it, mate."

Like everything else in this chamber, it feels out of kilter. You can't drink tea when your friend and mentor is stiff and cold directly behind you.

"I don't know, André. I don't know what to do."

"I'm not pushing you," he says, taking another sip, gasping with exaggerated pleasure.

I wait.

Have it.

Have a nice cuppa.

"Pour it," I say.

The new Life Support Technician, a man I've known for years, comes on through the speaker. "To confirm, the kitchen staff are being monitored at all times. All food and drink is being filmed as it transits through to you. The water is taken from sealed bottles."

I hold my thumb up to the camera and take the mug and blow into it.

Hot, sweet, stewed tea.

A tonic.

What do you do when your friends drop all around you? I've been in Britain for enough years to know. You have a cup of tea and try to make sense of it.

"It'll hit us completely different when we get home," says André, blowing into his mug. "Some base animal defense mechanism. Same as when we work in the water. You can't let yourself process it properly until you're in a safe place."

I look at the four boxes on the table in between us.

Antidote kits.

He's right. We're diving buddies but we also have to act as underqualified doctors and priests. We sew each other up and we keep the peace when there is disharmony.

André sits up straighter.

He pushes the mug away from him.

"Medic," he says, scratching his throat, holding it. "Medic. I don't feel right."

67

I RIP OPEN the cyanide antidote kit.

André is standing facing the porthole, his back as straight as a rod.

"Joe, talk to me. Can you breathe?"

He looks back over his shoulder at me, then to the porthole. "Yeah, I think so. I think it's all right. Give me a sec."

He takes several deep, raspy breaths.

"Brooke, can you check his vitals, please."

"Thirsty," he says.

Water is pushed through the Medlock. He watches eagle eyed, sweating, as I remove the seal in front of him and hold the bottle to his lips.

"Heart rate's OK," I say to the new medic, one eye on the clock.

The Super comes over to the speaker. "I've got an old friend here for you both."

Halvor's reassuring voice. "Take a minute for yourself, diver."

André smiles and stifles a sob. I watch him calm down with this instruction.

We sit together as he gets his breath back. I pack the antidote kit away so it'll be ready to use if we need it.

"Six hours remaining," says Halvor. "Six hours left. Over."

"Roger that," I say.

"Sixteen hundred hours. Four p.m. Then the door will pop open. Hold on until then, both of you. Over."

André lets out a deep sigh. "Roger that."

We decide not to drink any more tea. It could be that André's reaction was some unspoken fear at drinking again, a subconscious reaction, or it could be entirely unrelated. Although I have been daydreaming of a bacon roll with ketchup, we opt to stay fasted until we understand how the toxic substance is reaching us.

"In the Medlock, lads," says the new Betty, someone I vaguely recognize from a Norwegian DSV.

I open the hatch. Six fresh magazines. *National Geographic*, *FHM*, *Private Eye*, *Top Gear*, *Men's Health*, and a copy of *Cosmopolitan*. I almost smile, imagining one of the assistants running down the steep gangplank to the nearest newsagent, and then standing staring at the magazine shelves deciding what I might want to read.

Still no news, though. Not a single unfiltered update from the outside world. What are they saying about us?

The medic asks me to check on André again. She asks him questions via the speaker.

Jumbo is gone.

I eye André suspiciously but then I scold myself.

No logic to my thoughts.

Some of them aren't even mine to begin with.

We have lost track of our circadian rhythms. Sometimes when you are on a dive job in dark water, silt all around you, or glass sand like in the Gulf of Mexico, you lose the ability to tell which way is up. In neutral buoyancy, with no visual clues, you can find yourself spinning slowly in seawater not knowing which way faces the surface and which way the seabed. A spacewalk gone wrong. The umbilical is your only guide in those circumstances: you hold on to it and you follow it to the safety of the Bell.

My personal umbilical to the outside world is *complicated*. Halvor reassures me, as do the Super and, to some extent, the Night Super and the Life Support Technicians, but my virtual umbilical, my connection to reality, is more a thread than a sturdy tether. A single strand of spider-wool. When I attend talking sessions at the church group in Harrogate most of the conversations are aligned, as in we ask similar questions of each other and give vaguely similar answers. Grief is complex and simple at the same time. But one question I get that the others do not is: *Do you keep on deep-sea diving because you don't care anymore if you live or die?* I was taken aback by that question the first time it was asked, by a woman five years older than me who lost her son to suicide. She asked with kindness and genuine interest, but I couldn't answer her until the following week. In truth, I wasn't entirely sure. So I went for runs and I walked Gilly's dog, which always helps give me answers and reassurance, and then I went back into the church hall and told her I still worked because I wanted to live, not die, but I need the escape. I feel alive when I am diving. It is as if I can contribute to a large project, a bigger picture than just myself. I can help the guys and we can get something done. I tried to explain that while my own fear of death has diminished, and that a big part of me wants to rejoin my husband and children, even if that only means in the same burial site, I do still want to live on. I hold those memories. I keep my family alive by talking about them, by writing letters to them, by listening to Steve's voicemails, by making donations in their names. My lust for life has largely faded, some of that replaced by pain and emptiness, but what years I have left are a privilege and I do not take them for granted.

I will not waste the chances others never had.

68

I'M WATCHING ANDRÉ but I'm thinking about musicians. Imagine a band, let's say six members, and you tour together for a solid month with no breaks or off-days. Only you do not have a tour bus, not a full-size one, you have a minibus instead. Three bunk beds and a folding table. Now imagine all your gigs are suddenly canceled and yet you are unable to leave the minibus. If someone opens a door, you all die. Imagine the closeness, the annoyances, the smells, the comradery, the conflicts; only with our helium gas and humidity. That is just the beginning. The minibus is rocked by storms. Then the musicians begin to die inside the minibus, one by one.

There are only two band members left.

"If either one of you would like some counseling, or to talk with a chaplain from the ship company, we can have that arranged while you're still in saturation," says the Super.

"I'd rather you speed up deco, boss," says André. "Five hours left? How about we accelerate that down to three."

"We've already had meetings about it. That's a negative, I'm afraid. Over."

"Yes, it is," says André under his breath.

He starts to wipe down the surfaces, the walls, the area where the garbage liner hangs on the wall, the shelves where we store our bottles of hot sauce, vitamin bottles, and condiments. The wiping isn't required right now. He is half-hearted, no pressure from his hand, and his posture is terrible. He looks defeated.

We are a few hours from leaving and this place is cleaner than I have ever seen it. Perhaps it is because we are sharing the tight space with a corpse once again, or perhaps it is some form of autonomic action we struggle to switch off.

"When I reach home after a job," I say, "I keep on wiping."

"Are you telling me I'm not the only one?" says André as he spits into a tissue and places it in a clear garbage bag. Is he worried he consumed something?

"You are not the only one wiping like a maniac," I say.

"My ex-wife used to watch me clean, her arms crossed. Thought it was some kind of criticism of her housework."

"I used to get up and do it when Steve was fast asleep in bed. I'd creep downstairs and wipe down all the kitchen surfaces and then the fridge. I'd dust his watchmaker benches because he said they needed to be spotless. Always slept better after that."

"It's a tough profession to quit, isn't it? Once it has its hooks in you can't do much to wriggle free. The money and the brotherhood."

"My sister-in-law reckons it's the ultimate avoidance technique. Gilly says I keep doing this because it's the only way I can get away from what happened."

"Makes sense. We're all running away from something."

"What are you running from?"

He licks his peeling lips and talks as he wipes. "When I was a kid I'd do long hikes with my old man. Scotland, Peak District, Bodmin Moor. We'd thru-hike trails in all weather. He was a solid outdoorsman and, although he never really spoke much, I learned a lot from him. Those were probably the best days of his life. He never said as much, never talked in those terms, but I know he cherished the simplicity of quiet, simple nights under canvas. We survived on porridge, mostly, and the occasional pub lunch when we came across one. He was a serious man with a decent war record, and he clearly enjoyed eating straight from a pot while sitting on a tree stump overlooking a lake or a mountain slope. He enjoyed sleeping a bit cold and a bit damp, tired legs, condensation dripping from the canvas. He liked answering the call of nature behind a bush. He relished the chance to wash his face in a stream. Men back then had a lot of responsibilities and very little downtime. He used hiking like I use being in the chamber. It's different in a thousand ways, of course, but it's a repetitive, physical existence."

"Is he still alive?"

André shakes his head. "Three years ago I was working out in the Red Sea, making decent money. Mainly pipeline work: short Sat and Air jobs to pay back loan sharks. My sister called me and told me I should come home to see him. I told her I was too busy with the job, had to earn before I came back. Eventually her husband called me and told me it was time. He's a copper, her husband. A serious man. So I jumped on the next plane home and went straight to the hospital. He was only sixty-two. They were run ragged with tiredness, the lot of them. My sister, my cousin, and my mum. Exhausted. I told them to all go home and get some rest and proper food. I told them I'd take the night shift and they should come back in the morning. I said I'll work out a rotation so they don't get burnt out at the same time and then crash together. They don't understand the value of shift work like we do." André's eyes turn glossy. "I sat by his bedside all night. He was lucid from time to time but he was given a lot of pain medication. Ketamine, I think it was. I quoted some *Macbeth* to him, but I'm not sure any of it went in. Dad drifted in and out of sleep and I sat there holding his hand. He had big hands, my dad, fingers flattened by decades of manual labor. That was the first time I'd held his hand since I was a little lad. When he woke we would talk about our hiking trips, Dartmoor, the time he was chased by a bull that turned out to be nothing more than a big cow. We talked about how he once forgot to bring a stove, so we had to eat cold porridge each morning, and how he told me that's how the Scots do it and it'll put hair on my chest. He smiled through the pain when I told him that. He didn't say he was proud of me or anything that night, not his way. He didn't tell me he loved me like my son might tell me, but he asked me if I was still deep-sea diving and if I was enjoying it, and I told him I was. He said it's good money, isn't it, and I agreed it was pretty good. *I'm glad they're paying you a decent wage*, he said. *You deserve a decent wage, lad, the way you work.* That was the most powerful thing he ever said to me because I knew how much he respected hard work. He worked in teams his whole life and he could not abide anyone who, out of idleness, was content to let others take the weight for them."

"He sounds like a good man," I say.

André screws up his face and blinks. "When my sister and mother came in the next morning I told them I was leaving. They asked if I'd be back that night. I gave them the new schedule, the shift quota, and said I was heading back out to the Red Sea for work. My sister's lip started quivering. I told her me and Dad had already said our goodbyes. I told her we'd spoken more in the past twelve hours than we had in decades. Two days later I was onshore outside Hurghada when I got the call. I wasn't in Sat at the time, I was air diving. Dad had gone. I didn't feel sad to be honest with you. It is what it is. Ill for four weeks at the end. He would have hated a long, drawn out illness. We both talked about how we couldn't imagine old age. The quicker the better, right? He had lived a good life and I'd had the chance to say goodbye to him properly. To hold his hand. That's not a bad outcome, is it?"

"Not bad at all," I say, looking over at Jumbo's covered body.

69

AT THIS STAGE of a deco I would usually be spending many hours in my bunk. I prefer to withdraw, blanket drawn, music pumping through my headphones. I'll get up and out for meals and I'll open the curtain back to chat with the guys from time to time, but as the countdown progresses I usually hide. To process the transition I am about to undergo, from diver back to civilian, to reflect on the job completed, the close calls in and outside the Bell, and to emotionally prepare for seeing home again. The empty bedrooms. Their coats still on their individual hooks in the downstairs hallway because I can't bring myself to store them away or donate them.

Not yet.

Today I have no bunk. It's there, I can see it clearly, but I don't want to step over Gary to reach it. Not that he would care, he would tell me to get on with it, but I don't want to spend a single second in that end of the chamber, not until the moment the hatch hisses and opens and we are able to step outside.

"He had no pension," says André.

I frown.

He gestures to the body on the floor. "No pension, no investments, no house in his name after the divorce. He had no backup plan, Gary didn't. Spoiled his girlfriends, his daughter, his grandkids, and himself. But I'm not sure he would have enjoyed his old age, either."

I don't answer him.

Most divers don't reach old age. Not because the job itself is dangerous—it looks more risky than it is thanks to safety improvements and training—but because this line of work tends to attract thrill-seekers and outlaws. Life spans are shorter because we don't visit doctors unless we have to, and we won't take it easy when others would, and we tend not to plan for a long future.

"You want some music?" asks André.

"I don't know," I say, staring at his eyes, then at the antidote kits between us.

"What did Gary like?"

"Sorry?" I say.

"What music?"

I smile. "Boss?"

A Life Support Technician comes on through the speaker and says, "Hendrix?"

I nod. "You got it."

We sit flicking through our new magazines as "All Along the Watchtower" pipes through our speakers. My eyelids feel heavy and I can't focus on the pages. Hendrix sings about getting no relief. I open the hatch and retrieve new sealed water bottles and a bag of clean laundry. There is an eyeball at each porthole. They watch us constantly.

Four kits on the table. One of them already open and partly used.

If it's just the two of us left.

Then the odds are worsening.

I pick up my camcorder and hit record.

"Really?" says André. "Now?"

"We have to pass the time somehow. No other option."

Somewhat reluctantly, he talks about his courses, about his early days in Asia, about accidents and near misses, about more women coming into commercial diving.

"You know, I keep thinking about . . . all this," I say, placing the camera back down. "Four fatalities. All preventable with the correct antidote kit, so that must be a health-and-safety issue. There will be reports written about this job, just like there were after Piper Alpha and Byford Dolphin. But logically speaking, the cause of the poisoning is either internal and intentional, i.e., you or me; external and intentional, i.e., one or more people outside the chamber but on the ship; or it is accidental."

One of the people supervising us from outside moves and is instantly replaced by another shadowy figure.

Green eye to brown.

Slowly, André puts on his reading glasses. "Game of chess?"

70

WE TAKE OUT the magnetic chessboard, a set designed to be played by children in the back of station wagons while their parents bicker about routes and lunch stops.

I try, but I can't bring myself to play. I tell him the pieces are too small and I can't focus my eyes.

In truth, I need a little more distance from him.

"We can do it later," says André, clearly irritated.

We have about three hours left and the minute hand is dragging slower than it was before. Time really is relative after all. Relative and cruel. We sit watching the gauge on the wall and knowing that nothing can bring about our escape to safety, even if we brutally attack each other.

A thought comes to me.

"Still no Wi-Fi?" I mutter.

"Any updates on the Wi-Fi?" says André.

"We're still working on it. Over."

"They're not working on it," I whisper.

"They can hear you, you know."

"They can't have us reading the news," I say. "Or messages. Imagine if they know exactly what is going on inside here but they can't tell us. They might be hiding something. They might know how the cyanide is getting to us."

"We've been over this. But why couldn't they tell us? Let's not go over the same subject. I can't handle it."

He clenches his jaw and inspects an antidote kit.

"What if they know that it's you or me who is responsible for the deaths of four innocent men? What if they know that Gonzales is responsible?"

"She's not responsible," he snaps. "She's still working out there somewhere, I saw her awhile back preparing IV bags. Stop it, Brooke. Cut it out."

"You guys have enough water?" asks Halvor.

"Yes," I say, rubbing my eyes, incapable of forming coherent thoughts. "Let's just say it's *you* who is responsible." A prickling sensation on my arms. "They can't tell us that they know that, can they? Imagine the repercussions. They can't come in here and help me in any way, and they can't arrest you. So they have to keep us in an artificial state of stasis."

"How about we just don't speak for a bit," he says, rubbing his eyes with his knuckles.

"Bubble brain," I say, tapping my head. "Sleep deprivation and low blood sugar. Sorry."

He doesn't respond.

After a few minutes I can't help focus on the irritating way he is breathing. Exaggerated inhalations. His nostrils flare.

A wave of abject disgust.

And then guilt.

I couldn't rush to my son's bedside. I knowingly prioritized my job over my children. And then the deeper, darker guilt, the tiers and strata of it. If it had happened one week later it would have been me driving them both to school. If I had chosen not to take that job and instead taken a shorter, less lucrative dive off the coast of Holland, a job I never really considered because of the pay differential, I would have been driving and I would have died along with my children. And the complex, shameful guilt that perhaps I would have been able to swerve out of the way of the oncoming truck. My reactions are faster than Steve's ever were, he admitted as much. I was the better driver and perhaps I would have saved us.

71

THEY GIVE US various small tasks and drills to keep our minds busy. Two hours and forty minutes remaining.

As I check equipment and perform mental acuity tests I keep one eye on André at all times.

I keep watching his hands.

We do not need to be told to wipe down, to remove old garbage bags, to keep the space as orderly as possible, which is not a simple task with a corpse on the floor. I am not a cold person, I don't think of Gary as a *corpse*—he was instrumental to me getting into Sat and he invited me to the christening of his first grandchild—but he wasn't *my* family, and I have to maintain some emotional distance, and keep an even keel, if I am to make it out of this chamber alive. Disassociation? Is that what this is? I don't know the exact terminology but I do know that when working three hundred feet down I have to put everything else out of my mind so I can get the job done. This is the reason Mike never brought photos of Emily into the chamber with him, and the reason he often wandered off when a diver was talking at length about their kids. He wanted to focus on work when he was working.

They ask us to run through step-by-step drills of how to deploy the cyanide antidote kits. The kits themselves have now been supplemented with extra medical and resuscitation equipment, although the new medic has explained, at great length, that these devices are as yet untested under pressure. As we are about done with deco and the pressure is low I guess we are the guinea pigs they need right now.

Have Tea-Bag's parents been able to see his body? This question bothers me. He was young and I assume, for some reason, they still had a close family relationship. I suppose I gleaned it from our brief conversations. Intuition. I want for them to be able to say goodbye to their son in person. To touch his hand.

"Foot fungus and Rolexes," says André, looking at his watch, turning the dive countdown bezel as if timing something only he knows about. "Our world."

I nod, but then I have to clear my throat.

It is as if the gas in here is thickening.

A commotion out on deck. We hear a crash and then see a rush of people in the background. We watch them through the porthole window in the direction of the ship's deck. The eye at the window disappears. Nobody's watching us back. I pull away from him. André tries to make out what is going on as I keep an eye on him, his pockets, his long fingers. It looks like chaos out there. A Sikh police officer in uniform chases a man into the bowels of the ship. The man looks like Leo. I mean, he looks exactly like him: the same symmetrical dark features and wide lips. The same unusual cowlick in his hairline.

"What's going on, boss?" André asks, nervously.

"Situation on deck," the Super says, calmly. "Being taken care of."

"Hold on to a kit," says André, throwing one to me and grabbing another for himself.

"Why?"

"I don't know," he yells, taking me by surprise. "Just do it.

We might need help quickly. They're not in control out there anymore. Look."

Shouting outside. Another two uniformed police sprint past the chamber.

The Super says, "Unauthorized personnel on the ship. It's being handled. Over."

"Don't let them get close to us," I say, shaking.

Suddenly I am very cold.

"Police are dealing with it. Over."

My teeth begin chattering.

"Roger that," says André, clutching his kit to his chest.

We both watch the hatch.

The eye returns at the porthole. The anonymous person the eye belongs to offers us a less-than-reassuring thumbs-up.

I whisper to André, "He looked like Spock."

André shakes his head dismissively and sits back down on the bench.

I sit opposite him.

"Protestors?" he asks, ignoring my comment. "Anti-oil or Greenpeace?"

"Could be." I rub my arms to warm up. "Could be a reporter trying to get an exclusive? All they'd have to do is make their way to the docks and jump aboard when nobody's looking. It's not like there's much security."

"I'd sell my story for fifty grand," says André.

"Don't talk like that," I say, gesturing to Gary's covered body.

"He'd want me to, wouldn't you, mate? Listen, if you don't sell your story you're a fool."

I swear I can see my exhalation form a faint cloud in front of my eyes.

"Could have been enraged relatives," says André. "Come here to attack the Super for not keeping their nephew safe."

He might have a point. This could be furious parents or siblings or partners, driven to extreme action by their loss, by the horrific nature of their loved one's demise, here to seek their revenge. Did Leo have a twin? A brother? I rub my arms again and drag my sleeves down to my wrists. But what narrative have *they* been told? Who do *they* think is responsible for all this? Because it could be Dive Control or the DSV owner they are after.

Or it could be that they have traveled here to deliberately sabotage our chamber.

They might be here for one of us.

72

"THE DRAMA'S FINISHED, lads," says Halvor over the speaker. "My apologies. Over."

André perks up. "Protestors? People trying to get to us?"

"Negative," says Halvor. "Two reporters broke through a cordon and jumped on deck at great personal risk to themselves, then ran around half the ship looking for you two in the chamber. They have been apprehended and are being dealt with."

"Dealt with?" I say.

"Arrested or charged. Cautioned?" says Halvor. "DCI MacDuff can explain the technicalities. They obstructed police and they have been taken away in the back of a car. Apologies for the breach. We're working with police to make sure nobody else gets aboard without us knowing."

I have so many questions. What exactly do the reporters know that we don't? They're often the people who dig deepest. Investigative journalists. They might know, or suspect, that one of *us* is responsible.

Two hours and twenty minutes.

André sets up the magnetic chessboard on the table.

"No," I say, firmly, surprising myself.

"I'll play against myself then. You know they'll turn us in, right?"

"What?"

"For compulsory counseling." He spits out the words. "They won't say it's compulsory, but I doubt they'll let us work again unless we complete a long course of therapy onshore with over-educated shrinks."

"You'll work in Sat again after all this?"

He squirms on the bench and starts blinking repeatedly. "I have a mortgage to pay, mate. Payments that need to be made." He closes his eyes tight like he's fighting off pain.

"You OK?"

He nods but he is still cringing.

I found my counseling immensely challenging. Then, one Saturday, spontaneously, I walked down to the local church. I am not religious at all, or, rather, I wasn't back then, and it's not even the church where my beloveds rest, where I visit them every week when I'm onshore, it's the little one next to the pub. I walked there during a driving storm, my hair plastered across my face, expecting to be able to sit quietly at the back while a small congregation sang traditional hymns and the vicar gave a soporific sermon. I opened the ancient wooden doors to find eight people sitting in a circle in the nave, with the vicar being one of them. They had mugs of tea and coffee. They were talking about loss, grief, insomnia, the death of a loyal dog. Pain in all its myriad forms. Not my kind of thing at all, but the vicar, a man in his seventies, smiled. He didn't welcome me in with his words, but I understood from his demeanor, from his silent expression of acceptance, that I was welcome if I wanted to join. I walked toward them. If they had started asking questions I would have most likely turned on my heels, but they let me be. I notice André playing chess against himself, turning the diminutive board with every change of play, a crazed look in his eyes. I think back to the first session I participated in. I don't mean that stormy day when

I merely sat in the first pew and watched, and they let me do that, but the following week when I turned up before anybody else, and, after they had all spoken of spouses lost to breast cancer and strokes, or grown-up children lost to drug overdoses, I opened up about the accident. That was the first day I could let it all out. The pressure was immense, like the gates of a dam unlocking and water gushing out. They had shown their vulnerabilities. They showed themselves at their lowest, they shared their pain, and that generosity allowed me to do the same. I couldn't, as much as I tried, do this with people who were not actively grieving their own personal loss. In the church hall, a place I returned to multiple times, to listen as much as to speak, they helped me make sense of something senseless. Something larger than all of us. They helped me process and adjust, a little at a time. They helped me realize I would always feel a large, empty black hole inside my chest. It would never go away. But the rest of me could grow around the hole, the absence, and I could live on remembering them.

An unwanted flash inside my head, this one worse than whatever has come before.

A voice. Lisa's sweet voice: *Open the hatch, mum.*

I clear my throat to get it to go away.

Quiet, my love.

Or if you can't do it, go into the Wet Pot and open the valves.

I stop breathing.

Hush, darling.

Seize hold of André's hair and smash his face into the metal table.

I force the thoughts away. That's definitely not her and it is not me.

Do it.

Come to us.

73

I KNOW THE thoughts are not *mine*. I am quite sure I am in control and I would never hurt anyone, myself included. I have understood these thoughts, these voices, on a deep yet shameful level ever since I was a young girl. When I was seven my family went to a fortieth-birthday party in Prien, Louisiana. It was for my dad's best friend from college. The day was tranquil: a lakeside setting, bouncy castle for the kids, water guns, smoked meats, crawfish, gumbo and jambalaya, lots of laughter and high jinks. Caitlin was there. She was five—pigtails and blue eyes—the youngest daughter of our gracious hosts. She had a handsome room, a little larger than mine, and I remember she kept it ordered and neat. We'd finished lunch and the grown-ups were drinking beer and smoking cigars by the lake. Caitlin showed me the new board game her parents had given her and my mind *flashed*. That is the best way I can describe it. A thought flashed into my consciousness, as if a slide on a projector in front of my eyes. I saw what I was going to do. I literally saw myself strangle the little girl and take off with her new game.

I didn't do it, of course.

That is what's pertinent.

André takes a shower and I am left alone with my wayward mind.

You can't really talk publicly about intrusive thoughts. I have spoken openly about grief, I have talked about my mother's alcoholism, I have discussed how difficult it is for women to be employed in offshore jobs at the right rates. But you can't really talk about thoughts as dark and unwelcome as the ones I sometimes have. I am luckier than many in that my intrusive thoughts flash when I am stressed. Some kind of cortisol response, perhaps. My first deep dive, going down in the Bell, I was half-tempted to open the valves. When I was focusing all my strength, all my might, to hold it together long enough to deliver the eulogy, the *three* eulogies, because I insisted they each deserved a separate one, I fought against multiple flashes, multiple despicable thoughts, standing at that church lectern. I can't even talk to a counselor about them—they might call the police despite what you read about doctor-patient confidentiality. They might construe, however absurdly, that a crime was committed, or is about to be committed, and so that nullifies the privilege. I couldn't mention it to Gilly, my closest friend in the world, or the other grieving people in church group, how I kept imagining me working on the family car at night before I went offshore, modifying the brake lines, using my engineering knowledge to render them fragile. I shake the ugly image from my head. The one time I did share my thoughts, many years ago, with a classmate I considered my best friend and confidante, she went and told the most popular girl in our year and I was a social outcast for weeks.

I learned a very important lesson that day.

Startling me back to reality, André opens the Wet Pot hatch and slides through wearing his towel.

I can see his ribs.

He stands by the porthole. "More police officers out there now. They're trying to move around where we can't see them, but I can spot them in the window reflections and in the gas pipes." He turns his head to the microphone. "I said I can see all the coppers."

"Roger, Roger," says the Super.

André looks even more vulnerable now that he has showered. His hair is plastered to his skull, each contour and bump visible.

"We need to think about services," I say. "A memorial fund."

He clenches his teeth and says, "Not now, Brooke. Less than two hours to go, yeah. I want my mind somewhere else. We can deal with all that when we're out, yeah? Yes? Onshore-only. OK? Yes?"

He stares at me.

"Chess set in the Medlock," says a Life Support Technician.

"You ordered *another* chess set?" I ask.

He grinds his teeth and takes the set from the Medlock. "You wouldn't play me on the magnetic one, so I asked for a full-size board. Will you take me on or won't you?"

74

I TAKE THE wooden chess set from André.

"It's sealed," says the Life Support Technician. "We haven't opened it."

I peel off the cling wrap. A static crackle. The board is hinged in the center. Dark brown pieces and cream-colored pieces, all made from softwood.

I take my time to set the pieces down on the steel table. André moves the four cyanide kits farther up toward Gary's feet.

"Black or white?" says André.

"Flip for it."

André stretches over Gary's body and retrieves a penny from his bunk.

"Lucky penny. Heads or tails."

"Heads."

One wins. One dies.

Stop it.

I don't believe that.

It is what it is.

The voices are mixing.

Deep breath.

He flips the coin and lets it fall to the steel table and it spins in place, and we watch it spin for what seems like minutes. Eye at the porthole glass. The penny slows and trembles. We are hypnotized. The trembling intensifies. A metallic drone.

Its spin becomes irregular, and then it falls.

"Heads," he says.

I opt to play white. Starter's advantage. He looks deadly serious as we arrange the pieces, as if we were playing for money, but that look is tinged with abject dread. André is notoriously competitive and I sense he needs this escape, this chance. I will give him what he needs because it is in my interest to keep him calm. After four days of terrible losses, he needs a win.

"How much are we playing for?" he asks, looming over the board, his long back arched.

"No money."

He stares at me. "Loser has to speak with Leo's wife when we get out."

"No." I withdraw. Memories of being told they are gone. Flashbacks of well-meaning people trying to speak to me about what I was going through. "We can't play for that."

He seems puzzled by my reaction.

The lights on the walls flicker. Bright, then dull.

"Winner gets to step out first in . . ." I check the clock. "One hour forty-five minutes."

"Done."

The Super passes us a fresh camera through the Medlock. I am not sure if they have an endless supply of Sony camcorders, or if they merely replace the tapes and charge the batteries. They could have two, or two dozen, for all I know. A detective, not DCI MacDuff, supervises the camera handover process through the porthole over André's shoulder.

I move a pawn up two places.

André mirrors my move.

I push a knight forward.

André does the same.

"Zero points for originality," I mutter.

He keeps his focus on the board.

It is odd to look around and see the empty bunks, the covered body of our friend on the floor, the eyes at the glass. A chamber of this size, six-man, would usually be covered with clear garbage bags, headphone leads, hot sauce bottles, towels hanging up to dry, bunk curtains closed for privacy.

"My granddad was a chess player," he says, as if to himself. "He taught my uncle. My uncle taught me."

I move three pawns forward.

He counters by breaking out a bishop and two pawns.

I threaten with yet another pawn.

The heat has come back on. I can feel it in the gas we are breathing. It is hot in my throat. Thick and stifling.

He retreats.

I move my queen out in preparation for an attack.

"Brooke," he says, looking up at me. "What is going on here?"

75

I WATCH HIM move his knight, his fingers trembling. "What do you mean?"

He glances at me as I bring forward a rook to flank my queen. He feels outgunned and outmaneuvered; I can sense it in his breathing.

I begin to sweat.

Why is it so hot in here?

"What I mean," he says through gritted teeth, "is you and Jum, sitting down. What happened?"

I gesture to André and frown.

He nods.

"We don't . . . know," I say. "You know we don't know. We might not know for weeks."

He wipes his face on his forearm. "Don't play games."

"Everything OK in there?" says Halvor.

André ignores him. "What do you *think* happened, Ellen?"

I have to pull back my queen. He counters with both knights. Strong move.

Direct.

"I won't spout theories when we have no facts. When we're outside, fresh air, doors I can actually open, we can talk about it then."

He sets his jaw. "It stopped with Jumbo. Did you notice?"

"How could I fail to notice?"

I castle.

He does the same, a single bead of sweat falling from his straight, sharp nose to the steel table.

Not a single piece taken so far.

Even.

He wipes the sweat away.

"Three lads died," he says, holding his piece before committing to the move. "Then Jum died and it all stopped."

I take one of his bishops.

He moves his head closer to the board, covering more of it in shadow.

"We *think* it has stopped," I say, peering at the eye in the window.

He picks up his lost bishop and paws at it.

"You're losing momentum," he says.

"We still have an hour forty to go."

"At least we have this now," he says, taking my rook.

He doesn't think I saw that coming.

He *thinks* he outplays me.

I maneuver a pawn so that, in the coming minutes, it can be taken by him.

A planned sacrifice.

I lift my collar to vent.

He takes the pawn immediately.

Amateur.

Taking the bait.

"We don't know what Jumbo died of yet," he says, barely a whisper.

I edge closer. "I assume the same as the other three."

I move my knight next to his queen.

"Don't assume," he says, his breath sour, hot, his hair still clinging to the ridges and raised scars of his scalp. "I was as close to Jumbo as anyone here, but it could be that he had a grievance with Tea-Bag, Leo, and Mike. Poisoned their water or their food, then died of a heart attack from the guilt and the stress."

"You're insane."

I take his rook.

He looks upset about that move. Like he never factored my counter as a possibility. He *should* have seen me coming.

It was a textbook bluff.

Look strong when you are weak, weak when you are powerful.

"The natural causes part, I don't buy," I say, sitting up taller on the bench. "Not that I buy the rest of it. Why would Jum want to do that to three divers? No offense to him, but he wasn't the mastermind criminal type. That kind of thing takes planning."

"He had a record."

I consider taking a pawn, my fingers almost releasing, but then I reconsider.

"Everyone in Sat has a record from somewhere. I have a record in Louisiana."

"It stopped with him," says André, his face glistening. "Can't you see?"

"Enough," I say, taking his other bishop, further depleting his ability to attack.

He counters by taking my queen. "Roger that."

Was this a ruse to make me lose concentration? Was this him outflanking me while I *thought* I was outflanking him the whole time?

I ponder making my next move.

I do not rush.

"Good thing this isn't speed chess," he says.

"We can make it speed chess for the next game if you like."

His nose twitches. "Maybe *you* did something."

His stale exhalations sit between us in the heavy gas.

I stare at him, at his red eyes. "I did something? What did I do, Joe?"

He stares back at me.

His cheeks flush and he does not release me from his gaze.

"Everything all right in there, lads," says the Super over the speaker.

"Dandy," says André, still looking straight at me.

"Fine," I say, picking dead skin from my lip.

I push forward to threaten his king.

"Nobody would suspect *you*, would they," he says, almost under his breath. "A woman in Sat. A pioneer in the North Sea."

The structure creaks around us.

"Save your breath," I mutter, moving a pawn.

He takes that very same pawn. "You even have an alibi ready, don't you?"

I take my eye off the board and glower at him, my teeth clenched.

Taste of iron on my tongue.

He keeps looking down, and then moves his queen across the board.

I counter with my knight.

"Say it out loud," I urge. "If you've got something to say, say it out loud like a man."

His lips part.

He moves his rook while looking right at me. "Checkmate."

76

"YOUR ROOK WASN'T on that square," I say, trying, with all my might, to stay calm.

"It was. I moved it from g4."

My hackles are up.

He's not playing fair.

"Your rook was never on that square, mate."

"Wait one second, Brooke, mate. Are you suggesting I cheated?" He grits his teeth. "*Mate*?"

I wipe sweat from my upper lip.

The roof creaks again but the tone is different. A warping.

"Human error." I scowl at him. "I do it all the time."

"You're doing it now."

I glance over at the eye on the other side of the hatch.

"You want to play again, then?" I suggest.

"*What's done cannot be undone*. Why would I want to go again if you lie on the first game?"

"Lie?"

He nods, raising himself up to take up more space.

"Joe, Ellen, this is the Superintendent. I want to check on you both. We're approaching the final feet of pressure now." He sounds both authoritative and anxious. "Last lap of the circuit, as it were. Over."

I say, "I'm great," but my fists are clenched so tightly my trimmed fingernails are digging into the soft flesh of my palms.

André looks straight into my eyes and says, "No problems here, boss. Playing with a straight bat, as always."

A long pause.

"Roger that. Hang in there, both of you. I remember the last thirty feet, I know it's an arduous time even when things are going according to plan. Take it easy with each other. Over."

"Rematch?" I say, droplets of sweat emerging at my hairline.

He taps the steel table with his hand. "Glutton for punishment."

My stomach aches. No sugar in my blood. "I saw your attack ten moves before you made it. Relax, André, pal, this is just a game."

He stands up.

I stand up as well.

My nose is at his chest level.

"I want you two to remain separated," says the voice of the DCI, his voice urgent. I can tell he is struggling to maintain his composure. "We're almost through this. Ellen, I suggest you spend the next half hour in the Wet Pot so we can conduct some more questioning pertaining to the case. Joe, I'll ask you to remain in the chamber, please."

"We don't answer to you," says André, coldly, still standing, still looking right at me. We both know the police have no effective control over us. They would be unable to break up a fight. "We answer to Dive Control."

"Do what DCI MacDuff asks, please. Both of you," says the Super.

I stare at André. "I see you. I watched you do it. I'm always watching."

He snarls and knocks the chessboard as I step away, several pieces tumbling to the metal floor.

If he lunges for me and they conduct a rapid acceleration of the last stage of deco we could both get bent. We could die, even. I knew an onshore diver working on the tunnel under the River Tyne who, after his shift, died coming up too quickly from a seemingly harmless depth.

As I open the hatch and prepare to slide through into the Wet Pot, I turn to look at André and say, "Valve malfunction in the Bell. Want to get anything off your chest?"

I slide through without waiting for his response.

The Wet Pot doesn't smell like it usually does: salt water and gear. There are eyes at the portholes, whereas usually they afford us some privacy.

"How are you holding up, Ellen?" asks the DCI.

I take a deep breath and wipe my face. Odd to be called by my first name in here. "How would you be holding up?"

He nods. "Not long now."

"You know how the sixty minutes *feels*, Chief Inspector? It feels like days."

"I don't want any more friction between the two of you, is all. You're rubbing each other up the wrong way. I can't come in to help you if that happens."

"Why do you assume *I'd* be the one needing help?"

"I didn't mean it like that."

"I'm sorry. Cabin fever. *Chamber* fever."

"Have you noticed anything you missed before? Any feelings of nausea or dizziness? Any memories coming back of your fellow divers feeling strange after eating something?"

"Not that I can think of. I wasn't paying attention until we started dying one after the other."

He nods.

I focus on him through the thick glass.

"We overheard Joe tell you his theory," he says. "That Gary might have been responsible. What do you think about that?"

A loud clang from the main chamber.

MacDuff leaves the porthole.

"What's going on?" I say, straining to see.

He returns.

"It's nothing. Joe's theory about Jumbo."

"Absolute nonsense," I say. "And it's not right to speak ill of the dead."

"It might be tolerable if that deceased person caused harm, wouldn't you say? Morality is not absolute."

"I will not speak ill of the dead, Chief Inspector. Especially not Jumbo."

"I respect you for it. Do you maintain that position from your childhood, your upbringing, or has it become hardened since the passing of your immediate family?"

The *passing*? My *immediate family*? My face reddens. I loathe this nomenclature. They didn't *pass*, they were *killed*. My husband was murdered and my children were slain. A drunk driver *killed* them.

"Can you explain why much of the camera footage from the past hours has been deleted?" he asks.

"Sorry?"

"What is your explanation, Ellen? Twelve minutes have been wiped. We can ascertain from the surveillance camera footage that the camcorder was recording. The light was on. Twelve minutes is missing."

"I know nothing about that. By someone on the outside? It must be. There's someone out there doing it. Nobody inside has had access to the camcorder except me."

"Only you?"

"It's someone outside."

He shakes his head wearily. "No, Ellen, I'm afraid that is not the case."

"What?"

"Tell me what's going on, Ellen. It's just you and me. Get it off your chest."

The Super interjects. "I'm sorry to interrupt, Chief Inspector," he says. "But with your permission we need to move Brooke back to the living chamber immediately. We must transfer her back right now."

77

THERE IS ACTIVITY outside the chamber.

I can sense the vibrations caused by men in heavy boots as they run.

Some kind of alarm outside. Commands.

"Move back now, Brooke."

I open the hatch and slide through to the living chamber.

André crosses his arms. "They said we had to come together immediately. Did they tell you why? Is this your idea?"

"Boss, what is this?"

It is not Halvor or the Super or the Life Support Technician who answers me. Rather, it is the familiar voice of Gonzales. "We need you to stay together in the living chamber for the remainder of the deco. Fifty minutes. You must not split up again."

"What's wrong with the Wet Pot?" I ask. "Is the Super there?"

"*Fifty minutes?*" says André, snarling, jabbing his finger at the gauge on the wall. "We are well past that."

"Recalculation," says the Super, taking over the microphone. "Fifty minutes left now. Over."

I want to ask André about the missing camera footage. Ask him outright to his face. But something stops me. Maybe Mac-Duff plans to interrogate him on the subject.

"Stay on that side of the chamber," I say, gesturing to the sleeping area and the far side of the table.

"You don't tell me what to do."

"Poison," I say, frowning, looking around, probing all the shadows. "Cyanide. Is the Wet Pot compromised? Is that why I was moved?"

"The Wet Pot is fine but you need to stay together from now on. Same room. That's the protocol."

"Explain," says André, picking at his fingernails.

"Buddy system," says the Super. "You need to be in a position to help each other immediately if contaminated."

"We have four kits," says André.

"Sit down and let me talk you through it," says Gonzales.

We both refuse, standing our ground on each side of the table.

Gonzales points through the glass. "Inside your kits you have several components. I will talk you through them."

"We've already had the training," says André, slamming the palm of his hand on the table.

The chessboard shakes and several more pieces fall over, his king included.

"Then you'll understand that you may well not be in a position to administer the antidote medication to yourself if you come into contact with cyanide, in any of its forms. As you have seen with your colleagues, this substance can be fast-acting. You need to be in close proximity to one another at all times from now on in order to be able to medically intervene to save the other diver."

"A standoff," mutters André.

"Sorry?" says Gonzales.

"If one of us is doing the poisoning, then the other can't get away. We need to stay tethered together, no escape."

"You do need to stay together." Her tone is serious. "The police are aware of this protocol. They have signed off on it."

André shakes his head and rubs the sweat from his eyes.

"The kits you have on the table contain three active elements," says Gonzales. "If one of you experiences chest pain, shortness of breath, dizziness, confusion, the other diver should immediately administer the antidote. Time is of the essence. The affected diver may suffer seizures. The first step is to administer oxygen via the BIBS system and then find the amyl nitrate. Snap and hold under the nose of the patient for fifteen to twenty seconds every two to three minutes. Then you need to inject sodium nitrate. You'll find ten-milliliter ampoules in your kits. You also have sterile gloves, syringes, and needles in the kits. Then, inject sodium thiosulfate. You have fifty-milliliter vials. That is the complete course of acute medication. From that point onward I will advise on follow-up care and oxygen therapy. We will need to work together to track vitals."

"The way you're talking," says André, "it's like you expect one of us will need to do this. What is it that you know and we don't?"

78

THIRTY-EIGHT MINUTES.

Thirty-seven and a half.

So close. Unless they decide to reset the clock again.

I am watching André like a hawk but I am thinking about life after. At the moment all I have is a mini troupe of ducks: one parent and two ducklings, and Gilly is looking out for them while I'm in here. Feeding them every now and again. She thinks a puppy might do me some good: a living, breathing pet to look after, and she is probably right. She says I can drop off the pup with her if and when I need to work offshore. She says *if and when* because she would love me to stop working in Sat. According to her, a nice office job would be far more suitable, and, with the insurance money from Steve's policy, and potential proceeds from selling my now-too-large home, I won't even need a good salary anymore.

But would it be fair to the dog?

André stretches over Jumbo's body, careful not to touch it, and begins to pack away his belongings, periodically glancing at me over his shoulder as he does so. DCI MacDuff has asked us each to sort everything we have into one clear plastic bag. He says we can't take our belongings with us until they have been checked and the chamber has been photographed.

He deleted the camera footage.

You shouldn't let him get away with it.

I let the thoughts wash over me. I am too exhausted to push them away.

"You know this is just the beginning?" says André, a little breathless. "You ever been involved in a health and safety executive inquiry?"

I scratch my scalp and shake my head.

Thirty-three minutes until the hatch opens.

My throat is burning from heat and thirst.

"You ever been part of an inquiry?" I ask.

He nods, ties up his clear garbage bag, and sits down heavy on the bench.

I gesture for him to elaborate.

"*Estonia*. I can't talk about it."

"OK."

He scratches at his own head, angrily digging his nails into his scalp, and then he knocks an antidote kit off the table and bends down to retrieve it. "The shipping company and rescuers all gave their testimony. They knew what had gone wrong—the bow door separating from the ship, pulling the ramp away—and the horrors of that dark night, whereas we only talked about what we saw in the aftermath, when we went down thinking we knew what to expect."

"Something down there you didn't expect?"

"Don't push it," he yells, scratching at his neck now.

I flinch. Push my back into the curved chamber wall.

"I get night problems if I start thinking on what I saw." He shakes his head violently from side to side, flakes of skin falling away, and then he starts smiling. "I prefer the good stories, you know? Happy endings."

I bring an antidote box closer to myself. "How do you mean?"

Thirty-one minutes.

My breathing quickens.

A thought so black I cringe as it enters my consciousness. I have to pinch a raw section of cuticle to banish it.

"Quiet," I mumble, to myself. I look at the kit in my hands, then at the eye in the porthole.

"You telling me to be quiet?" he says.

Twenty-nine minutes.

Something feels off. More off than before.

"Can you open the hatch, please?" I say.

"Twenty-eight minutes," says Halvor.

My joints and tissues are fizzing.

Tingling.

My chest tightens.

You can't last that long.

I look deep into his eyes.

You can't trust him.

You know what happens next.

79

TWENTY-FIVE MINUTES.

"Delta P keeps me up at night," says André. "Not drowning, not freezing, not getting disconnected from the ship. Delta P."

"Divers, just checking you're both feeling OK. Only twenty-three minutes left in the chamber. Over."

I want out.

Buzzing in my ears.

I remember explaining Delta P to Steve in the early days. I told him it was pressure differential, and how it was the number one fear for many divers.

"India," says André, wearily, his shoulders slumped. He pauses to equalize. "Midnineties. A Russian diver called Oleg, big man, must have been six five, taller than me, was standing on a grate at depth. He was a bear of a diver, one of the hairiest men I ever worked with, broad shoulders. There was a screwup in terms of the order in which things should have been done. Supervisor absent for five minutes. Human error. The pressure was enormous." He shudders at the memory. "It was over in seconds and I will never forget the noise. The only thing left on the grate was Oleg's helmet. Sitting there on its own. Everything else had been shredded and pulled down through the metal grating."

"Raspberry jam."

"Have some fucking respect."
Don't make any moves, André.
"That's what you call it."
He stands up.
The chess rematch without the board.
He's manipulating me to do what he wants.

80

SICKNESS.

I feel like I will vomit.

"I'm sick. I need the Wet Pot."

"Negative," says the Super. "Hatch is locked. Use a bag. Over."

My head feels like it might burst, but if I admit to that fact we'll likely be blown down again, maybe all the way back down to depth, maybe just to 150 feet. I cannot tolerate that. I must leave.

Twenty-two minutes.

"Check the kits again, please, divers."

We run through a safety check of the four antidote kits, keeping as much space between us as possible. We run through what we will do if one of us shows symptoms of poisoning, but the truth is that we only need to make it another twenty minutes or so and then the medics and trained personnel outside will be able to treat us directly. These kits looks smart enough, and they might work well, but I want the ability to go straight to the Aberdeen Royal Infirmary if the worst was to occur.

"That vial," says André, his voice straining.

I look at him, puzzled.

"The small one. Check it."

I hold it up to the yellowish chamber light.

The glass has a crack.

It has been compromised.

"This kit is a no-go," I say, almost shouting, but not quite. "Can we have a replacement ASAP, please. Over."

"Please confirm: Kit not satisfactory? Over?" says the Life Support Technician.

"Affirmative. We need a replacement now. Over."

André looks at me and opens one of the other kits. It looks sealed to me. He takes out the amyl nitrate ampoules and inspects them. The gloves and syringes and needles.

"The ampoules are cracked in this kit as well."

He smashes the kit on the table.

Is this the pressure change coming through the Medlock? Or have these all been tampered with?

81

"DON'T TRUST ANYONE or anything," says André, his hands trembling, his eyes darting around the chamber. "These could all have cyanide in them."

I stare down at the antidote kits, my palms clammy. He was alone with them when I was in the Wet Pot. He could have done something with his back to the camera.

"Boss," I say. "We're going to need four new kits. New source, if you can, and they should be supervised from pickup to Medlock. Is that possible?"

"Roger that," says the Supervisor. "We'll make it happen. Over."

Twenty minutes left on the clock.

We stare at each other.

The pressure gauge is almost back to surface level.

"I bet the kits are fine," I say, mainly to calm myself, shallow breaths not helping my state of mind. "We're being paranoid."

"Four divers out of six dead," barks André through gritted teeth. "We have good reason to be fucking paranoid, no?" He stands up and yells, "Work together, lads. We need you on top of your game."

He is shaking with rage, or fear, as he speaks these words. A rash is developing on the back of his long neck. Sleeplessness and rage.

I find myself picking at the loose skin on my hands. A coping mechanism. When life is too much to cope with, or my thoughts become too overwhelming, I tend to pull at the thin skin covering my knuckles and at my cuticles. After a month in a chamber, when most of our surface hand skin comes loose and flakes away in what we call *diver's hand,* the process is made much simpler and more satisfying.

"Nineteen minutes," I say.

"Four men dead and we're sitting here waiting for a fucking clock."

"Fresh kits are on their way on the back of a bike," says the Super. "Five minutes, I'm told. Over."

Eighteen minutes.

André starts wheezing.

"Are you feeling OK, Joe?" asks the Super. "Joe?"

"I'll live," says André, wiping his mouth on his sleeve.

I am twitchy.

"My mate had a baby on the way," he says.

"What?"

André continues, not looking at me. "The storm came in and the barge captain made the call to abandon ship. The divers watched out of the windows as everyone fled. Then the barge sank. When they reached the seabed all the hatches popped open and the lads drowned, my mate included. They were later found with goodbye letters strapped to their chests."

He comes at me, his eyes wide.

I pull back. "What is it?"

"I haven't written a fucking letter." He looks like a madman. His eyes are burning. "I should do one. Fuck. Do you have paper and a pen?"

"We have fourteen minutes left, André."

"A lot can happen in fourteen minutes, *Ellen,*" he says, spitting out my name. "I have things I need to say."

82

THIRTEEN MINUTES LEFT.

I pull on a sweater because the air has cooled suddenly inside the chamber now that deco is almost complete.

"I need paper." He scurries around, hunched, looking for materials. "Ellen? Paper?"

I tear off ten or so sheets from the back of my notebook and hand them to him.

Twelve minutes.

We sit opposite each other, awkwardly, the same way we did when playing chess, and we write.

I keep glancing at the hatch, willing it to pop open, and then sneaking a look at his paper.

André writes furiously, his hand zigzagging and darting. He is in a crazed rush to put words down. In contrast, I take my time. I write to Steve, like I have done many times before in past years. I write about losing four colleagues and about how I know, without any doubt, that now my days in the bin will be numbered, whether I want it or not.

André turns a page over, peers at the clock, then at me, then keeps on scribbling. His handwriting is impossible to decipher from this angle. His words slope at an angle and he hums as he writes.

I tell Lisa and Henry I have been playing chess, although not as well as their father can play, and that a newspaper reporter tried to break onto the ship to take photos of our chamber.

A brief pause to observe André again. He is in a different realm. Absorbed and energized, like there is a ticking bomb beneath the table, a fuse that has been lit, a deadline that cannot be extended.

Murderer.

He looks up. "What?"

He is manic.

"Nothing."

"You said something. What did you say?"

"I need to concentrate."

He grits his teeth and keeps on writing, licking the tip of his pen to make the ink flow faster, stabbing it into the paper.

Separately, I write a short note to Halvor and a short note to Mike's girlfriend, one to Jumbo's grown-up daughter, and the same for Tea-Bag's parents and Leo's wife.

Then I write a one-liner to André, over the way from me, except I address it to *Joe.* I use my arm to screen the cursive script from his eyes in case he looks over.

All the notes are similar in tone.

They all begin with the same words.

I am sorry.

83

I FOLD THE letters and stack them neatly on the table in front of me.

André completes his note, signing the bottom of the paper with a flourish, and immediately begins work on a new one.

I watch him and I try not to make a noise. He needs peace and quiet to put his thoughts down on paper. This is the least I can do.

"Five minutes," says the Life Support Technician.

André finishes writing, as if completing an examination paper just in time for the deadline, and pants as he folds his papers. He has written three times as much as I have. Most likely because I have already made peace with most of my demons.

He is still wrestling with his.

"We should strap them to our chests," he says, his voice raspy.

"What?"

"Whatever happens, this way they'll know who said what. They will always have our letters."

"It's five minutes. Four and a half. We're in port. We're not going to sink."

"I'm not taking any more chances." He uses duct tape to secure the notes to the front of his T-shirt, moving the tape around his torso again and again to fix them in place.

I do the same thing. First I tape the notes together in a tight bundle. Then I place them against my torso, just beneath my ribs, and wind the tape around and around. It is a tradition and we are following it.

"I need to brief you on what will happen when the hatch opens," says the Super. "As I'm sure you can imagine, this won't be the usual setup. You will not be required to do anything in the chamber when it comes to cleaning or taking out rubbish. None of that today."

"Let us out, boss," says André, straining to adjust his tape. "Open it now."

"Roger that, very soon. When the hatch opens you will be divided, and then you'll both be given immediate health checks. The medical team wants to make sure you're healthy and fit, and the police will be here supervising. Everyone on the ship is primed and ready for action. They will look after you both. We ask that you do not remove anything from the chamber beyond the clothes that you are wearing. Please don't bring out your wash bags or personal effects."

"Can I bring my photos?" I ask.

A long pause. "I've been told you should leave all your photos in situ, same with any magnets holding them to the walls. Just step out in your clothes and your sandals. Nothing more."

"Roger that," says André, breathless. He gestures for me to pass him a cup of water.

I do as he asks.

"Once your initial health checks are complete you will be taken to talk with DCI MacDuff and his team from Grampian Police. He will fill you in on the details when you're out in the fresh air. Over."

"Two minutes," says André, his hand trembling as he points to the clock on the wall. The pressure gauge shows no variation from what is outside. We are waiting for the hiss that accompanies the hatch unlocking. His voice stuttering, he says, "I don't know what's on the other side."

I've seen this before. Cabin fever in reverse. Perversely, it is sometimes difficult to leave.

"You're all right, Joe," I say. "I've got your back."

84

WE WILL NEED to step over Jumbo's body to move bunks and access the exit hatch.

Intense hissing.

A flurry of activity outside. Footsteps. Talking. Can I hear sirens?

The final moments.

André approaches Jumbo's body.

"About one minute, lads, give or take. Prepare yourselves. Over."

The hissing is growing in volume.

The portholes darken.

Will one of us be arrested on release? Are they telling us the whole story?

"We should be the ones who take him out," says André, looking down at the covered corpse. "It's our job."

"That's a negative, Joe. The police have asked for you to keep the body as it is, as far as that is possible, please. Acknowledge."

"Roger that," mutters André.

"Any moment now," I whisper.

"Departure lounge," says André, a little slurred. "Final Call." He always says this as the hatch is about to pop open.

The hiss changes in tone.

It is deeper now.

Vibrations.

My pulse throbs in my ears. Pins and needles. My jaw begins to ache and I feel scorching-hot pain behind my eyes.

The hatch pops.

85

I APPROACH, STEP over Jumbo, and help adjust the bunk. First in line. There are a dozen or more people outside waiting for us. I can see Gonzales. She is with three other medics and they have blood pressure readers and other diagnostic machines. She looks stern. Anxious.

I hold on to the rail above the hatch and slide out.

"Are you OK?" asks Halvor, his expression surprised or puzzled.

I nod. "I am now."

My voice begins to change back to normal.

The mood on deck shifts. People rush to the hatch, barging me out of the way, and I turn to watch André crouch down. He collapses slowly to the floor inside the chamber, half on top of Jumbo's body.

"Medics!" yells Halvor.

The Superintendent continues to pull me away but I fight to move closer. "He's convulsing. He needs a kit."

I am held back.

"The antidote!"

They bring him out and lay him on the ridged metal floor of the chamber deck. Oxygen. Glass breaking. Amyl nitrate under his nose. Paramedics in uniform, a defibrillator on standby.

"Ellen Brooke," says a woman's voice behind me as handcuffs are placed securely around my wrists. "I am detaining you under Section 14 of the Criminal Procedure (Scotland) Act 1995, because I suspect you of committing an offense punishable by imprisonment . . . namely, murder."

86

I STRAIN TO see André. "Amyl nitrate. Give him oxygen." My voice has no strength.

A policeman pulls my wrists tight and pushes me away from the scene.

"What are you doing to me? You need to save him."

The look of disgust on the face of the Superintendent, on the face of the Life Support Technician, on the face of DCI MacDuff.

Flashing lights and jarring sirens as I emerge into natural light for the first time in almost a week.

A helicopter hovers overhead.

My voice is normal now: helium replaced by air. I squint as I am taken away.

"You are hurting me."

The deck crane stands still. No operator. The winch cables and equipment are stowed away neatly and they have erected screens to shield me from the reporters on the dock, but they are insufficient for the task. The photographers have long lenses that flash in my field of vision as I am walked toward the gangplank. My wrists burn and the tendons in my forearms feel like they could snap. Why do they suspect that I am responsible for any of this? The policeman loathes me; I can feel it through every tug and push.

"Why are you taking me away?"

He does not answer.

A woman in plain clothes walks in front of us holding up a jacket to shield me from the waiting reporters. I can hear people screaming hate slogans on the other side of the barriers. What narrative has been formed over these past days? What forces have been at work here while we were kept in the dark? Women scream slogans against the shipping company, against the government, against me and André. What do they know? How long have they been aware?

They don't know about André yet.

Rain begins to fall.

Fresh, clean rain on my eyelids and on my cheeks.

I angle my head to take a drop of something real, something unsealed and natural, something safe, reliable, and the policeman drags me onto the gangplank.

I stumble.

We walk down together, him at my back, and the angle is steep. It is the first incline I have stepped on in days.

I turn my head. "Is he OK? Did he make it?"

The policeman ignores my questions.

Rain drips off the tip of my nose.

I step up onto the granite dock, the first solid piece of land in days, and there is a van waiting with its door open, ready to accept me.

No.

Not another sealed, confined space.

I drag my feet and stiffen.

"What happened in there, Ellen?" yells a deep voice. "Where is Joe Atkins? What did you do to him?"

The policeman places his large, flat palm on top of my head

and pushes me down into the van, making sure I don't knock my forehead.

Camera flashes split through raindrops as they move down the window.

The door slides shut.

FOUR WEEKS LATER

I LIKE TO sit here quietly, thinking, remembering, at this time of the morning.

One confined place swapped for another.

No fresh air.

No space.

The school is busy.

I enjoy watching the bustle as teenagers disembark buses and other younger children squirm as they try to avoid their mothers' precious kisses. I smile from the safety of my car. Henry used to tell me I could kiss him at home if I wanted to, but not outside school. Brief hugs were acceptable. Lisa never minded, despite being at that age when she wanted to go to the mall with friends and claim some level of independence for herself. I must have dropped them off at this curb a thousand times over the years. And then, when I was working offshore, I would *imagine* them rushing through the metal gates, huddling with their friends, heavy bags pulling at their shoulders, skirts and shirts flirting with regulation uniform standards, and I would tell them both, sometimes from the seabed, that I loved them.

A van's horn wakes me from my daydream, and I notice someone on the other side of the road staring, and then pointing, so I signal, check my rearview mirror, and move out into the road. They are not journalists surely, that's stopped. They were most likely looking at someone on the far side of the road. Or else they recognized me from when I used to come here regularly in the good years, and they have seen my photo on the news, and they ponder why on earth I would come here again when I have no children of my own.

I *do* have children of my own.

I will always have them.

When I return home I wonder how I even drove back. Operating on autopilot, like I sometimes do underwater. The human brain is a curious organ: miraculous, powerful, misunderstood. It is as dark and deep as any ocean, and we can only analyze it *with* it. That must be a conflict of interest. The brain can also turn on you without notice. We all have days like this, driving through countless sets of traffic lights, dealing with intersections, where we never consciously know or acknowledge what we are doing.

The mind takes over for a while.

A glitch.

My real estate agent's sign is up by the laurel hedge. "For Sale. By Appointment Only." I have been quite clear I don't want to show anyone around myself, but I've agreed to keep the house tidy and clean. They said that was fine, and that they understand my circumstances and will work with me to make the sale process as frictionless as possible. They do not understand my circumstances.

Nobody does.

Me included.

The gentle coo of a wood pigeon from a neighbor's neatly trimmed holly tree.

I walk down to the pond at the end of the garden, and they are waiting for me. A beautiful, protective mother duck and her two ducklings. Their feathers gleam and rustle in the cool breeze. The little ones have grown so much since I returned home.

A plane passes overhead and the mother duck fusses over her offspring.

I leave them in peace.

An ache deep inside myself. A hollowness, a yearning.

I smile to myself, remembering the real estate agent's reaction when I told them I would keep the place absolutely spotless. I have never cleaned so much in my life as I have this past month. Lady Macbeth washing her hands: I am scrubbing and wiping as if I never left the saturation chamber. I order takeout because I relish the delivery of food in aluminum containers, my front door a makeshift Medlock. When I boil the kettle to brew tea in the morning—bottled water, sealed—I ask myself out loud for a pot of hot. I am not insane, I am merely learning to cope. It is similar yet different. My garbage bags are translucent, and I remove them to the outside bins as soon as they have the smallest dirty item inside them, keen to avoid any infection at depth.

Leave it how you found it.

Halvor refuses to talk with me about my next job. Nobody in the industry will countenance it. I have contacted him ten or twenty times to be considered for various contracts and he tells me it is far too soon. I say I know it is too soon but I need some kind of timeline, some plan, some hope that I may be able to dive in the future, or else I may have to work farther afield.

The police say I may need to come in again to answer more questions. I don't see why. I've told them everything I know. MacDuff has requested I keep him updated if I leave the area.

Halvor and his colleagues have referred me to a counseling service.

They have asked me not to contact them again.

André is still in the hospital. They will not permit me to visit.

He is stable and recovering, being held under arrest on a special ward. I imagine him handcuffed to his bed. He is good with confined spaces. He was quick-witted and calm in the Bell when we had the unusual valve issue with the bilge drain. He's a survivor and he will muddle through, but I will never understand what possessed him to do what he did. He claims he didn't do anything wrong. Sometimes that claim enrages me and sometimes I understand it. Agree with it, even. André claims he has no idea why police found cyanide capsules secreted inside the hollow rims and arms of his tortoiseshell reading glasses. Apparently, in the background of footage I recorded trying to explain how to equalize pressure, André can be seen in the bunk area manipulating the arms of his glasses. That might be useful evidence, or it might be deemed innocent behavior. Police believe he poisoned Tea-Bag, Leo, and Mike as they slept, but the attack on Gary was quite different. Their working hypothesis, in the absence of a confession, is that Jumbo collapsed from exhaustion and then, when we assumed André was working to save him, he took the opportunity to poison him instead. A minuscule tablet, whole, or crumbed up, placed on Jumbo's lips. When the newspapers started to dig into André family life—his divorce, his documented threats, unhinged text messages, the testimony from one of his estranged adult children, his mounting debts owed to several notorious loan sharks—a picture began to emerge: that of a man with nothing left to lose. A diver coming to the end of his working life, bitter at the world, especially saturation divers with a future in front of them.

I still don't know what to believe.

My lawyer is even starting to question the actions of police, and whether they followed procedures correctly when I was arrested and then released. There was so much media attention during those days of decompression. She suspects they were under intense pressure to act decisively.

André helped me. He helped all of us. We were a tight unit, on the whole: a decent set of lads. He told me multiple times how he preferred diving with me. I'm not sure if that had anything to do with my gender, my character, my proficiency, or how much he trusted me. Perhaps that is why I was spared.

This is already being labeled the worst diving incident in recent memory, not because of the body count, but because it was intentional homicide.

The authorities may not reach the same conclusion, but I believe it was partially a result of bubble brain, a niche and largely undocumented condition: the effects on his psyche, on his physical neurology, from decades spent living at pressure, saturating and decompressing, and dealing, or not dealing, with trauma. In recent days retired divers George Seyton and Samuel Fleance, two characters well known and well-liked in the community, have come forward to claim that André made threats and spoke incoherently about revenge, witchcraft, evil, and missed opportunities—during a drinking binge earlier this year in Inverness. They put it down to inebriation and thought nothing more of it.

Until, that is, they watched the news.

It turns out André's uncle drank himself to death, in debt, with people after him, at exactly André's age. There are rumors he might have been a hit man in his thirties. And André's paternal grandfather, a traveling thespian specializing in Shakespeare's plays, strangled his second wife and then hung himself from a tree. He was André's age when he died.

I open a fresh, sealed pack of antibacterial wipes and clean down the granite countertops of the kitchen island.

Church group didn't go well. I went there same as always, to share, to open up about grief, about loss, about 8:40 a.m., but they looked at me strangely. Suspiciously, almost. Perhaps because of the rumors on the internet, and the blog posts, and the theories. Three group members didn't ask me about the chamber outright, but I could tell some of them desperately wanted to. They don't believe all the facts have been released yet.

I understand now that I will never go back there.

Check outside.

I check the kitchen window for people lurking out on the street. It is clear. The man from one of the national papers was the worst. He persuaded me to answer the door under false pretenses, and then proceeded to tell me how I won't be working for a long, long time, probably never again in Sat, and he could ease any financial burden—he had heard I was selling the family home, regrettable—with a sizable payment for my exclusive story.

I told him to never, ever come back here.

The thing Halvor and the others don't quite grasp is if I don't go back to work eventually I really will lose my grip completely. I must go down in order to sleep. Jumbo and Mike understood the concept. They experienced the same thing in the military. There is a certain luxury in going to work each day and never having to worry about cooking, washing up, jealous partners, homework, the police, unpaid bills, neighbor disputes, or anything else complicated, like unthinkable grief or guilt. *Work, eat, sleep.* I need that routine to keep my head straight and ensure the thoughts stay that way: *thoughts.* Perhaps I have adapted and evolved so now I can only truly sleep properly under extreme pressure. I desire the squeezing—the push of it from all sides, like a cover-all weighted blanket—to truly rest my fractious mind.

I have spent countless hours in formal interviews. With the police, suffering flashbacks to my brief stint in the Oklahoma County Jail, and then with the health and safety executive, and finally, the company men. We've been through the tapes, including the footage salvaged from my camcorder. They told me the other lads in Sat, the lads working as far away as Brazil and Malaysia, are requesting pre-chamber gear checks, sniffer dogs, cyanide antidote kits, and closer surveillance. They are even requesting cameras in their sleeping areas.

I'm glad some good can come of all this.

Some progress.

I won't lie, the thoughts come and go. I will be hanging wash out on the line in the garden and suddenly a flashback to buying six cyanide pills two years ago when I was out of Sat following the accident: my darkest, longest days. *Flashback* is the wrong word. An intrusive and utterly false memory. Not sure if they were intended for the drunk driver, his family, or for myself to take the easy way out. Then I went a few days with my head straight before having another flashback image of me working on a pair of spectacles, the brand and model André always wears, using Steve's Bergeon fine watchmaker tools, carving and hollowing out the stems, breaking four identical pairs before trying again on a fresh set. Never happened, of course. Wearing latex gloves and pushing the six pills carefully into the stems. Three on each side. Bubble brain. *Too many hours in the bin*, Halvor would say. *Time to move up in the world.*

When I met up with Spock's wife for a coffee in a chain hotel outside Leeds I suddenly had the idea of dropping something into her cup. I shook the horrid notion away, of course. Too much stress. She was absolutely distraught, the poor woman, and she was furious with André for taking away her soulmate. I know *exactly* how she feels. Your partner being ripped away like that, your life changing in an instant. I am not dreaming of the body on the beach anymore, thank goodness. That is one relief. I am not dreaming of digging with my hands to find its pallid, bloated torso, only to realize the body was my own. But last night, when I was trying and failing to sleep, I had the vision of slipping something into André's water immediately before we left the chamber. I am hoping the thoughts will fade after I move. I urgently need some distance from this place.

My phone beeps.

A text from Gilly. *I'll be with you in 20 mins. I found the photos you wanted. Picking up pizzas on the way. And WINE xx*

Maybe Halvor is right after all. Could it be time for my career to move on?

Yes, it's time.

Much to do.

André did this to himself and we may never fully understand the *whys* and *hows*, no matter how many inquiries are launched. It may be time to heed Halvor's advice and transfer out of Sat. It might be time to start supervising divers instead of being one. I think I'm probably ready now. To watch them 24/7 in the chamber, in the Bell, in the water. To operate the cameras and microphones, and give them instructions. To base myself in Dive Control and oversee every operation and pressure change.

To look after divers so this can never, ever happen again.

My letter to Steve

I am sorry for everything I have put you through.

It is nearly the end.

The hatch will open soon. They all will.

I miss you three so much I can't put it into words. But you have sustained me in here. I couldn't have survived this without you.

What will happen now? I don't know. There will be questions and interviews, inquiries and papers written. I know I must help their families in whatever way I can. It would be the least I can do. If they have questions for me I want to answer them. I remember those darkest of days. They will be craving detail. I will give them that gift.

I also know I will return to the offshore world if it is an option. I need it. In order to carry on I must have the vacuum it affords me. The peace and quiet, and the distance from my own thoughts and demons. If you three are in heaven, then the bottom of the sea is truly the closest I can be to sharing it with you.

I miss you all more than I can say.

Everything I have done, I have done for you.

Kiss them both good night from me.

Love, E.

André's letters (this text in triplicate)

She should have died hereafter;
There would have been a time for such a word.
To-morrow, and to-morrow, and to-morrow,
Creeps in this petty pace from day to day,
To the last syllable of recorded time;
And all our yesterdays have lighted fools
The way to dusty death. Out, out, brief candle!
Life's but a walking shadow, a poor player
That struts and frets his hour upon the stage
And then is heard no more. It is a tale
Told by an idiot, full of sound and fury
Signifying nothing.

Macbeth (Act 5, Scene 5)

. . .

Be bloody, bold, and resolute.
No regrets, lads.

Fair is foul, and foul is fair.
The quicker, the better.

There's nothing serious in mortality.
We laugh at everything.

What's done cannot be undone.
It is what it is.

ACKNOWLEDGMENTS

To my literary agent Kate Burke, and the team at Blake Friedmann (Isobel, Julian, Conrad, Anna, Juliet, Sian, Lizzy, James, Susie, Nicole, Daisy, et al.): thank you.

To my editor Emily Bestler, and the team at Emily Bestler Books & Atria (Hydia, Megan, Maudee, Jolena, David, Megan, Morgan, Lara, et al.): thank you.

To my international publishers, editors, translators: thank you.

To all the booksellers and bloggers and librarians and reviewers and fellow authors: thank you. Readers benefit so much from your recommendations and enthusiasm. I am one of them. Special thanks to every single reader who takes the time to leave a review somewhere online. Those reviews help readers find books. Thank you.

To my family, and especially my parents: once again, thank you for letting me play alone for hours as a child. Thank you for taking me to libraries to borrow books. Thank you for allowing me to build (so many) dens, and then letting me read and draw and daydream inside them. Thanks for not censoring my book choices (too much). Thank you for allowing me to be bored (a lot). It was a special, and increasingly rare, gift.

To my friends: thanks for your ongoing support (and patience, and love).

To librarians: again, thank you. Without libraries I wouldn't be a writer. You helped me find this life.

To the brave saturation divers who have worked, and who continue to work: thank you. I couldn't do what you do. I am in awe.

To Marc Sebastian: thanks for dazzling, and for making *The Last One* kind of real.

Special thanks to my late granddad for teaching me many valuable lessons. He urged me to treat everyone equally, and with respect. To give the benefit of the doubt. To listen to advice even if you don't then follow it. To take pleasure from the small, inexpensive things in life. To protect nature, and to appreciate it. To read widely. To never judge or look down on anyone. To be kind. To grow food, even if that means herbs on a windowsill. To spend time with loved ones. To keep the curious child inside you alive.

To every shy, socially awkward kid: I see you. I was you. It will get easier, I promise. You will make it through to the other side.

To my wife and son: Thank you. Love you. Always.